FROM THE HEART

ALSO BY BARBARA HINSKE

Available at Amazon in Print, Audio, and for Kindle

The Rosemont Series

Coming to Rosemont

Weaving the Strands

Uncovering Secrets

Drawing Close

Bringing Them Home

Shelving Doubts

Restoring What Was Lost

No Matter How Far

When Dreams There Be

Novellas

The Night Train

The Christmas Club (adapted
for The Hallmark Channel, 2019)

Paws & Pastries

Sweets & Treats

Snowflakes, Cupcakes & Kittens

Workout Wishes & Valentine Kisses

Wishes of Home

Novels in the Guiding Emily Series

Guiding Emily (adapted for The Hallmark Channel, 2023)

The Unexpected Path

Over Every Hurdle

Down the Aisle

From the Heart

Novels in the "Who's There?!" Collection

Deadly Parcel

Final Circuit

CONNECT WITH BARBARA HINSKE ONLINE

Sign up for her newsletter at **BarbaraHinske.com**
  Goodreads.com/BarbaraHinske
  Facebook.com/BHinske
  Instagram/barbarahinskeauthor
  TikTok.com/BarbaraHinske
  Pinterest.com/BarbaraHinske
  BookBub/Barbara Hinske
  Twitter(X)/Barbara Hinske
  Search for **Barbara Hinske on YouTub**e
  bhinske@gmail.com

FROM THE HEART

BOOK FIVE OF THE GUIDING EMILY SERIES

BARBARA HINSKE

CASA DEL NORTHERN PUBLISHING

ISBN: 9798987694268

Library of Congress Control Number: 2024905440

Casa del Northern Publishing

Phoenix, Arizona

To my incredible group of readers: you've supported me, encouraged me, rejoiced with me, and assisted me with unfailing enthusiasm. I am honored and more grateful than I can express. You've made this author journey a joy.

CHAPTER 1

*G*rant Johnson rolled the suitcase out the door and hoisted the duffel bag filled with kibble, dog bowls, and toys onto his shoulder. He turned back to face the three sets of eyes staring at him. "Martha," he addressed his mother-in-law of only five weeks, "I can't thank you enough for coming in on such short notice to stay with the girls."

Martha Main stood on her tiptoes to give him a quick hug. "Nonsense. It's my pleasure. I always love spending time with my granddaughters."

The girls standing on either side of her grinned with pleasure at the description of themselves.

"You don't think I'm off base—taking Emily on a surprise second honeymoon?"

"Of course I don't." Martha's tone was firm. "The two of you have been on the go from dawn until dusk, ever since the wedding, what with the holidays and moving into this place." She waved a hand behind her head to indicate the interior of the luxurious home in Presidio Heights that Emily and Grant had purchased. "You need this time as a couple, before these two start fourth grade in their new school." She looked from Zoe to Diedre. "This family is going to be busier than ever."

Grant turned his face aside, lines furrowing his brow. "I owe it to Emily. Taking her to the beach for our honeymoon…well…it was a stupid idea. Thoughtless."

Martha reached out and took his shoulder, turning him to face her. "You listen to me, Grant. The fact that going to the beach brought up unwelcome memories for Emily was not your fault."

"Come on, Martha. She lost her sight in a horseback riding accident on the beach. I should have seen that coming."

"It was Emily's idea to honeymoon at the Hotel del Coronado. She loved hearing about Stephanie and Dhruv's honeymoon there. Emily told me so herself. If she didn't think the beach would be traumatic for her, why would you?"

Grant shrugged.

"You can't shield the people you love from everything that might hurt them," Martha said quietly. "As much as we'd like to. Life doesn't work like that." She squeezed his shoulder and released it. "Now go pick her up from work and have the most wonderful time. Sedona, Arizona, is one of my favorite places on the planet. It'll be lovely this time of year."

"I know how much Emily likes to control things. I hope I'm not getting off to a terrible start by surprising her."

"If you'd have asked her about going away this weekend, she'd have rattled on about how much unpacking remains to be done. You'd never have gotten her out of here."

"That's what I'm afraid of." He smiled at Martha. "This surprise second honeymoon seemed like a good idea when I booked it, but now I'm not so sure."

"It's a genius idea. If that headstrong daughter of mine balks, just ignore her. I know she's going to love it—it's exactly what you both need." Martha put her arms around the girls. "We're going to finish unpacking while you're gone and clear away all the boxes. Aren't we, girls?"

"We sure are," Diedre said. She squared her petite shoulders.

Zoe bobbed her head emphatically, her dark eyes shining with determination.

"Your mother should be here any minute," Martha said to Grant, looking at her watch. "Sylvia's spending the weekend with us. And Doug Roberts is coming over Sunday afternoon to hang pictures. Between the five of us, we'll put everything to rights around here."

"You know where to hang things?" Grant asked.

Martha rolled her eyes. "You told me yesterday you'd placed everything on the floor against the walls where they're to go. I think we can figure that out."

Grant's shoulders relaxed as a smile spread from ear to ear. "You're the best, you know that? All of you." He turned his attention to his daughter and stepdaughter. "I want you

3

both to be on your best behaviors. Make sure you mind Martha and Sylvia."

"Oh, Dad," Diedre moaned. "We will."

"I'll have you know, my granddaughters are model children," Martha said with mock indignation.

"Have I got everything I need in here?" Grant hoisted the duffel higher on his shoulder and pointed to the suitcase.

"I packed the duffel for Garth," Zoe replied to her stepfather. "You've got everything for him, with enough for an extra day. Just in case." She straightened. "You can trust me."

"I know that. You're mature and dependable—far beyond your years." He patted Zoe's shoulder. "Both of you are."

Zoe nodded in satisfaction, and Diedre grinned.

"I packed for Emily," Martha said. "Casual clothes with one nice little black dress—just like you requested."

"And her hiking shoes are in there?"

"They are. I took a peek at the weather report. It's supposed to be sunny and in the upper sixties all weekend. Ideal weather to hike."

"I'd better get going." He bent his six-foot-six frame to hug each girl. "We'll call as soon as we get to our hotel room."

"You'll do no such thing," Martha said, placing her hand on his back and steering him over the threshold. "Text us when you arrive, but you don't need to call from your honeymoon."

Grant looked at the girls.

"We're going to be too busy to talk to you anyway, Dad," Diedre said.

"We've got a lot to do here," Zoe added.

"We'll be back Tuesday afternoon so we can take you to

your first day at your new school on Wednesday." He turned to Martha. "If you need anything, give one of us a call."

"Of course. But we won't need anything. Now...go!" Martha began closing the front door.

Grant picked up Emily's suitcase and headed to the car. He placed it in the rear cargo section next to his bags. He'd be waiting for Emily at the curb when she exited her office building. Once more, doubts about the wisdom of his surprise crowded his mind. He shook his head to banish them. It was too late for second thoughts.

Grant slid behind the wheel and started the car. He'd know whether he'd been a genius or a fool within the hour. He'd just have to wait and see.

CHAPTER 2

I led Emily out the large glass door of our office building. Other people—some I recognized from our company and others I did not know—pushed through the doors with us. I'd heard people say TGIF earlier in the day. I've been working in an office long enough to know that TGIF was a good thing.

Emily commanded me to go left instead of the usual right we took when heading for our bus stop. I knew what this meant. Someone was picking us up.

My tail began to wag before Emily even gave the command.

"Find Grant," Emily said.

I'd spotted Grant right away. His car was pulled to the curb, and he was standing on the passenger side, waving his hands over his head at me. I raised my muzzle and quickly brought it down again to signal I'd seen him.

He continued to wave.

I picked up my pace to show I'd already seen him.

Grant continued to motion to us.

When we were close, I uttered a soft bark to assure him I'd seen him so he could stop waving like he was trying to hail a cab in Manhattan.

Grant got the message. He stepped toward us and uttered Emily's name in the way I knew she loved, before sweeping her into his arms.

I looked away to give them some privacy while they kissed. I understood that newlyweds acted this way.

Grant opened the rear door for me. Emily removed my working harness and I jumped with my usual fluid grace into my spot on the floor. He opened the door for Emily, and she tucked herself into the passenger seat.

"You didn't have to drive in to pick me up," Emily said. "I mean…I appreciate it, but Garth and I are fine on the bus."

"I know you are," Grant said, sliding behind the wheel. "The only problem is that the bus would take you home. And we're not going home." He buckled his seat belt and pulled into traffic.

Emily's brows furrowed in concentration. "Have I forgotten something? Do we have plans tonight?"

"No. You haven't forgotten anything."

"Thank goodness. It's been a long week and I'm pooped. I'm always happy to support you, but I'd hate going to a client dinner tonight."

"There's no client dinner." He put on his turn signal and changed lanes.

"Well…then why aren't we going home?"

"We're headed to the airport."

"What? Are we picking someone up?"

I glanced at her from the backseat through the space between the two bucket seats. I suspected by her tone of voice that she was growing impatient with their game of twenty questions. The rigidity in her neck confirmed my suspicions.

"We're taking a trip."

I heard her sharp intake of breath. Evidently, Grant heard it too.

"We're having a redo of our honeymoon," he continued quickly. "Only this time, we're headed to Sedona, Arizona—famed for its healing vortex and peaceful tranquility."

Emily pursed her lips and paused before speaking. "You don't have to do this, sweetheart. We had a lovely honeymoon. You let me pick the place and I had a great time."

Grant reached over and put his right hand over her left one. "You put on a brave face, but I know that being on that beach brought back unwelcome memories of your riding accident and..."

"Vision loss." Emily finished his sentence. "I was reliving memories from my honeymoon with Connor, but not about the accident and all that followed. All I could think about was how much I wanted to please Connor. I knew I shouldn't have gone riding—I knew my retinas were precarious. The people pleaser in me ignored all of that." She shook her head and ran her hand through her hair. "I may have been successful in my profession, but I was awfully insecure in my relationship with him. Why in the world did I let that happen to me?"

"Don't beat yourself up..."

Emily swung her right hand over to place it on top of their clasped ones. "Let me finish. I realized how much happier I am now—with you, but also with myself. I'm a more secure and better person. It sounds ridiculous to be grateful for my vision loss, but without it, I wouldn't have you and Zoe and Diedre in my life. I wouldn't trade my current life for anything."

Grant brought her hand to his lips and kissed it.

"I'm sorry if I spoiled our honeymoon for you by being so introspective," she said.

"You didn't spoil anything. I want us to have a relaxing getaway—just the two of us—before the girls are back in school and we're juggling all the balls that make up our wonderful life together."

I glanced from Emily to Grant and back again.

Emily rubbed his hand, then released it. "Mom loves Sedona and raves about how relaxing it is. I've always wanted to go." Emily relaxed into her seat.

I rested my head on my paws.

"You're not mad that I didn't consult you first?"

"As a rule, I'm not big on surprises."

They both laughed.

"I guess you already know that about me. I have to admit, the sound of a weekend away from unpacking and the hustle and bustle of our household is very appealing."

"Whew." Grant blew out an exaggerated breath. "I was worried you'd be so upset I'd end up sleeping on the sofa."

"Does our room have a sofa?"

"Our creek-side suite has a sofa. And a fireplace. With an extended deck at the edge of the creek. We'll fall asleep to rushing waters and wake up to birdsong. That's what the website says."

"Gosh. Sounds perfect. And you've got everything we'll need for Garth?"

"I do. Zoe packed a duffel for him. Your mother packed a suitcase for you."

"Seems you've thought of everything."

"I hope so. If there's anything we need, I understand Sedona has wonderful shopping."

"Who's staying with the girls?"

"Both our mothers. They're planning to finish unpacking for us. Doug is coming over to hang pictures."

"I'm delighted Mom has a man in her life." Emily chuckled. "It's doubly nice that he's so handy."

"I thought we could bring each of them a thank-you gift from Sedona."

"Good idea. I'll put that on our to-do list," Emily replied.

"I've got one request," Grant said.

"Anything."

"Let's spend the next few days without a to-do list."

Emily sucked air between her teeth. "Fair enough. You've got it. No lists."

"We'll fly into Phoenix, pick up our rental car, and drive the ninety minutes to Sedona. I figure we'll be there well before midnight."

"Sleeping in tomorrow morning will be the first order of business," she said. "I'm not making a list," she added hastily. "Just saying."

"I, for one, am looking forward to spending a long morning in bed."

I opened one eye in time to watch Emily flush. I wasn't sure what we were doing or where we were going, but that didn't bother me in the least. A guide dog is always ready for anything. I closed my eye again. I wanted to be as rested as possible for whatever Emily needed.

CHAPTER 3

*E*mily woke to the sound of Grant's deep breathing on the pillow next to her. Garth's muffled snore emanated from the corner of the room where they'd placed his bed. She stretched her toes toward the foot of the bed and nestled herself deeper into the curve of Grant's body, his arm holding her close. *My life is perfect*, she thought.

She opened her eyes and was greeted with the blurred light and dark shadow that her limited vision allowed her. She rotated the pinhole of usable vision in the center of her left eye around the room until she located a bright slash of sunshine penetrating the room from a crack in the blackout curtains. They hadn't pulled them completely shut in their hurry to fall into bed and each other's arms. Her skin warmed with memories of the night before.

Emily shut her eyes, determined to go back to sleep. She breathed deeply and tried to calm her mind, but it didn't work. Once she was awake, she couldn't go back to sleep. It had been this way her whole life. There was nothing for it but to get up.

Grant continued to breathe rhythmically, deep in sleep.

Emily carefully moved his arm aside and noiselessly rolled to the side of the bed. She sat up, slid her feet into her slippers, and donned the luxurious plush robe furnished by the hotel. She reached for her phone to check the time, then thought better of it. What difference did it make? They weren't on a schedule. Emily pulled her thick auburn hair out from under the collar of her robe, and picked up Garth's harness and leash.

Garth's ears perked up at the barely perceptible sounds that signaled his assistance was needed. He hopped to his feet and trotted to Emily's side, giving himself a good shake once he reached her.

She bent over, as she did every morning, to kiss the top of his head. "You are my remarkable, brilliant boy," she whispered in his ear, as she rubbed his chest.

He inserted his head into his harness, and Emily secured the strap and attached his leash with practiced precision.

"Let's take you outside to do your business," she whispered as she stood.

Garth understood what doing business meant and led her directly to the front door of the creek-side cabin they'd settled into just before midnight. There was a grassy area to the right of the door where he'd relieved himself the night before. He took her there now. Emily removed the harness but kept hold of the leash. He promptly accomplished his task.

Emily turned her face into the dappled sunshine coming

through a stand of Arizona ash trees. She slowly inhaled the crisp morning air and listened to the gentle breeze rustle the leaves. Grant was right—they needed this time away to celebrate their marriage and connect with each other.

She wrapped her arms around herself, savoring the sensations of the quiet morning.

Garth settled at her feet.

Emily wondered if they were close enough for guests in neighboring cabins to see her. They'd arrived very late and had been eager to get inside their cabin. She and Garth hadn't done any exploring, and Grant hadn't described their surroundings to her. She told herself she should go inside but remained rooted to the spot, cataloging all the things she was grateful for.

Grant stepped out the door, pulling her out of her reverie.

"Hey, you," he said, coming up behind her and circling her with his arms. "I thought you wanted to sleep in."

"I woke and couldn't go back to sleep. I tried not to disturb you, but I guess that didn't work. What time is it?"

"A little after eight."

"That's late for us."

"Not if you don't get to sleep until after two," he said, his voice husky.

"You're right about that. I'm sorry I woke you. I'm loving being out here, but you can go back to bed."

He yawned and stretched. "It's a beautiful morning. I'll go back to bed later—when you come with me. I'll make coffee and we can settle on the deck in back. The hotel brochure extols the virtues of relaxing on our private deck in generous upholstered chairs while listening to the rushing waters of the creek. Let's see if we agree."

"Capital idea," Emily said.

The three of them headed toward the deck through the living area, when Emily slowed down.

"Didn't you say there's a fireplace in here?"

"If you executed a sharp left turn right now, it would be ten feet in front of you. It's floor-to-ceiling stone and is natural gas."

"I'd love to sit by the fire tonight."

"If we have to leave the doors to the deck open so it gets cool enough in here, we'll do just that." Grant escorted Emily and Garth to an oversize chair that he positioned in a sunny spot. He moved the other chair and a low coffee table next to them. "I'll be right back with our coffee."

"You are a dream of a husband," Emily called after him.

Grant soon returned with two steaming mugs of coffee. "I've got another surprise for you. Be right back." He returned with a cellophane-enclosed gift basket secured with a large blue bow and set it on the coffee table.

"What's that? Sounds crinkly." Emily leaned over and reached out until she touched the basket. She ran her hands over it and scooted forward in her chair. "I thought it sounded like cellophane when you set it down. It's a gift basket, right? Did you have it sent for us?"

"It's a gift basket, but I didn't send it." He plucked a card from an envelope taped to the cellophane and read the message. "Have fun and don't worry about a thing! Love, Martha and Sylvia."

"Gosh—that's so nice! We have the best moms ever."

"We certainly do."

"What's in it? Is there anything to eat?" As if on cue, Emily's stomach gurgled.

Grant removed the bow and tore off the cellophane. "There's a bottle of Veuve Clicquot, cheeses, crackers, cookies, biscotti, and a tin of caviar." He unpacked the basket. "Plus, a small bag of Crunchy Cheetos."

They both burst out laughing.

"I'm so glad they included Garth's favorite snack. I'll bet the girls suggested that," Emily said.

"I think you're right." Grant got to his feet. "Let's order room service breakfast and save this for happy hour by the fire tonight."

"Genius idea."

"I'll find the room service menu," Grant said. "Then we can decide what we want to do today—go on a hike, go shopping, have massages?"

Emily extended her hand to him.

He took it, and she pulled him in for a lingering kiss. "Or we could just go back to bed."

"I'm in favor of that," he said, pulling her even closer.

Emily's stomach growled again.

"After breakfast. I'll feed Garth now, too." He stood and went in search of the menus, motioning for Garth to join him.

CHAPTER 4

"They're still asleep." Sylvia Johnson inserted a pod into the coffeemaker and pushed the brew button. "Would you like a second cup?"

"Why not?" Martha rose and brought her mug with her. "I'd like to sit and enjoy a few minutes of peace and quiet with you before those two bundles of energy bound out of bed."

Sylvia removed her now-full cup and replaced it with Martha's.

"You can reuse that pod," Martha said. "I like to dilute the dark roast that's all the rage right now."

Sylvia started the coffeemaker. "I'm surprised the girls still sleep in the same room. I thought when they moved into this house and each decorated their own room, they'd stay apart."

"It's sort of sweet, don't you think?" Martha asked.

"I do."

"It's a good thing their parents bought twin beds for both of their rooms," Sylvia observed. "Emily and Grant thought it would be useful for when the girls had friends sleep over. Little did they know their daughters would continue to sleep in the same room, switching rooms every night."

"Did they tell you why they're doing this?"

"Zoe said that she and Sabrina are used to being with Diedre, and Diedre said she's nervous about being in this great big house."

"I'm sure it's just a phase. They'll get over it soon enough." Martha brought her brimming cup to the kitchen table, reclaiming her seat in front of her laptop.

Sylvia sat down next to her, blowing across the surface of her steaming cup of coffee. "How do you want to tackle our day?"

"I thought we should finish taking everything out of the boxes and putting things away if we can—or at least placing them in the correct rooms. We can then move all the empty boxes to the garage."

"That's how I'd approach it. The girls can finish their bedrooms and we'll do the rest. I thought I'd handle the kitchen while you put away Emily's clothes, makeup, and toiletries. It looks like Grant has finished organizing his closet."

"Perfect. Then tomorrow, Zoe and I can use Emily's braille label maker and her PenFriend to label things. Zoe helped Emily label things in both of her prior apartments, so she knows what to do," Martha said.

"Diedre and I will spend the morning in the garage, breaking down all the boxes. We'll stuff as many of them as we can in the recycle bin and stack the rest against the wall of the garage. We should have plenty of time to finish that by the time Doug gets here after lunch to hang pictures." Sylvia patted Martha's hand. "That's so nice of him to offer to help. He's such a great guy. I'm glad you've found each other."

A flush crept from Martha's neck to her hairline. "Thanks. He's very special."

Sylvia arched a brow at Martha. "Any developments you'd like to report?"

Martha waved a hand in front of her face dismissively. "We get along great and are taking things slowly. That's good enough for both of us." She purposefully focused her attention on her laptop screen and turned it toward Sylvia. "I've been looking at bedding—duvet sets and sheets—for the girls' rooms."

"What a great idea. Emily and Grant were smart to let them each pick the color of their new room, but none of the bedding they already had works."

"It's nice to get new linens for new rooms, anyway. Plus, they need two sets of bedding for each room instead of one." Martha tapped the keyboard. "There's lots to choose from for Diedre's pink bedroom, but not much selection for Zoe's yellow one."

Sylvia reached over to Martha's trackpad and scrolled through several pages. "I see what you mean. Were you going to order online?"

"I was checking to see what's available. I thought that if we get everything done here by Sunday night, it would be fun to take them shopping on Monday to pick out what they'd like."

"Brilliant idea." Sylvia tapped the tabletop. "I always like to touch and see things in person. Can I tag along?"

Martha put her hand to her chest. "Gosh—I was counting on it. I don't want to wrangle these two on my own."

"Great. And I have one more request."

"What?"

"Will you let me split the cost with you? So the gift can be from the two grandmas?"

"Sure, but that's not necessary. It can be from both of us, regardless of whether you split the cost."

Sylvia put her arm across Martha's shoulders and gave them a squeeze. "That's very classy of you."

"What's classy? Of who?" Diedre asked from the doorway of the kitchen.

Zoe stood behind her, rubbing the sleep out of her eyes. Sabrina, Zoe's miniature schnauzer, stood at her heels.

Martha closed her laptop and pushed herself out of her chair. "We were just planning out the next few days. There's a lot of work to be done, but we," she pointed to Sylvia and then herself, "have a nice surprise for you if you work hard and finish everything."

The girls looked at each other, then back to their grandmothers.

"We'll work really hard. Can you tell us what the surprise is?"

Sylvia walked to the kitchen counter and pulled a box of pancake mix from the cupboard. "I'll make us all a nice breakfast. We can't work on empty stomachs. Go get dressed and be back here in ten minutes."

"That's a wonderful idea. Over breakfast, we'll outline

everything we need to accomplish, and we'll tell you what the surprise will be if we work together to get it all done." Martha cracked eggs into a bowl and whisked them.

The girls turned on their heels and raced to their bedrooms.

Sabrina glanced at her mistress as she retreated but stayed put in the kitchen doorway.

"And I'll feed you, Sabrina," Martha said. She scooped kibble into a bowl and set it in front of the dog. Sabrina picked at her food instead of hoovering it down, as usual.

Martha stroked Sabrina behind the ears. "You miss your buddy, Garth, don't you? He'll be home soon, don't you worry." Sabrina moved her tail in a microscopic arc. Martha patted her again, then reached into the bag of kibble and gave the sad dog another scoop. There wasn't much she could do to comfort Sabrina, but she could do this.

CHAPTER 5

$\mathcal{E}$mily inhaled deeply as she rubbed the lather between her hands, filling her lungs with the aroma of the eucalyptus and spearmint soap that was the hotel's signature fragrance. The past two days of lazing around the resort had done her a world of good. Grant had been right— they'd both needed this time to unplug from their busy lives. Emily dried her hands and padded out of the bathroom on bare feet. "Is that coffee I smell coming my way?"

"It sure is," Grant replied. "Slip back into bed and I'll bring in our breakfast tray."

"Ahh…breakfast in bed is the best." Emily's voice was rich with contentment. "I'd better take Garth out and feed him first."

"Already taken care of."

"Wow—what time is it?"

"Almost ten."

"Whoa. I really slept in."

"Yes. This is the first time since we've been married that I got up earlier than you." Grant leaned in and kissed Emily. "I'm savoring the moment. Now get back into bed."

Emily did as instructed and accepted the coffee from him. She carefully arranged her pillows behind her without spilling her coffee.

Grant soon returned with a tray

Emily inhaled deeply. "Smells divine. A girl could get used to this."

Grant got into bed next to her. "Let me know when you're ready for your plate."

"Eggs Florentine, right?" Emily asked.

"Your sense of smell is impeccable," he replied.

Emily reached for her nightstand and set down her coffee cup. "Ready."

Grant handed her silverware and a plate of the eggy delicacy. "There are croissants and fruit, too."

"Lovely. Is there room on my plate?"

"I can squeeze them on."

"Please do. I'm famished."

Grant accommodated her request. "What do you want to do today? Shall we hike along the creek and nap in the hammock below the deck again?"

"As wonderful as that's been, I think two days is enough of that. This is our last day here. I thought we should go out of the resort."

"I'm up for that. Any suggestions?"

"Mom used to come here all the time and she always loved the pink jeep tours. She never got tired of seeing the red rocks."

"Sedona is famous for them. They really are spectacular."

"You'll enjoy seeing the rocks up close and I'll love zooming along in a jeep with the sun on my face and the wind blowing my hair to pieces."

Grant laughed. "Sounds good. I'll call the concierge to book a tour at noon. They'll pick us up right here at the hotel. I read that they're two hours long."

"After that, we can go into town to do some shopping. I'd like to bring little gifts back for our mothers and the girls, and I want to pick up something for Stephanie, too. She's had such a hard time with stomach issues lately."

"Has she seen a doctor?"

"As a matter of fact, she's seeing a gastroenterologist tomorrow morning. Dhruv is taking the morning off to go with her."

"That's good. Hopefully, it's something they can easily treat."

"Yes. Sounds like acid reflux to me, but I'm no specialist."

"Let's finish breakfast and get ourselves together."

"These are the best eggs Florentine I've ever had," Emily said, covering her mouth with her hand as she chewed. "I'm already feeling full, but I'm going to stuff down every morsel of this."

"Maybe we should skip lunch and go for an early dinner. We'll have to be up and out of here at the crack of dawn for the ninety-minute drive back to the airport in time for our flight home."

Emily took a large bite out of her croissant and gave Grant the thumbs-up sign.

Silence descended as they cleaned their plates.

"OMG," Emily cried. "That was so much fun." She clawed at a strand of hair stuck to the side of her face.

Grant helped her tuck the hair behind her ear. "You really loved the pink jeep tour, didn't you?"

Emily chortled. "Totally. I'd do it again in a heartbeat. What about you? Did you enjoy it? You were awfully quiet." She ran her hands along his forearms.

Grant paused, choosing his words. "I was moved by it. The depth of color and the patterns of those rocks was... architectural. Almost spiritual. Seeing the beautiful formations confirms—for me—the existence of God. I understand why this place is a mecca for mystics."

"Wow. I'm thrilled you found it so meaningful."

Grant took her in his arms and kissed her. "I kept thinking about how blessed I am to have you and Zoe in my life. And Garth."

"Speaking of which...we need to go back to our room to get him. I didn't think he'd enjoy being jolted around on the jeep tour, but I'm sure he has serious cabin fever after the last two days hanging around our room. I want to take him shopping with us."

"Of course. Let's pick him up and head into town."

CHAPTER 6

"*D*o you girls want help with your new bedding?" Martha asked as she pulled into the driveway.

Zoe and Diedre looked at each other in the back seat and then said "no" in unison.

"I want to set up my room and surprise you," Diedre said.

"Me too," Zoe chimed in.

"You've got all afternoon," Sylvia observed. "That should give you plenty of time. We can have the big reveal right before dinner."

Both girls bobbed their heads in agreement.

Martha parked the car and she and Sylvia helped their granddaughters carry the bags of duvets, shams, sheets, and decorative pillows into the house.

"I've never picked out my own duvet before," Diedre said, trudging up the steps to the front door, an oversize shopping bag bumping against her thighs. The bag held two twin-size duvet sets strewn with a smattering of deep pink flowers against a light pink background, accented with spring green stems and leaves.

"I love flowers."

"They're fresh and modern," Sylvia said. "Pink is trending right now."

Martha unlocked the front door and set her bags on the floor inside the foyer. "Let's put everything down here so you can sort through them to find what belongs to each of your rooms."

"Great idea," Sylvia said. She dumped her bags beside Martha's and began unpacking them.

"Both of my duvet sets are in here," Diedre said. She hoisted the bag higher and headed off in the direction of her room.

"This is really sharp, Zoe," Sylvia said, holding up a clear plastic zippered bag containing a geometric print duvet in soft yellows and cream. "I may go back to see if they have this in a king size, for my room."

"Thanks. I don't like what other kids do," Zoe replied.

"You've got very sophisticated taste," Sylvia said. "That's something to be proud of."

Zoe's face erupted in a smile.

A faint "woof" emanated from the family room.

"I'd better release Sabrina from her crate and take her outside," Zoe said, heading to her beloved pet.

"Sounds good," Martha said. "I'm going to peel veggies and start a pot of soup for supper."

"I'll help you," Sylvia said. "Then I plan to put my feet up and read."

"I may take a nap," Martha said, stifling a yawn.

"That's an even better idea," Sylvia said.

Zoe found Sabrina wagging her tail in her crate and opened the door.

Sabrina stretched and got to her feet, following Zoe outside. After making quick work of her business, Sabrina trotted at Zoe's heels as she ferried her new bedding from the foyer to her room.

Martha and Sylvia were busy in the kitchen.

Sylvia directed the virtual assistant to play Broadway show tunes. "Is this okay with you?"

"Perfect," Martha said. "I could use a dose of upbeat music. This morning's shopping trip wore me out."

"Me too. What do you have in mind for supper?"

"Classic chicken noodle. Both girls love it. Does that sound all right?"

"Comfort food at its best," Sylvia said, picking up an onion from the vegetable basket and pulling celery and carrots from the refrigerator.

"I thought I'd make a big pot of it," Martha said, "so we can freeze some for Emily and Grant."

"I like the thought of that. I don't know how the two of them keep up with their busy schedules."

"They'll make adjustments and learn to cope. We did when our kids were young," Martha said, filling an enormous stockpot from the pot-filler above the stove.

"That's true."

"And they've got both of us to help."

The song "It's a Hard Knock Life" from *Annie* blared from the speakers and both women burst out laughing as they set to the task of making the soup.

Zoe carried her purchases to her room, pausing in the doorway of her stepsister's room. "Do you want to help each other make our beds and put stuff away?"

Diedre pursed her lips, considering her best friend's suggestion. "We can make our own beds—we know how. I thought it would be fun to surprise each other with our rooms when they're all done."

"Like we're doing with our grandmothers. That's cool. But if you need my help with anything, come get me."

Diedre nodded emphatically. "You too."

Each girl spent the rest of the afternoon behind the closed door of their room. They unzipped packaging, cut off tags, and unrolled tightly folded items. After being laundered, fitted sheets were wrangled into place, duvets were unfurled, and pillows plumped. Diedre arranged her collection of stuffed animals on the shelf Doug had hung across the length of the room above the beds, while Zoe placed books on hers.

Zoe finished positioning Sabrina's bed, blanket, and toy basket in the corner next to her bed and stood back to admire her handiwork. Satisfied with the results, she went to Diedre's room and knocked on the door. "Can I come in?" she called.

"Sure," Diedre replied and opened her door. "Are you all done?"

"Almost. I can't figure out how to put those sham things on my big pillows."

"That's tricky, but I got it. I'll come help you."

"Thanks," Zoe said.

Both girls walked into Zoe's room.

"This looks awesome, Zoe." Diedre turned in a circle in the middle of the room, taking it all in. "It looks like you." She walked to the bed and picked up the pillow insert, folding it in half and holding it against her body with her arm. "Hand me the sham and I'll show you."

Zoe watched as Diedre pulled the sham over the pillow, stuffing the insert into the corners and then zipping it shut.

"There," Diedre said, setting the sham into position. "Now you try it."

Zoe accomplished the task with ease. "Thanks! Do you need help with anything?"

"I'm rearranging my stuffed animals," Diedre said. "I'm grouping them by color."

"That'll look good."

"I also can't find my American Girl doll boxes," she added, turning away quickly.

"They're in the basement, remember? We put them there because you decided we're too old to have dolls in our rooms."

Diedre kept her back to Zoe. Her shoulders sagged and she didn't respond.

Zoe noticed the change in her stepsister. "I think that's stupid. You *should* have your dolls."

"You don't have any in your room," Diedre said and walked back to hers.

"That's because I never got into dolls, like you did." Zoe followed her. "I also never had an American Girl doll like your Samantha. She's really cool. I love her bed and furniture you had in your room at your old house." Zoe pointed to the corner near Diedre's bed. "You could put Samantha over there. That's where I put Sabrina's bed in my room."

Diedre faced Zoe. Her chin quivered.

Zoe raced to the doorway. "I know where they are," she said. "I'll be right back."

Diedre swiped across her eyes with the back of her hand.

"It's almost dinnertime," Zoe called back over her shoulder. "If you let me help you unpack your dolls, we can finish before we show our grandmas our rooms."

Happiness wrapped Diedre in its warm embrace and she tore after Zoe to reclaim her beloved dolls.

CHAPTER 7

I loved shops. And shopping. Except escalators. Those were still a little scary for me, but Emily knew how to direct me to get on and off so my paws wouldn't get caught. We didn't go on escalators very often. If there was an elevator, we preferred that.

There weren't escalators in Sedona. Just airy shops that smelled of incense, flowers, and food.

Grant drove us to a place with an odd name that called itself an arts and crafts village. Two-story pink adobe buildings with red tile roofs covered with vines snaked around a series of courtyards. Large terra-cotta pots containing small trees or vibrant red, blue, or yellow flowers were everywhere. I made note of these obstacles, so I could steer Emily away from them.

Staircases with tiled steps hugged the sides of buildings. Emily and I were experts at stairs.

The cobblestones under my paws were warm in the sun

but cool in the shady areas. Most of the shop doors were propped open and almost all of them had water bowls tucked against the outside of the building next to the door. I found that very thoughtful. Everyone wasn't considerate of dogs. I approved of this arts and crafts village.

"So, this is Tlaquepaque?" Emily said.

"The one and only."

"Mom loves to shop here."

"I can see why. It's beyond charming."

"I can hear a guitar in the distance."

"Someone's playing flamenco. They're good. I think it's coming from the next courtyard over. Would you like to go over there?"

"Maybe on our way out. After we finish shopping. Is there a fountain off to the left of us?"

"Yes. Maybe ten feet tall. Pigeons are perched along the edge, taking drinks. People are sitting on benches facing the fountain—relaxing or eating ice cream."

"Ice cream sounds like a good idea before we leave, too."

Grant rubbed her back. "I was thinking the same thing. Where do you want to start?"

"Is there a shop that sells home decor items? I thought that would be good for our moms."

"Looks like there's one directly across the plaza. Do you want to proceed with Garth on his leash and me as a sighted guide?"

"I'd rather work Garth. I'll have him follow you. Is that okay?"

"You bet. Ready?"

I felt Emily tighten her grip on my harness.

Grant began walking away from us and Emily commanded me to "Follow Grant."

We were soon weaving our way through a maze of glass shelves.

The shop owner approached us to tell us about her stock of hand-blown glass bowls, pitchers, and vases. She didn't say anything about me, but I could tell I made her nervous. I kept my tail in check—no wagging in this place.

"What do you think? Is there anything here that Sylvia or my mom would like?"

"I'm not too sure. It seems like they've both got all the fine glassware they need. I see a couple of vases that would be nice for the girls."

"That's interesting. They're getting old enough to enjoy nice things. I still have a Johnson Brothers china pitcher that my mom and dad brought back for me from a trip to Niagara Falls. I've always loved it."

"Then these might be perfect. They're small—only a little bigger than a bud vase. One is pink and lavender and the other is yellow and cream. Both are swirly patterns."

"Those are the colors they chose for their new rooms." Emily ran her hands over the curved sides of the vases. "The shapes feel well proportioned. The glass has ripples. I like that. These vases will be perfect." She nodded at Grant. "We can put up shelves in their rooms for knickknacks like these."

"Excellent." Grant picked up the vases, and we followed him to the register.

When we exited the shop, I swear I heard the proprietor sigh in relief.

"What about gifts for the others?"

Emily pulled up a directory of shops on her cell phone, and they listened to the screen reader. Her head came up at the mention of one that boasted fine imported woolen and silk scarves, shawls, and throws. "This sounds promising. It's January and San Francisco is so cold. You can always use another throw."

"Easy to pack to bring home, too," Grant said. "Let's look."

Emily and I again followed Grant through the shop. Emily rubbed fabric after fabric between her fingers. "This one," Emily finally said. "I adore the feel of this. So smooth and soft."

"You've got great taste. These are the most expensive items in the shop."

"How much?"

"It doesn't matter. I agree—these are the nicest."

"What colors do they have?"

Grant lifted the stack from the shelf. "There's a camel, a charcoal, an apple green, a burnt orange, a burgundy, and one in teal."

"I love teal, but I think your mother would like burgundy and my mom would want the orange. That leaves Stephanie. Is the green pretty?"

"Yes. They're all very nice."

"Let's give the green one to Stephanie. Sometimes—in very bright light—she can see colors. The main thing is that this feels so luxurious against the skin."

Grant pulled out the three throws Emily had selected, plus the teal one. We made our purchase and returned to the plaza.

"I heard the sales clerk give you the total," Emily said, her brows furrowed. "That's too much. She overcharged us. We need to go back."

"I bought the teal throw for you since you liked it so much."

Emily squealed with delight. "You spoil me, Grant."

"That's my goal. Now, let's find the ice cream store and listen to that wonderful guitarist before we go back to the hotel."

"It sounds to me like someone's now dancing the flamenco to the guitarist's accompaniment," Emily said. "That's really cool."

We found the ice cream shop, and I heard the words I was hoping for.

"They sell puppy cups," Grant said. "Peanut butter and vanilla. Garth's favorites."

I glanced up at him with appreciation. I loved that my new dad attended to my needs, just like Emily did.

CHAPTER 8

*S*tephanie Wolf sat rigidly in the waiting room chair, fidgeting with the white cane folded in her lap.

Dhruv reached over and put a reassuring hand on top of hers. "It's going to be all right. The doctor will find out why you're so sick and fatigued all the time. And fix it."

"What if I have to have an endoscopy or colonoscopy?" She crossed her legs at the knee.

"Those tests are safe and effective. The prep isn't much fun, but you'll get through it. I'll be with you every step of the way."

"You're not spending the evening in the bathroom with me!"

"No. That's true." He sighed, considering this. "We don't know what the doctor is going to recommend. Let's wait until we know."

Stephanie's foot jiggled.

A middle-aged woman holding an electronic tablet called Stephanie's name as she opened the door into the waiting room.

Dhruv rose, extended his elbow to Stephanie, and guided her to the exam room.

"You can leave your purse here, with your husband," the nurse said. "We'll go down the hall to get your height and weight, and the doctor would like a urine specimen."

Stephanie stood and extended her cane.

"Oh...I didn't realize," the woman sputtered. "Would you like your husband to go with you?"

"I'm good with my cane," Stephanie said. "Please keep talking to me to give directions."

"Sure," the nurse said, and they set off. When they returned to the exam room after recording Stephanie's height and weight and collecting the specimen, the nurse placed a folded rectangle of fabric on the exam table. "Please take off your clothing from the waist down. There are hooks for your slacks on the back of the door and there's a drape on the exam table to your left. The doctor will be in to see you shortly." She left the room, closing the door behind her.

Stephanie did as instructed and Dhruv hung her clothes on the hooks. She positioned herself on the exam table.

Dhruv sat on a molded plastic chair against the wall.

They waited.

"What's taking him so long?" Stephanie rubbed the tops of her thighs through the thin cloth drape. "It's freezing in here."

"It's chilly, but I think it's mostly your nerves." He took off his jacket and laid it over her knees. "Does this help?"

Stephanie nodded.

Dhruv rested a hip against the exam table and circled Stephanie with his arms. "It's all going to be fine," he murmured as he rested his chin on the top of her head.

Stephanie leaned into his solid embrace.

A sharp knock on the door drew them apart.

The nurse stood in the doorway. "I'm sorry for the wait," she said, looking from Stephanie to Dhruv. She narrowed her eyes. "The doctor would like to see both of you in his office."

Stephanie lowered her feet to the floor and clutched the drape firmly with one hand. She took Dhruv's elbow, and they started for the door.

"You can get dressed first," the nurse said curtly. "He's not doing an exam. I'll wait outside the door." She shut it without another word.

Stephanie's chin quivered. "This can't be good," she said in a shaky voice. "I must have cancer. The blood test I took last week must show it."

Dhruv handed his wife her clothes. "Don't be silly. You have no reason to think you have cancer."

Stephanie stepped into her panties and slacks. "Then what could it be?" She zipped her slacks and swung her right foot in front of her, searching for her shoes.

Dhruv assisted her as the nurse knocked on the door again. "Ready?" she called through the closed door.

Dhruv gave Stephanie a quick hug. "We'll know soon enough," he said, then opened the door.

He and Stephanie followed the nurse to a cluttered office at the end of the hall. Framed anatomical drawings of the human gastrointestinal tract were scattered across the walls. A bookcase stood in the corner, stuffed full of textbooks and medical journals. An oversize desk held a computer and dual monitors, and was littered with logoed merchandise from pharmaceutical manufacturers.

Dhruv directed Stephanie to one of the two chairs in front of the desk.

"The doctor is finishing with another patient and will be right in," the nurse said. She stood in the doorway, frowning at them, then stepped away.

Stephanie and Dhruv settled in once more to wait.

"She's not very friendly, is she?" Stephanie said.

"Who?"

"That nurse. She's all business."

"Oh." Dhruv rubbed his hands together. "I didn't notice."

"What's it like?" Stephanie asked. "His office."

"I dunno. Like any other doctor's office. Full to the brim with stuff."

"Can you see a file with my name on it? Like on the desk? Or computer?"

"I'm not going to snoop, if that's what you're hinting at. I know it's hard to…"

Heavy footsteps sounded in the hall, crossing the distance to them rapidly.

"Dr. Mills," the man said, bounding into the room. He shook both of their hands with great enthusiasm. "I'm sorry we kept you waiting so long, but I wanted to be sure."

Dhruv reached over to hold Stephanie's hand.

"I think this may be one of the best days of my professional career. I've never had this happen before."

Dhruv and Stephanie stared at the doctor with perplexed expressions.

"I'm afraid I'm not the right doctor to treat you," he continued. "I'm going to have to refer you to another specialist." He stifled a chuckle.

The young couple leaned forward in their chairs.

"I'm afraid you'll have to see an obstetrician," the doctor said.

Dhruv and Stephanie froze in place.

"You're pregnant, Stephanie. Your gastric distress is morning sickness. Being extra tired is part of the process, too. That's as far as my expertise takes me. Congratulations."

A sob escaped Stephanie's lips.

Dhruv swept her into his arms.

"I gather this is unexpected?"

Dhruv nodded. "We didn't think we would ever..." his voice broke.

"Why don't I give the two of you some privacy to process this? We'll send you home with a list of obstetricians. I suggest you see a doctor as soon as possible for prenatal vitamins and recommended tests."

"Thank you," Stephanie spluttered. "You're sure? There can't be a mistake?"

"I'm positive. I take it you're pleased."

A fresh wave of tears poured from Stephanie. "We are," she choked out the words.

The doctor stepped to the doorway. "Take as much time as you need here. There's no rush for you to leave. My nurse will give you those names on your way out." He paused to admire the couple who were overwhelmed by the unexpected—but joyful—news. "Congratulations, again." He closed the door behind him.

Stephanie and Dhruv clung to each other.

"I've always wanted to be a mother," she finally said in a whisper.

"You'll be the world's best," Dhruv replied, pulling back and brushing her damp hair off her face.

"Are you worried about me being blind with our child?" She held her breath as soon as the words were out.

"Of course I'm not. You'll do the same things everyone else does, but in different ways. Just like you do now." He planted a kiss on her palm. "Are you worried about me being a father? I'm...well...you know me. I get hyper-focused on things and don't read social cues well."

"You are the most loving, thoughtful man on the planet, Dhruv. The way you support and care for me is incredible. You'll be a fabulous father."

"You don't wish you'd married someone else? So they could be the father of your child?"

Stephanie took his face in both of her hands. "You listen to me. You are everything a woman could ever dream of in a husband and father. I've never been more thankful for anything in my life than to be your wife and having your baby."

They kissed deeply—then Stephanie stood. "Let's get out of here."

Dhruv gave her his elbow again. "We need to make an appointment with an obstetrician."

"And we've got people to tell. Our parents will be thrilled. They should hear it first."

"Agreed. Then Emily and Grant," Dhruv said.

"Definitely. I'd love to tell them in person. They're coming home from Sedona this afternoon. Let's see if they can drop by our apartment. It's on their way home from the airport."

They stopped at the reception desk and asked for the promised list of doctors on their way out.

The receptionist stepped away from her post to find the nurse. She intercepted her in the hallway.

The nurse handed the receptionist a sheet of paper and leaned in to whisper in her ear, gesturing to the folded cane that Stephanie held in one hand.

The receptionist's eyebrows shot up and she nodded, her mouth forming an "O."

The nurse shook her head and stalked away.

The receptionist returned to the desk and handed Dhruv the list of obstetricians without making a comment.

"Thank you," Dhruv called to the retreating back of the nurse, too overcome with happiness to notice the disapproving shake of the nurse's head.

CHAPTER 9

I was ecstatic as we started our descent. My ears felt funny, so I knew we were on our way to the ground.

Emily and Grant switched their phones off of airplane mode as soon as we landed.

"I'll wait until we deplane to have my screen reader read my messages to me. What've you got?" Emily asked.

"There's one from Diedre asking us not to come home until they text us," Grant said.

"What's that all about?"

"I've got a text from my mom," he said, opening Sylvia's message. "She says the girls are working hard on a surprise for us and they should be done by three. She asks if we can run an errand on the way home."

"Huh," Emily replied. "That sounds terribly sweet. I'm itching to get home and unpack before we jump back into the swing of things, but we shouldn't mess up their surprise for us."

The plane bounced to a halt at the gate and the cabin lights flashed on.

"I sense Garth has to go," Emily said.

She was always in tune with my every need.

"Can you step into the aisle to let me out so we can get off this plane fast?"

Grant flung himself out of his seat and removed their carry-ons from the overhead bins with lightning speed. "Good thing we're near the front of the plane." He leaned back and let Emily and me step into the aisle. "I'll manage our luggage. As soon as the line starts to move, head for the door and I'll be right behind you."

We quickly exited the plane.

Emily pulled out her phone and navigated to the app for the airport. She raced through the selections at top speed. "There's a pet relief area two gates from here," she said to Grant as he joined them.

She shouldn't have bothered to search for it. My nose told me where to go. We set off. I moved at a quick pace through the crowded terminal.

I attended to my business while Emily listened to similar messages from Zoe and Martha. Her final two text messages were from Stephanie and Dhruv. They each asked if she and Grant could stop by their apartment on their way home from the airport. Neither one specified why they requested an in-person visit. They both said it was important.

"I guess that settles what we're going to do before

heading home," Grant said. "Do you think it might have something to do with your work?"

Grant cleaned up after me. I wagged my tail vigorously to thank him, but he didn't notice. He and Emily were engrossed in their conversation.

"I don't think so. Stephanie wouldn't have texted about that. She saw a gastroenterologist today. Dhruv was going to go with her and work the rest of the day from home. It must be about that."

"I hope everything's all right."

"Me too."

We continued the long walk to the parking garage.

"I'll respond that we'll be there in thirty minutes," Emily said. She dictated the text.

We were soon zooming along the freeway, and I might have dozed off in the back seat. I knew where we were the minute Grant opened the rear passenger side door to let me out. I could smell my buddies Sugar and Rocco—and my best friend (next to Sabrina)—Biscuit. We were at Stephanie and Dhruv's apartment, in the building where Emily and I lived before we moved to the big house with Grant. I was on top of things.

Emily grasped my harness. I knew I was working and restrained myself from bounding up the steps and into the building to see my friends. I'd missed them since we'd moved.

Dhruv answered the door as soon as we knocked, as if he'd been watching for us to arrive.

Stephanie hovered behind him. "How was your trip?"

"Perfect," Emily said. "Sedona is beautiful. Exactly what we needed. I'll tell you more later."

We entered the apartment. Emily removed my harness and told me it was okay to go play.

The other three dogs and I all politely sniffed each before Sugar, Biscuit, and I thrashed across the floor, wrestling. Tiny Rocco looked on from a safe distance.

"I remember you went to a specialist this morning." Emily got straight to the point. "Your messages concerned us. Is everything okay?"

"Em?" Stephanie's voice overflowed with excitement.

Emily moved toward her friend until they could touch each other.

Stephanie took Emily's hands in hers. "I'm not sick, Em. *I'm pregnant.*"

"Stephanie!" Emily squealed in delight and pulled her friend into a tight hug. "That's the most incredible news. It explains all your symptoms. I can't believe we didn't think of this."

"They've been telling me since I was in my early twenties that I'd never get pregnant."

"Famous last words. How are you feeling?"

"Still nauseated and unbelievably tired. But now I'm thankful for it."

Emily released Stephanie and held out a hand. "Dhruv," she said.

He stepped toward her.

"Group hug," Emily said, throwing her arms around both her friends. "I'm beyond thrilled for you."

"Thank you," Dhruv murmured.

Grant clapped Dhruv on the back. "Congratulations, man. This is awesome news." He reached for Stephanie and bent to kiss her cheek. "We should have known you were pregnant. You've been glowing for weeks."

"How far along are you? Do you know?"

"We've got an appointment with an obstetrician at the end of this week," Stephanie said. "We'll get our due date then."

"Any ideas…when?" Emily pressed the point.

"My best guess is that we got pregnant right after our wedding." Stephanie's cheeks colored.

"Then we're looking at a June baby." Emily bit her lower lip. "That means a March or April baby shower. The girls will be beyond thrilled."

Stephanie chuckled. "I think we've got time for all that."

"What did your parents say?" Emily asked.

"I thought my mother was going to faint." Stephanie grinned. "She and Dad are so eager to become grandparents. It's a shock for them, too. Mom's called at least every half hour since we told them. She's already online, shopping for baby stuff. She'll completely outfit this child by the end of the day unless my dad can talk some sense into her."

Emily laughed. "Don't you dare rain on her parade. She deserves to celebrate this joyous news."

"How about your family, Dhruv?"

"My mom said she suspected it when they visited us at the Hotel del Coronado. She's been praying for it."

"I love hearing this," Emily said.

"My dad is a bit more reserved," Dhruv said.

The temperature in the room seemed to drop. Biscuit

quit wrestling with Sugar and me and went to stand next to Stephanie.

"What do you mean, Dhruv?" Emily asked in a quiet voice.

"He began to ask how we would manage a baby," Dhruv said. "I'm not sure whether he was questioning my ability to be a parent or Stephanie's. My mother took over the phone and put an end to that discussion."

The four friends stood quietly together.

"It's easy to misread things in emotional situations like these," Grant said. "Best not to worry until you know you have something to worry about."

Dhruv put his arm around Stephanie's waist and pulled his shoulders back. "We love our baby. He or she will have the best of us and everything that they need."

Sugar, Rocco, and I trotted over to our people. Something big was happening, and we needed to be part of it.

"We're here to help and support you in any way you need," Emily said. "I can't imagine anyone being better parents than the two of you."

"Would you like to have something to drink?" Stephanie took a step back. "Where are my manners?"

Grant checked his watch. "We have half an hour before we can head home."

Stephanie and Biscuit led the way to the living room.

Dhruv peeled off toward the kitchen and I soon heard the crinkly sound I loved best. He'd opened a bag of Crunchy Cheetos. I settled down next to Biscuit, knowing I'd soon taste my favorite snack.

CHAPTER 10

Grant pulled into the driveway and pressed the garage door opener.

"Do you think they cleared out the garage enough to let us park the car inside?" Emily asked.

"Mom texted me this morning to tell me they did," Grant replied. He let out a low whistle. "I don't believe it. All the boxes are gone and there's plenty of room for our car. It looks like they've even swept the floor."

"That's so nice. I bet they got everything done."

Grant pulled into the garage.

"I feel guilty about leaving our moms to finish unpacking, but I'm relieved."

"I don't think they minded. All the heavy stuff had been taken care of. I know my mom loves any sort of organizing project."

"Mine too," Emily chuckled. "They're both so good at it, too."

"We'd better get upstairs," Grant said. "I'll bring our bags in later. Diedre texted me twice to tell me they're ready for us."

"They must be eager to show us their rooms." Emily got out of the car and opened the rear door for Garth. "We should at least bring in the suitcase with our gifts for everyone."

"Good call. I'll get it."

Emily put Garth into his working harness and commanded him to take her to the door.

Sabrina's muffled woof on the other side of the door in from the garage announced their arrival.

Grant, Emily, and Garth stepped into the hallway that led past the laundry room and into the living area.

Emily took off Garth's harness and he and Sabrina raced ahead of them.

Diedre and Zoe were waiting in the family room and threw their arms around one parent and then the other.

"Did you miss us?" Zoe asked.

"And how," Emily replied, rubbing the back of the girl who had become her ward after the untimely death of Zoe's grandmother. She pulled the girl into a second hug, remembering how Zoe's inquisitiveness and tenacity had encouraged her when she had first lost her sight.

"But you had fun?" Diedre asked, circling Grant with her arms.

"We did," Grant said. "Sedona is beautiful and there's lots of fun things to do. We thought we'd go there for a family vacation. You'll both love it."

Zoe whipped her head around to look at Diedre.

Diedre nodded her agreement.

"That'd be cool," Zoe said.

"Where are Martha and Sylvia?" Emily asked.

"In the kitchen. They're making us an early dinner so we can all eat, and they can get out of our hair," Diedre said.

"They're never in our hair," Grant protested.

"That's what grandma said, not me," Diedre replied defensively. "We told them they can stay forever."

"We like it when they're here," Zoe added.

"We do, too," Emily said. "I'll bet they're eager to get home and back to their own routines though. They're both busy ladies, you know." She made her way to the doorway to the kitchen. "Hey, guys. We're home. How did it go?"

"Beautifully," Martha said, sliding a pan of chicken thighs into the oven.

"Those girls are so well-behaved," Sylvia said. "They're no trouble at all."

"I'm glad to hear it. I can't tell you how grateful Grant and I are to both of you."

Sylvia pulled a large salad bowl from a cabinet under the kitchen island. "Did you have a good time?"

"Great time," Grant said, joining Emily. "This trip was exactly what the doctor ordered."

"I can't wait to hear all about it." Martha filled a pot with water and set it on the stove.

"We'll tell you everything over dinner," Grant said. "Right now, there are two girls who are eager to show us their rooms. I'm here to tear Emily away from you."

"You go," Martha said. "They've been excited about that— and their surprise—all day. I imagine they're about to burst."

"We've got a surprise to share with you at dinner, too," Emily said as she and Grant rejoined the girls.

"We'll do our rooms one at a time," Zoe said. "And we're each going to verbally describe our room to you, Emily."

"We've practiced it with each other—to make sure we don't leave anything out," Diedre added.

Emily blinked rapidly. "That's perfect, because I want to know every detail. I remember how important my room was to me at your ages." Her voice was husky.

"My room is first," Zoe said. "You had it painted the soft yellow of morning sunshine."

"What a good descriptor," Emily praised.

"Morning sunshine is the name on the paint can, but I added the word 'soft,'" Zoe said, pride evident in her voice. "My sheets are the same solid yellow and my duvet cover has a cream background with white curvy lines that Sylvia said are flourishes. It has yellow circles of different sizes and yellow triangles all over it, too."

"Geometric shapes sound like you," Emily said.

"Sylvia said it's very sophisticated, and she's going to look for a set in king size."

Emily could hear Zoe's confidence growing as she continued to describe her room.

"I have a matching pillow sham on each bed, plus a round yellow decorative pillow on my guest bed and a triangle one on mine."

Zoe took Emily by the hand and led her to the closet. She opened the door and put Emily's hand on a blouse. "I hung all my clothes up real neat. You can feel them."

Emily ran her hand lightly along the row of hangers.

"You certainly did."

"I'm gonna keep them that way, too," the girl said with conviction. "Diedre's room is always clean. I like that."

Emily grinned at Zoe.

"Doug put up a long shelf close to the ceiling over the beds in each of our rooms. I put my books there. Sabrina's bed and toys are in the corner by my bed. My desk is on the wall by the closet and my school backpack is on top of the desk, ready for tomorrow."

"It all looks great, Zoe," Grant said. "You've done a terrific job."

"Now Diedre's room," Zoe said. "You're going to love it."

Diedre took over as tour guide and perfectly described her pretty-in-pink room.

Emily was especially interested in Diedre's doll corner.

Diedre gave Emily her Samantha doll to hold and described every detail about it, including its clothes, furniture, and accessories.

Emily cradled Samantha gently. "I would have loved having her when I was a kid. I'm so glad you showed me all this."

Diedre paused, then said, "Zoe told me to unpack her. I thought it might be too babyish to have all this doll stuff in my room."

"Never! No way," Emily cried.

"That's what I said," Zoe chimed in.

"Zoe knew where the boxes were in the basement. We brought them up here, and she helped me unpack them."

Grant put his arms around both girls' shoulders. "I love

hearing this," he said. "That's what families—and friends—do. They support each other."

"I'm so proud of you," Emily said. "Mom and Sylvia told us you were extremely helpful the whole time we were gone, too."

"I understand you have another surprise for us?" Grant asked.

Zoe tore back to her room and returned with her tablet. "We made a family calendar," she said proudly.

Diedre added, "We heard our grandmas talking about how busy our family is—how they can't keep track of us. We decided we could help with that."

"We've got rows for each day of the week, separated into thirty-minute sections, and each of us has our own column. Including Garth and Sabrina, since they have to go to the vet sometimes. We've put in our school times for next week already. All four of us can update it. And Emily's screen reader can read it to her." Zoe scrolled through the screen, holding it out to Grant.

"That's fantastic," Grant said. "The two of you did all this by yourselves?"

Zoe hesitated. "We called Rhonda twice for help. She told us to keep her number after Dhruv and Stephanie's wedding and call her if we ever needed her."

"She was super nice and kept saying she loved talking to us," Diedre said.

"She's a peach," Emily said. "I'll thank her when I see her tomorrow at work. That calendar is exactly what this family needs. I'll update it with my schedule after dinner."

"Speaking of which," Grant said, "something smells really great."

"I'm starved," Zoe said. "Let's go see if it's time to set the table."

They exited Diedre's room and headed toward the kitchen.

"We've got a wonderful surprise to share with all of you, too," Emily said. "Plus, we brought all of you gifts from our trip."

Both girls stopped walking.

"Dinner's about ready," Martha called from the kitchen.

"We'll share our surprise over dinner and give you your gifts during dessert," Grant said.

"How do you know there's dessert?" Emily asked.

Grant chuckled. "With our mothers in charge of the meal? How could there not be dessert?"

"Good point," Emily agreed as they stepped into the kitchen.

CHAPTER 11

I leaned back in my best downward dog pose and stretched, splaying the toes of my front paws and digging them into the plush bath rug. The bubbles from the tub tickled my nose and I sneezed twice in rapid succession.

"Gesundheit," Emily said.

I wagged my tail and sneezed again. Whatever she'd poured into that water didn't agree with me. I was off duty, so I decided to join Grant. He was probably in the family room. He liked watching programs where men and some-times women ran up and down a floor, bouncing and throwing a ball that looked too big for my mouth. There was always a lot of whistle-blowing which bothered my ears, but it would be better than all this sneezing.

We'd had a busy day. After all the excitement at Dhruv's, we'd come home to an early dinner with the moms. Dessert had been interesting. Everyone had become suddenly ecsta-tic. They'd been talking over each other, and I noted the occasional mention of Dhruv and Stephanie. Maybe it had something to do with our earlier visit to their apartment.

After that, the moms left and the girls got ready for bed. They'd each gone to sleep in their own room, for the first time since we'd moved in together. Emily had gotten into the tub for a "long, restorative soak," as she'd told Grant.

I padded past the girls' rooms. Both doors were slightly ajar. I could hear their breathing and knew neither of them was asleep.

I paused to listen. Zoe's sheets rustled as she turned over in bed. Diedre's breath came in fits and starts. I detected a slight moan.

Was she crying? I needed to find out.

I pushed Diedre's door open with my nose and quietly entered her room. I walked to the side of her bed.

She was definitely crying.

I rested my muzzle on her bed.

She fished a hand out from under her covers and patted the top of my head.

I licked her hand, then moved on to her damp cheeks, mopping up her salty tears.

"Oh, Garth," she said, a small chuckle slicing through her tears.

I wagged my tail, and it thumped against the bed.

Before I knew it, Sabrina was racing into the room and had launched herself onto Diedre's bed.

Diedre pushed herself into a sitting position and greeted the effervescent Sabrina.

Zoe soon stood in the doorway. "Can I come in?"

"Sure."

"I can't sleep," Zoe said

"Neither can I. I'm too nervous about tomorrow."

"Me too. I wasn't scared when I transferred schools after moving in with Emily, but this time is different."

"Maybe it's because we're older now."

"I know. Middle school is next year."

"We'll make plenty of friends," Diedre said.

"You'll make plenty of friends," Zoe replied. "Everyone likes you. You're a popular kid."

"They like you, too," Diedre said.

Zoe climbed onto the other twin bed in the room.

Sabrina abandoned her perch and hopped onto the bed with Zoe.

"I'm a brainiac," Zoe said. "We both know this. The other advanced kids like me, but most of the class doesn't want anything to do with me."

"They're jealous, that's all," Diedre said. "And at least you know you'll have a group to fit into. I was popular at our old school, but what if nobody at this one likes me? Your brainiac friends don't want anything to do with me, either. I could end up with no friends."

"That won't happen," Zoe said. "Besides—you always have me. We're going to be friends—best friends—our whole lives."

"That's true. Makes me feel better." She snuffled and dried her eyes on a corner of her sheet.

"Can we sleep here tonight? Sabrina's not ready to sleep alone in our room."

"Yep. I don't want to be alone, either."

Zoe pulled back the duvet and slipped her feet under the

covers. She arranged the duvet on top of herself.

Sabrina circled three times, then curled into a ball against the curve of Zoe's small body.

"That's so exciting about Stephanie and Dhruv," Zoe said.

"Emily said we'll give them a baby shower this spring. I'm happy about that."

"Me too."

"We should start planning right away," Diedre said.

"I already have," Zoe said. "I went online before I got into bed."

"We've got plenty of time to order decorations. Stephanie hasn't even picked out her colors yet."

"I was looking at baby products for the visually impaired," Zoe said. "There's a ton of accessible stuff—from baby carriers to lightweight strollers and car seats, and braille marked medicine droppers."

"That's great!"

"I figure we can help Stephanie fill out her registry with the things she wants."

Diedre propped herself on one elbow. "That's so helpful. You know what, Zoe? You're even nicer than you are smart."

I couldn't understand the words they were saying to each other, but I felt the tone in the room change. We'd gone from fear and sadness when I'd walked in, to happiness and appreciation.

Diedre planted a kiss on the top of my head, then yawned and burrowed into her pillow. "I'm pooped."

"We'd better get to sleep," Zoe said. "First day at a new school is a big deal."

"I'm glad we're going in together, even though we're not in the same homeroom."

"Same here. Goodnight, Diedre."

"Nite, Zoe."

My work here was done. I turned and padded out of the room.

I found Grant in the family room. The game was on the television, as expected, but he wasn't watching it. Grant was sprawled on the leather sofa, sound asleep. His laptop sat open on the floor next to him and a sheaf of papers lay on his chest, raising and falling with his rhythmic breathing. An annoying buzzer sounded from the television.

Grant didn't need me. I continued on, into the kitchen, and found my bed in the far corner. I had four beds in this house and this one was my favorite. You couldn't beat a kitchen for smells.

I curled up. Emily would wake me when it was time to go to bed with her. I was soon snoozing the evening away.

CHAPTER 12

*G*rant pulled into the school parking lot twenty minutes before the first bell. The lot was almost full, but they found a spot in the last row. On either side of them, students with backpacks and parents were getting out of cars. "Looks like we're not the only ones arriving early on the first day of winter semester," Grant said.

"Are you walking us to our rooms?" Diedre asked from the back seat.

"We sure are," Emily said. "And we'll keep doing that until you're comfortable being dropped off."

"I remember how to get to our homerooms," Zoe said. "You don't have to."

Grant opened his car door. "We want to—at least this once."

Zoe and Diedre climbed out of the backseat, shouldering their backpacks.

Emily got out and put Garth in his harness.

"Do you want to wait here?" Grant asked.

"No way. I'm going to teach Garth to find their rooms. We'll follow you."

They set off, and their new homeroom teachers welcomed both girls. The fourth-grade wing contained eight classrooms aligned along a hallway, with four pairs across from each other.

Emily read the braille display at the entrance to each of their homerooms with her fingertips. She named each room for Garth as either Zoe's homeroom or Diedre's homeroom and gave him a treat. She repeated the naming and treating process two additional times.

They said a quick goodbye to each girl and set out for the car.

"No hugs or anything," Grant grumbled.

"They're getting too old for PDAs," Emily replied.

"Huh?"

"Public displays of affections. By the time I was in fifth grade, I hardly acknowledged my mother in public."

He groaned. "I'm not looking forward to that."

"I'm not either, but it's part of the growing-up process."

"I hope that stage doesn't last long."

"Are you kidding? They'll go from tweens to teenagers. It's going to get worse before it gets better."

"I envy Stephanie and Dhruv."

"Who knows? Maybe we got pregnant this weekend."

"I'm ready for a baby whenever it happens," Grant replied.

They emerged from the fourth-grade wing onto the busy schoolyard.

A group of younger boys approached them.

"Hey—look at that dog!" said a boy.

"Let's pet him," said another.

The tallest boy in the group stepped forward and put his arms out to stop them. "He's got a harness on." He looked at his friends. "See it?"

The boys behind him nodded.

"That means he's working. He's a service dog." He addressed Emily. "Is that right?"

"It sure is. I'm happy you know that. I'm blind and Garth is helping me right now. He's friendly and loves to play when he's not working, but we can't disturb him right now."

"Can you bring him back when he can play?" said the first boy.

"I'd love to do that," Emily said. "What grade are you in?"

"Second," replied the boy.

"I'll contact the school to see if we can visit the second-grade classes," Emily said.

"Cool," said the boys and continued on their way.

"You're a celebrity here already," Grant said as they proceeded to their car.

"I'm not," Emily said, "but Garth is one everywhere he goes."

"Speaking of Garth—will he remember where the girls' homerooms are based on that one lesson?"

"Maybe. We'll see. I trained him to find the break room at work, plus Rhonda and Dhruv's offices in one session."

"Garth," Grant said, "your mother's right. You are the smartest boy in the world."

"Both of their teachers seem nice," Emily said. "I'm looking forward to parent-teacher conferences so we can get to know them."

"This school is highly rated," Grant said. "The girls should do well here."

Grant opened the rear door for Garth, and he and Emily slid into their seats.

"I wonder if Dhruv will have shared his good news with everyone by the time you drop us at the office?"

"I'll bet he has," Grant said. "He was so excited yesterday."

"I'm thrilled for them."

"I detect a note of hesitation," Grant said, glancing over at her as they drove away from the school.

"I sometimes think you can read my mind. I'm beyond thrilled for them—of course. Stephanie thought she couldn't get pregnant and now she's having a baby. That's the stuff of Hollywood movies. I worry that having a newborn will draw some of Dhruv's focus away from the job."

"That doesn't sound like you. It's a bit..." he paused, selecting his words carefully.

"Selfish." Emily completed his sentence. "I know. I agree. It's only because I just took on the whole cybersecurity tech team from Denver and promoted Dhruv to help me manage the new workload and employees. I was counting on his over-the-top work ethic to see me through this transition."

"From what you've told me, Dhruv, working at half capacity, is still far more productive than anyone else's full-time output."

"True. I'm being completely selfish, worrying about how this pregnancy might affect me. I'm ashamed of myself for even thinking this. I need to refocus on being thrilled for them. Work will be fine."

"Maybe someone from the Denver team will be a super-star. You've said great things about the woman you promoted to team lead in the Denver office and who now reports to you."

Emily shifted in her seat to face Grant. "Kari's terrific. This might give her a chance to shine. Thanks for pointing that out. I feel better now."

Grant reached across the console and squeezed her hand.

Emily asked, "What's on your agenda for today?"

"I'll complete and submit the firm's bid for that private residential complex south of Los Angeles."

"The one on twenty acres with a 20,000-square-foot main house, three pools, two guest cottages that are twice the size of the average home, tennis courts, and a helipad? For that East Coast billionaire who won't let you reveal his name to anyone?"

"The same. This has been an exciting project to work on, but I'm not sure I want to win the bid."

"I can understand that. This client sounds extremely high-maintenance." She furrowed her brow. "Why are you going after the business in the first place?"

"One of my professors recommended me highly. The client reached out to us and only two other firms. I appreciate the referral and don't want to seem ungrateful to my professors."

"Makes sense. You're in a tricky situation."

66

"I just hope we aren't selected. We're bidding everything at top dollar."

"Doesn't sound like this client is price conscious."

"I'll be in front of your building in under a minute," Grant said, slowing the car.

Emily reached for her purse at her feet. "I hope you don't win the bid," she said and chuckled. "That's an odd thing to say to my husband."

"It's exactly what I wanted to hear." Grant stopped at the curb and leaned over to kiss Emily. "Have a good day. See you tonight."

Emily and Garth got out of the car. "Go mess up that proposal," she said before she and Garth headed into her office.

CHAPTER 13

$\mathscr{D}$hruv refilled his coffee cup for the third time that morning and headed back to his office. He intercepted his coworker, Rhonda, coming out of Emily's office.

"Are you looking for Em?" he asked.

"No. I was returning the scissors I borrowed last week. She'll be in late this morning—she and Grant are dropping the girls off at their new school."

"She said she'll be here by 9:30," Dhruv said.

"Can I walk with you back to your office?" Rhonda fell into step next to him. "I wanted to ask how things went at the doctor yesterday. With Stephanie? I don't know her well, but since I officiated at your wedding, I feel very connected to the two of you."

"Wait until you hear." He took three large strides into his office and set the brimming cup onto his desk with such abandon that coffee sloshed over the sides.

Rhonda followed him into his office.

He turned to face his coworker. Happiness exuded from every pore.

Rhonda reflexively reached out a hand to touch his elbow. "You're positively glowing, Dhruv. This must be good news."

"The best. A miracle, actually." He sucked in a deep breath.

Rhonda nodded encouragingly.

"We're having a baby!"

Rhonda cocked her head to one side.

"Stephanie's pregnant."

"Gosh..." Rhonda cleared her throat. "That's...that's wonderful news. Congratulations."

Dhruv grinned and bounced on his toes.

Rhonda drew him into a hug. "Really...that's spectacular news." She stepped back. "I thought...I didn't know you wanted kids."

"That's the miraculous thing. Stephanie's been told she couldn't have children since she was in her twenties. We accepted we wouldn't have a family. But now we will."

"Are you excited about it?"

He bobbed his head vigorously. "Stephanie will be the most remarkable mother. You should see her in her third-grade class. All of her students adore her."

"I can imagine. You're going to be a terrific parent, too, Dhruv."

"You think so?" He stopped bouncing. "I worry that I won't know what to do. Especially with a baby."

"Not many of us know what to do with a baby. When we took our first child home from the hospital, I wondered why they weren't sending a pediatrician home with us. It's natural to feel this way."

"I'm serious. I've never even held a baby." He stifled a yawn. "I stayed up really late reading on the internet about the care of infants."

Rhonda chuckled. "You can take parenting classes, but you'll mostly figure out what to do as you're doing it. Parenting is on-the-job training."

"I hope that's true."

"You've got all the right instincts, Dhruv. You're great with kids—very intuitive."

"Why in the world do you say that?"

"You spent lots of time with my boys at the company picnics over the years. They all adore you." She smiled, reliving the memories. "They're grown men now, with families of their own, but they still talk about you. That sort of lasting memory is unusual, Dhruv. You connected with them, and you'll do the same with your child."

A crimson flush rose from Dhruv's collar to his hairline. "I'd forgotten all about that. Your sons are wonderful. We had a ton of fun at those picnics. I always looked forward to seeing them."

"It's going to be fine." She patted his elbow. "How's Stephanie feeling? I guess all that gastric distress was morning sickness."

"She still feels queasy in the mornings, but now that we know nothing's wrong with her, it's easier for her to bear."

"It may go away at the end of the first trimester. Do you know how far along you are?"

"That's what we're hoping. And we're not sure. We see

the obstetrician on Friday afternoon. She'll give us a due date."

"That's exciting! Have you told the others?"

"We told Emily and Grant yesterday, but decided we'd wait to tell our coworkers until we have a due date."

"Then mum's the word. Your secret is safe with me."

"Thanks, Rhonda. For helping me feel I can do this."

Rhonda swallowed hard and brought him into her for another hug. "You can do anything you put your mind to, Dhruv. I'm behind you, one hundred percent."

"Hi, RHONDA." Emily turned her face to the door of her office.

"How did you know it was me, hovering in your doorway?"

"I know the cadence of your walk." Emily relaxed against the back of her chair. "I can identify all of my team members, plus the receptionist and a few others, by their footsteps. It's like a signature."

"You never cease to amaze me, Em."

"What's up? I'm sorry I haven't left my desk to check in with each of you. I was only out for two days, but I didn't touch my email while I was gone and it's out of control."

"I'm proud of you for unplugging," Rhonda said. "All of this work stuff can wait. Did you two have a nice time?"

"The best. Let's go to lunch next week and I'll fill you in on all the details. I think you and your hubby would love a long weekend at the resort we stayed at."

"We're overdue for a getaway. I'd like to hear about it."

Emily moved her hand back toward her keyboard. "Anything else you need? I'm still digging out."

"We can talk about this later." Rhonda remained in the doorway.

"Something's bothering you. I can tell. What's up?"

Rhonda stepped into the office and closed the door, to help keep the news a secret. "Dhruv told me he and Stephanie are pregnant. He said that you know."

"Yeah. Stephanie's one of my best friends. Grant and I stopped at their place on our way home from the airport yesterday and they told us. Isn't that wonderful? A miracle, really, since they didn't think Stephanie could get pregnant."

"Dhruv called it that, too."

"You don't sound excited about it." Emily straightened in her chair.

"It's just that...Oh, Em." She stood in front of Emily's desk, wringing her hands.

"What?"

"Can Stephanie take care of a newborn? Forgive me for asking. I hate even thinking this. Will the baby be safe with Stephanie? I know she'll want to be a good mother, but..."

Emily cut her off. "Of course she can care for the baby. I took care of Gina's newborn the night he came home from the hospital. In Gina's new house, which was unfamiliar to me. I changed a diaper and gave a baby a bottle for the first time in my life that night."

"That's right. I don't know why I'm even asking. I feel terrible for mentioning this to you." Rhonda fidgeted with a button on her sleeve. "You cope with a million things around here—every day. To tell you the truth, I sometimes forget you're blind."

"I love hearing that," Emily said. "I can do everything in my job that I used to do. I just do it in a different way."

"You must think I'm terrible for bringing this up—"

"Not at all." Emily interrupted Rhonda again. "You simply didn't know. So you asked. I'm sure everyone else will wonder about the same things when they hear the news. Heck—I would have before I lost my sight."

"Really?"

Emily leaned across the desk and held out her hands, palms up.

Rhonda put her hands into Emily's.

"Yes. Now we need to make sure everyone else knows that blind people can be parents just like anybody else. And be thrilled for Stephanie and Dhruv."

"Without reservation," Rhonda said, squeezing Emily's hands, then stepping back. "Thanks for talking to me about this, Em. I'll let you get back to work."

Before Rhonda left the office, Emily said, "Email me some dates when you're free for lunch."

CHAPTER 14

*Z*oe took a place at the end of the line as her teacher escorted their class toward the cafeteria. Her stomach growled. She'd been too nervous to do more than nibble at a piece of toast at breakfast. Her class was assigned to the last of the four lunch periods, and she was hungry.

The morning had dragged for Zoe. She'd finished the book they were reading for her language arts class when she was in second grade. The math problems in the next section were easy, and she'd completed them without error during the first ten minutes of class, leaving her plenty of time to assess her fellow classmates.

Her home room of thirty students was evenly divided between girls and boys. The girls separated themselves into two groups. Based on their clothing and mannerisms, one group was sporty and the other very girly. The sporty ones seemed nice, but she had never been athletically inclined.

Zoe couldn't be sure, but she thought one of the girly girls had made fun of her appearance.

She smoothed an errant strand of her curly dark hair and tugged at the long sleeves of the oversize dark green sweater that was her favorite item in her closet. Her late grandmother always said green was Zoe's best color. She suspected one girl had said she looked like a pickle—a stinky dill pickle. The girl had pointed at Zoe, and the other girls had laughed.

The boys weren't much better. Most of them hadn't noticed her. With an exception: one boy finished his math assignment almost as quickly as she had. They'd exchanged glances when he'd turned over his paper on his desk, but then he'd pulled a sheet of paper from his backpack and started drawing. Their eyes hadn't met since.

Zoe stood on her tiptoes as they filed into the cafeteria. With any luck, Diedre had last lunch, too. She could sit with her stepsister and her friends. Diedre was outgoing and friendly. She got along with everyone. Zoe was certain Diedre would be invited to sit at someone's lunch table.

She craned her neck, searching from one corner of the large, high-ceilinged space to the other and back again. Diedre wasn't in the room.

Zoe lowered her heels to the floor and caught up with the boy in front of her. She took a tray from a rack and proceeded down the line. The macaroni and cheese with a side of carrot and celery sticks didn't look too bad. The lunch lady put it on her tray. Zoe picked up a carton of milk and stepped into the noisy lunchroom.

One last look around the room confirmed that Diedre wasn't there. Zoe would have to find someone to sit with.

She squared her shoulders, thinking of what Diedre would do—she'd walk up to a table with an open seat and ask if she could join them. That wasn't so hard. She could do that.

Zoe approached the first table of girls from her class. The girly girls were deep in conversation. There was one vacant seat. Just as she was about to set her tray on the table, another girl came rushing up with her tray and claimed the spot.

Zoe turned away. The table with the sporty girls was already full.

She moved to a wall on the far side of the room. A lone girl occupied a table to her right. Zoe walked over and set her tray down on the other end of the table from the girl.

The girl leaned toward her and stared at her intently.

"Do you mind if I sit here? There's nowhere else."

The girl's eyes were locked on her lips as she spoke.

"Sure. That'd be great," the girl said.

Zoe pulled out her chair and sat.

"You're new here, aren't you? I haven't seen you before."

Zoe nodded. The girl's voice sounded muffled—almost like she had a stuffy nose.

"My name is Ava," she continued. "I'm in third grade. I could be in fourth because I'm smart, but my parents won't let me skip."

"I'm Zoe. This is my first day and I'm in fourth."

Again, Ava watched Zoe carefully as she talked.

Zoe slid her tray down the table until she sat next to Ava.

"Do you like it here?" Zoe asked, spearing a forkful of the macaroni and cheese.

Ava twisted around so she could see Zoe. "I'm deaf," she said. "I'm reading your lips."

Zoe's eyes widened. "I thought you sounded like that actress Marlee Matlin. Do you know who she is?"

Ava nodded vigorously while she chewed.

Zoe picked up a carrot stick, then replaced it on her plate. "Would it be easier for you if I sat across from you? Then you don't have to twist around to see me."

Ava nodded wordlessly.

Zoe leapt out of her chair and moved to the other side of the table. "There. Much better." She picked up her fork again and glanced at Ava. "Are you crying? Did I hurt your feelings?"

"No," Ava responded, blinking rapidly. "You didn't."

"I don't know anything about being deaf," Zoe said. "My mom…" Zoe paused, unsure if she should apply that appellation to Emily, her legal guardian, appointed after her grandmother died. She decided she should. Even if Emily wasn't Zoe's biological mother, Emily was her mother now. "My mom is blind, so I know how that is. But not being deaf."

"Do you really want to know?" Ava asked, suddenly shy. "The other kids don't want me around."

Zoe leaned across the table toward Ava and spoke distinctively. "I.Want.To.Know."

Ava smiled for the first time since Zoe had sat down. "I'll tell you what it's like to be deaf if you tell me about being blind."

"Deal," Zoe said. "One of the coolest things is that blind

people have guide dogs. Mom has the coolest dog. His name is Garth."

"Some deaf people have dogs to help them," Ava replied. "I don't have one—yet. I want one."

The girls tucked into their meals and talked until the bell signaled the end of lunch hour.

"Can we sit together tomorrow?" Ava asked as they slid their trash into the bin and returned their trays.

Zoe bobbed her head in agreement. She'd made a new friend—all on her own. "See you tomorrow."

Both girls rejoined their classes, with an extra spring in their steps.

CHAPTER 15

*G*rant turned into the school parking lot.

Emily pushed the button on her smartwatch and it told her the time was 5:57 p.m. "We made it with three minutes to spare."

"We're not the only parents cutting it close to pick up a child from the after-school program," Grant said. "There's a line of cars following me. Sorry I was so late picking you up. We made some last-minute modifications to our proposal, and we had to submit it today."

"I understand," Emily said as he parked the car. "I'm sure the girls are fine. We just don't want to be this late every day."

"I agree. We won't be." He opened his door. "You and Garth can wait here. It'll be quicker if I run in to sign them out. I'll leave the car running."

He was gone before Emily could respond. The warmth from sunlight shining through the car windows had dissipated. The sun was setting. She reached her hand toward the climate control vents and felt a faint puff of warm air.

Emily pulled her thin sweater around her shoulders. She was nestling into her seat when a thought struck her. Grant answered his phone, adjusted the fan speed and cabin temperature, and changed the radio station with voice commands. If she remembered correctly, he pushed a button on the steering wheel before voicing his command.

She released her seat belt and leaned across the center console. Emily ran her hands around the circumference of the steering wheel. The leather surface was unbroken except for a small rolling ball on each side of the steering wheel.

This had to be what she was looking for. She pressed the ball on the right side of the steering wheel and said, "increase fan speed."

She waited and listened, then felt along the dashboard until her hand was over the vent. Nothing had changed.

Emily reached for the steering wheel and found the left rolling ball. She pressed it in and repeated her command. This time, the whoosh of air from the vent told her she had been successful. She pushed the ball again and told the car to increase the temperature.

Grinning, Emily swiveled to address Garth in the back seat. "I did it, boy. I may not be able to drive—yet—but I can still operate part of Grant's fancy car."

She was re-buckling her seat belt when the car doors opened, and Grant and the girls joined her.

Garth army-crawled along the floor to the middle of the back seat to make room for Zoe and Diedre.

Zoe was the first to greet him, planting a row of kisses along the top of his head.

Diedre massaged his shoulders. "I was freezing," she said. "It's nice and warm in here, though."

"It's supposed to rain tomorrow," Emily said. "You'll both need your puffer jackets with hoods."

The girls buckled their seat belts and Grant backed out of the parking spot. "Did you adjust the fan and temperature in here?" he asked Emily.

"I sure did."

"I didn't think I'd told you how."

"You hadn't. I thought about what I've heard you do and figured it out on my own."

"Well done, you."

"Thanks. I was proud of myself, I must admit."

He shook his head. "I'll make a note that you notice and remember everything."

Emily chuckled. "That's an exaggeration—but a good plan." She turned toward the back seat.

"I'm dying to know: how was your first day?" She waited, expecting a torrential response from each girl.

The warm air from the vents supplied the only sound in the car.

"Come on—are you having trouble deciding where to start?"

There was still no response.

"Do you like your teachers?"

Each girl responded they did.

"How was lunch?" Emily prodded. "Did you eat together?"

"No," Diedre said. "I have first lunch."

"And I'm last," Zoe said. "The food was okay. I liked my macaroni and cheese."

"That's what I had, too," Diedre said.

"I met a cool girl at lunch," Zoe said. "We sat together. She's in third grade but is super smart and could be in fourth, but her parents won't let her skip. She's deaf."

"That's interesting," Grant said.

"Yep. We're going to sit together tomorrow, too. I'm going to learn about being deaf."

"Were there other kids at your table?" Emily asked.

"No. Just Ava. She said she doesn't have other friends."

Emily pursed her lips. Being different was hard—especially if you were a child. "How about you, Diedre? Did you make new friends?"

"A bunch of girls in my class are on a swim team. It's not through school. They get picked up by their parents right after school to go to practice. One of them asked if I swim."

"Do you want to do that instead of going to the after-school program with me?" Zoe asked.

Diedre shook her head no. "I'm not a good swimmer, and I like staying with you. I didn't see you even once during the day."

"I know," Zoe said. "I kept looking for you when we changed rooms for different sections."

"It's only the first day," Diedre said. "Maybe we'll see each other tomorrow."

"I like knowing that you're there," Zoe said. "At least we see each other as soon as school is out." She turned to her stepsister. "You were talking with a couple of girls and a boy when I got there."

"Those are theater kids. They're part of a youth theater near us. It's doing *Mary Poppins Jr.* this spring."

"You're a good singer," Zoe said. "And I know you love that play. You should try out."

"Maybe. Those kids seemed really nice."

"I'm happy that you both made new friends today," Grant said. "What about homework?"

"I've got some," Diedre said.

"Zoe?" Grant asked.

"I did it all during class. The math was super easy, and I finished the book we're reading when I was in second grade."

"Maybe you should read it again," Emily suggested. "I'm sure you'll get more out of it now."

"I guess," Zoe replied. "What's for supper?"

"We're in luck," Emily said. "Your grandmothers left a meal for us in the refrigerator. It'll take thirty minutes to warm up, and then we'll have the best lasagna in the city for our dinner."

"Yeah!" the girls cried in unison.

Grant nodded his agreement.

Emily reached across the console and rubbed her hand along Grant's arm. They'd all had good days and were soon to sit down together to a home-cooked meal. It was all any working parent could want.

CHAPTER 16

*D*iedre opened the door to the back patio for Sabrina and me after dinner. We raced across the decking and down the short flight of stairs to the lawn. Running off-leash from one end of the yard to the other made my heart happy. We both loved the freedom that this new fenced-in yard gave us.

Sabrina's legs were much shorter than mine, but they pumped like pistons on a race car. She kept up with me, stride for stride. When we'd finally worked off the tension of the day, we both did our business and wandered to the door. I waited patiently to be let back in.

Sabrina scratched at the door and yipped. I knew this would get her into trouble. I settled myself a respectable distance from her. There was no point in both of us getting reprimanded.

Zoe came to the door and let us in. She didn't admonish

Sabrina about her bad behavior. I followed them into the kitchen.

Grant started the dishwasher.

Emily rinsed out the dishcloth and hung it up to dry.

"I'd like to catch up on the emails I ignored today while I finished that proposal. Do you mind?" Grant asked.

"Go ahead. That soaker tub in our bathroom is heavenly. I think I'll take another bath."

Sabrina and I looked at each other. This was when we usually curled up together for our after-dinner naps. Neither of us made a move toward our beds in the corner of the family room, however. Something seemed off with our people that night. Their words were relaxed, but their energy was all wrong.

"I'll check on the girls first," Emily said, heading toward their bedrooms.

We followed her.

Sabrina cast a longing glance at her bed as we passed by the family room but continued to follow Emily.

We reached Diedre's room first. She sat, elbows on her desktop and head in her hands, her long hair falling over her petite shoulders like a shawl. Her ankles were crossed under her chair, and she jiggled one foot.

"Diedre," Emily said from the doorway. "Can I come in?"

"Sure." The response sounded sulky to my ears.

"Everything okay?"

"I don't really understand fractions." The girl released an exasperated sigh. "Zoe can multiply and divide them, which we really don't do until next year, but I don't get them."

Emily paused, her hands on her hips. She did that when she was thinking.

I sat down next to her. Whatever was wrong with Diedre, Emily was figuring out how to fix it.

Sabrina took her cue from me and sat.

"You understand fractions, honey. You just don't know it. Come into the kitchen with me."

The four of us were soon back in the room we'd recently vacated.

"Pull out the measuring cups, please," Emily directed.

Diedre put them on the counter.

Emily instructed her to find the 1 cup measuring cup. "Now take the cup marked 1/8th—that's with a 1 on top of the line and an 8 on the bottom—those are called the numerator and denominator."

"I know that much," Diedre said.

"Great. Now fill the 1/8th cup and pour it into the 1 cup measuring cup. Be careful not to spill."

Diedre performed the task.

"Now repeat that until the 1 cup measure is full of water. Count the number of times you fill it. We've already done one."

Diedre continued until she reached the count of 8. "It's full," she said, excitement creeping into her voice. She dumped the water from the 1 cup measure and duplicated the process with the 1/3 cup measuring cup. "OMG. This makes so much sense to me. It's easy. I can't believe I didn't understand this."

Sabrina and I got to our feet and wagged our tails. We

weren't sure what we were celebrating, but we knew there was something to be happy about.

Diedre's mood changed in an instant. "I'm such a dummy for not seeing this."

Emily's response was swift and firm. "You're no such thing. We all learn in different ways. You may be a spatial learner, and no one presented fractions to you this way. There's no contest here. The only important thing is that you now understand fractions."

"I guess. I don't think Zoe has problems understanding anything."

"Zoe's extremely academically advanced, but she struggles with other things."

"Like making lots of friends?"

"She's not as gregarious or outgoing as you, Diedre. Relating to people is as important a life skill as mastery of any academic subject."

"I hope this doesn't mean I'll always be bad at math."

"I think you'll find this was an anomaly. You'll sail through everything else—but if math is hard for you, so be it. You'll master all the concepts in the end."

"Thanks, Emily," Diedre said. "Can I watch TV before bed?"

"Sure. What's Zoe doing?"

"She was re-reading that book, like you suggested."

"I'm headed for the tub. I'll check on her now and tell her you're in the family room, watching a show."

We walked into Zoe's room to find her at her desk, hunched over her laptop, tapping at the keyboard."

"What're you up to?" Emily asked.

"I'm researching assistive technology for deaf people." Zoe remained focused on her computer screen.

Emily smiled. "You want to understand your new friend's world, don't you?"

Zoe nodded, then quickly responded audibly, "Yes."

"Like you did with me when I lost my sight. You're looking for things that might help her."

"Yep."

Emily walked to the desk and bent to hug Zoe from behind. She kissed the top of her head. "You're a remarkably kind human being."

Zoe shrugged, but I could see the flush of pleasure redden her cheeks.

Emily straightened. "Diedre said you were re-reading that book."

"Already finished it. I picked up more details, like you said."

"Good." Emily rested one hand on Zoe's back. "Are your classes too easy for you?"

"I already knew everything they taught me. I was very bored today."

"Maybe you should skip a grade. Like your friend Ava was talking about."

"No!" Zoe's response was swift and sure. "I don't want to go to fifth grade. Those kids seem so much bigger—and meaner. I want to stay where I am. In the same grade as Diedre."

"I'll talk to your homeroom teacher about putting you in advanced classes," Emily replied. "I've already got appointments to talk to both of your homeroom teachers next

Monday about the best ways to communicate with each of them. We'll discuss it then."

She smoothed Zoe's dark hair down her back. "Can you hang in there until then?"

"Sure. I already went to the school library and checked out biographies of women physicists."

"I love the sound of that. Like who?"

"Marie Curie and Maria Goeppert Mayer—they were the first two women to win Nobel Prizes in physics."

"Very impressive," Emily said.

Zoe yawned and shut her laptop.

"Diedre's watching TV before bed, if you want to join her."

"Can we have the last of the chocolate chip cookies Sylvia made us as a snack?"

"Sure," Emily said. "As long as you brush your teeth before bed."

"We always do, Mom."

Zoe and Sabrina peeled past us, out of the room, in search of the snack.

Emily stood rooted to the spot. She reached out a hand to me and I touched it with my muzzle. "Did you hear that, Garth?" Her voice was thick with emotion. "That's the first time I've heard Zoe call me 'Mom.' "

The faint scent of chocolate chip cookies reached my nostrils. Under normal circumstances, when I was off duty, I'd hurry to investigate the source of the smell. These weren't normal circumstances.

Emily was about to cry. Happy tears—but tears, none-theless.

I followed her into her bathroom. Sometimes she needed me as her guide, and sometimes my presence was required as her best friend. This was one of those latter times.

I settled myself on the rug next to the tub, nose pointed away from the mound of bubbles growing under the stream of water from the faucet. Even if my nose itched and I sneezed up a storm, I was staying by my Emily's side.

CHAPTER 17

"*I* love that May 24 is my due date." Stephanie and Biscuit trotted next to Dhruv on their way to the car. "That's my grandmother's birthday. It would have been her 100th."

"That's a good omen," he replied.

"I may not actually give birth on my due date. A lot of first-time mothers are late."

"You won't be," he said with conviction. "Your grandmother will see to it."

"I'm not sure it works like that." Her tone was playful.

"It does. You'll see," he replied, undeterred.

"Now that we have a date, should we tell the rest of your family? I need to let my school know that I'll be on maternity leave at the end of the school year so they can hire a substitute teacher."

"My mother is bursting to tell her sisters," Dhruv said. "I

don't know how much longer she can keep the news to herself."

"I was thinking we could invite your family over for dinner on Sunday night."

"Just my parents or my uncles and aunts and cousins? And their spouses and children."

"The whole gang. It's already Friday, so I realize it's short notice, but it would be nice to share our news with everyone, all at once."

"Are you sure you're feeling up to it?"

"I haven't been sick in the late afternoon or evening for almost a month. It'll be fine. I'll make a big pot of chicken noodle soup and you can fix your chili. We'll buy artisan bread from the bakery on the corner and a couple of pies, too. That should be plenty."

"We can do that. I'd like to talk to my uncle about moving down the hall into the big three-bedroom apartment that Emily just vacated. With a baby on the way, we need the room." He pressed the button on his key fob to unlock the car. "I agree to this—on one condition."

He opened the rear door for Biscuit to jump into the back seat.

"Oh?" Stephanie got in on the passenger side.

"You go straight to bed the minute everyone leaves. I'd take care of all the cleanup."

"I won't say no to that. Do you think everyone will be surprised?"

Dhruv bit his lower lip. "Some of them may be wondering. Especially my aunties. They notice everything."

"What're you talking about?"

"Even those loose, flowing dresses you've been wearing are getting a bit..." He chose his words carefully, "snug."

Stephanie's hands flew to her belly. "You mean...I'm showing?" A smile erupted from ear to ear.

"Yes. You are." He swiveled to face her. "And you're the most beautiful woman I've ever seen."

THE COMPETING aromas of chicken soup, spicy chili, and warm bread wafted out of Dhruv and Stephanie's apartment into the hallway. Slashes of crimson and gold were visible from every window as the winter sunset arrived in the late afternoon. Candles on the mantelpiece enhanced the cozy scene.

Lining the kitchen counters were two crock pots with different chilis, together with baskets of crackers and warm bread. Chicken noodle soup simmered on the stovetop. A tray of vegetables and a bowl of fruit balanced the offerings, with an apple, a lemon meringue, and a cherry pie promising a sweet end to the meal.

Dhruv's extended family arrived on time. They had all accepted the last-minute invitation. Soon everyone was sitting in the living room with a plate perched on their knee and a soup bowl clutched in their hand.

Dhruv's well-mannered golden retriever, Sugar, acknowledged the guests respectfully. His enthusiastic dachshund, Rocco, was more effusive, jumping up onto people's legs until they finally bent to accept his welcome.

Biscuit wasn't in her working harness, but she stayed close to Stephanie.

A cacophony of voices elevated the noise level as people greeted each other when they arrived, but died down as they ate.

Dhruv's mother was wedged into the sofa with her three sisters. The aunties were leaning across each other, talking over one another, and casting surreptitious glances at Stephanie.

Stephanie ladled herself a serving of chicken noodle soup. She rested her back against the kitchen counter and raised a spoonful of soup to her mouth.

Dhruv approached his wife. "There are two open chairs along the wall. I'll help you find your seat." He reached for her hand.

"I can navigate my own apartment without help," she said.

"Not with this crowd," he said. "Rocco is racing around, people have their feet outstretched, and there are purses on the floor everywhere. I'll be lucky to cross the room without tripping."

"Good point." Stephanie took his arm, and he led her to a chair.

He looked at his mother, who was shrugging her shoulders and raising her hands, palms up, in the universal gesture of I Don't Know while the aunties barraged her with questions. "I'm going to make our announcement now," he said to his wife.

"Good, I'm ready to be out in the open with our news."

Dhruv stepped to the middle of the room and waved his

hands to get everyone's attention. "Thank you for coming. We're very glad you could all be here. Stephanie and I have remarkable news to share. Life-changing news."

The aunties each swung to look at his mother, then returned their attention to Dhruv.

"Stephanie and I are going to have a baby."

No one made a sound.

Dhruv cleared his throat, then repeated himself.

No one moved.

After what seemed like an eternity, his uncle jumped to his feet and came to Dhruv. "Congratulations, my boy," he said, shaking his hand.

Dhruv's father began clapping, and soon everyone joined in.

His favorite female cousin pulled Dhruv into a tight embrace before kneeling next to Stephanie's chair to hug her. "I'm thrilled for both of you. When are you due?"

Stephanie told her.

"That'll be here before you know it," she said.

"Yes. We…we didn't think we could have children. This is a complete shock." She leaned toward Dhruv's cousin and lowered her voice. "I thought his family would be thrilled for us. You could have heard a pin drop when he first told everyone. Aren't you happy for us?"

"Of course we are." The cousin glanced over at her mother and the other aunties. "It's just that we didn't find it surprising. You've been showing since before the holidays."

"Fair enough," Stephanie said. "I guess I'm not the best judge of my appearance, and Dhruv doesn't notice that sort of thing."

"Exactly," the cousin said, an unmistakable note of relief in her voice.

The auntie group huddled around Dhruv's mother, talking nonstop and gesturing wildly with their hands.

"Is the family upset with us?" Stephanie asked. "I may not be able to see, but I can still read a room. This isn't the joyful response I expected."

The cousin remained quiet.

"Do you wonder if we're capable of being parents?"

The woman put a protective arm around Stephanie's shoulders. "Don't jump to conclusions," she advised.

"The blind woman can't care for a baby?" Stephanie's voice rose in volume. "Her own child won't be safe with her. Is that it?" Stephanie sunk into her chair, like a balloon that's been popped with a pin.

Dhruv's cousin turned her face to the floor. "There may be some of that. It's ignorant. Dhruv's mother supports you both a thousand percent. And so do I, Stephanie. We'll educate the others."

Stephanie nodded, her expression miserable.

"Let his mom and me work on this. Your job is to rest and grow a healthy baby all of us are going to love."

Stephanie nodded. "Okay. I'm just so disappointed..." her voice quavered. "Where's Dhruv?"

"I think he and my dad went down the hall to see the three-bedroom apartment. Dhruv told me earlier that the two of you want to move into it."

"Dhruv thinks we should."

"Me too. I'll help you pack your stuff and my brothers

have already told Dhruv they'll come over to move your furniture down the hall."

"That's nice," Stephanie said, her voice steadying.

"Put all the naysayers out of your mind. You and Dhruv are going to be fabulous parents. That's one very lucky child in there." She pointed to Stephanie's abdomen.

Although Stephanie couldn't see the gesture, she knew what Dhruv's cousin was doing. Stephanie patted the cousin's arm, hoping she and Dhruv would be fabulous parents.

CHAPTER 18

*E*mily threw her arms around Gina. They rocked back and forth in a tight hug.

"I can't believe I haven't seen my best friend since her wedding," Gina said when they finally pulled apart. "I'm so sorry."

"You're tied up with a new baby, for heaven's sake," Emily said. "We've both been far too busy."

"Let's promise each other that we'll talk on the phone at least once a week," Gina said.

"I've got an idea." Sylvia stood in the doorway to her kitchen, observing the two daughters-in-law she loved like her own children. She pulled a tissue from the pocket of her apron that sported the saying "Food is my Love Language" and dabbed at her eyes. Craig and Grant, her twin sons, could not have married more perfect women for them. That Emily and Gina had been close since grade school was an added benefit.

"What's that, Mom?" Craig asked, taking his infant son Alex out of his baby carrier.

"Both of your families are so busy that it's hard to stay connected. Let's have dinner here once a month. Maybe the first Sunday?" She turned to Martha. Emily's mother had become one of Sylvia's best friends. "Martha—you need to be here, too."

"That's a genius idea," Grant said. "We can take turns hosting. All the work shouldn't fall on you."

"Nope. You're too busy to add this to your schedules. Having you over for dinner once a month isn't too much for me."

"I can help," Martha chimed in.

"Perfect," Sylvia said. "You can come into the city and spend the weekend with me, if you want. We can go shopping on Saturday—see a movie—go to a gallery opening."

"I'd love that," Martha said.

"How could we say no to this?" Emily's smile unfolded like a flower blooming on a time-lapse video. Her mother was living a happy life again after the devastation of losing her husband—Emily's father—in a tragic car accident several years earlier.

A timer buzzed from the kitchen. "Are you ready to eat?" Sylvia addressed the question to no one in particular.

"Sure are," Grant and Craig responded in unison.

"I've never known the two of you *not* to be hungry." Sylvia chuckled. She walked over to Alex and planted a kiss on his forehead, then straightened and spoke to Zoe and Diedre.

"Will you help me bring the food to the table? We're eating family style."

The girls followed Sylvia and Martha into the kitchen as the two brothers and their wives took their seats at the long dining room table. Garth found his spot under Emily's chair.

Craig looked around the room of his childhood home with fresh eyes. From the detailed crown molding, to the heavy doors that shut with a satisfying click, everything about the space spoke of soundness and implied security. "Did you ever think we'd be sitting here, as adults, with our own families?"

"It's surreal." Grant's voice caught in his throat. "It seems like only yesterday we were at this very table, with Dad."

Emily reached under the table and put her hand on Grant's knee, giving it a comforting pat.

"I hope we can give our families the happy life our parents gave us," Craig said.

Grant nodded. "I think about that a lot. We were both in Boy Scouts and sports. Things were busy, but it always felt like we had family time."

"We want that, too," Gina said. "We've only got one child —and Alex isn't even crawling yet. We're keeping our heads above water—barely. I'm not sure what's going to happen when I go back to work in another four weeks."

"A baby is a ton of work," Emily said. "You're coping beautifully. What will you do with Alex when you go back?"

"Sylvia insists she can take care of him two days a week," Gina said. "I'm going to be working four ten-hour days, so that only leaves two days. We'd like to get a part-time nanny."

"That's a good idea," Emily said. "Have you found someone?"

Zoe and Diedre each approached the table with a pitcher of water and began filling glasses at each place setting.

"We both like to babysit," Diedre chimed in.

Gina and Craig exchanged a glance.

"We know you'll be fabulous babysitters," Gina said. "When Alex is older," she added quickly. "We need someone to take care of him during the day, anyway—when you're in school."

"You'll be too busy to babysit this semester," Grant interjected.

Martha entered the dining room with a large wooden salad bowl and a basket of steaming garlic bread, and set them on the table.

Sylvia followed with a pan of eggplant Parmesan she'd just pulled out of the oven, its cheese still bubbling. She placed the pan on a trivet on the table in front of her seat and removed her oven mitts. "This is too hot to send around the table. Pass me your plates and I'll dish up a serving for everyone."

"Tell us all about your new school," Gina said. "I can't wait to hear. Emily and I were your ages when we met. I wonder if things have changed much since our day."

Zoe and Diedre launched into detailed reports about their new school.

"How are things at your firm, Grant?" Sylvia asked.

"Busier than ever," Grant said. "Architecture is booming." He launched into a detailed description of the large residential compound in Los Angeles that his firm had bid on. The enthusiasm in his voice was unmistakable.

"It sounds surreal," Gina said. "It'd be so fun to work on

that project. Your ideas are out of this world."

"But in LA!" Sylvia exclaimed. "How would you handle that from San Francisco?"

"I'm not going to win the job," Grant said. "I don't want it, frankly, because someone would have to be on-site the entire time. The firm submitted a proposal out of respect for the person who recommended us. Our bid is far too high to be successful."

Grant turned to Emily, who had stopped eating, her fork frozen in mid-air like a sudden malfunction of a Ferris wheel.

"I promise you, Em. It's not going to happen. Don't worry."

The happy dinner conversation continued to float around the table.

A classic chocolate layer cake concluded the family meal.

Sylvia walked both families down her front steps to their cars in her driveway.

Both Emily and Gina hugged her tightly. "Mark your calendars," she reminded them. "We'll do this once a month."

"Thank you, Sylvia," Emily said. "We loved this. And I'm so happy you've included my mom."

"She's like the sister I never had." Sylvia kissed Emily on the cheek.

"This was great, Sylvia," Gina said, moving off to where Craig was strapping a fussy Alex into his car seat. "Time to get someone to bed. I'll call you this week."

Martha finished saying her goodbyes and the two women stood arm in arm as they watched the young families head home.

CHAPTER 19

"Hi. I'm heading into a meeting with my team. Can I call you later?"

Grant sucked in a breath. He could tell Emily was walking at a fast pace. "Sorry to bother you. I remember you have a busy day."

"I want to make sure we're all set for the meetings with the Denver team. They arrive tomorrow right before our get-acquainted dinner. That'll be purely social. We need to hit the ground running on Wednesday morning. I want to redistribute duties and integrate both teams by the end of the week."

"I'm glad I caught you before you went into your meeting."

Emily stopped walking as she reached the conference room door. "Why? What's up?"

"You know that bid we just submitted?"

"Of course I do. You said you wouldn't know anything for at least a month."

"I was wrong about that. We just heard...we won the contract."

"Oh, Grant! I'm so happy for you. Congratulations."

"Thanks," he said.

"For someone who was just awarded a ginormous, career-changing project, you don't sound the least bit happy."

"No...I'm thrilled. Just surprised, since we bid it out at really high costs. Everyone in the office is on cloud nine. You'd think we'd won the lottery."

"If this is thrilled, I'd hate to hear disappointed." Emily retreated a few steps. "Come on. What's wrong?"

"It's just that they want to fast-track this project. It'll be a ton of work and I'll have to travel much more than I do now."

"We talked about this. We'll figure it out."

"It turns out we'll have to figure it out, starting now." Grant inhaled audibly and continued in a rush. "I have to be in Los Angeles the rest of the week to interview contractors and consult on permits."

"Whoa. I'm going to be working longer hours than usual with the Denver team in town. You know this." Emily couldn't hide the irritation bubbling up inside her. "I can't take the kids to school or pick them up. You were going to handle all that this week."

"I know and I'm sorry, but I fly out first thing in the morning. They're just getting started on this project and they want me to be there. After things are up and running, I'll be able to send someone else from the office. I'm taking Dave with me tomorrow so the client will get to know him."

"That's great, but what are we going to do this week?"

"You're sure you'll have to work late?"

"Grant!" Emily put her palm to her forehead. "*Yes.* I'm sure."

"I'm sorry, honey. I wanted to make certain. This is my fault—I'll figure something out."

Emily blew out a breath. "There's no fault here. And I'm sorry if you're not feeling as happy as you should be about winning this bid. I'm very proud of you. Why don't you call your mom? She told me she'd be happy to let the girls come to her house if we're running late at the end of the day."

"I'll…I'll make some calls." Grant didn't tell her he'd already called his mother, only to learn that she had plans to babysit Alex that evening. He'd also talked to Martha, who was hosting her mah-jongg group in the afternoon and couldn't drive into the city until early evening.

"I've gotta go," Emily said. "I can hear that people have finished filing into the conference room. They'll be waiting for me."

"Have a good day," he said. "Don't worry about this. I'll get coverage for the kids."

"Thanks, sweetheart," Emily said and tapped to end the call.

"Garth, forward," she commanded. "Find conference room."

"Sorry to have kept you waiting." Emily entered the room and took her customary seat at the head of the table. "I know you're all really busy, so we'll get started."

"Em," Dhruv leaned across the table toward her. "Can I say something before we start?"

"Sure." Emily smiled inwardly. The news that he and Stephanie were having a baby would thrill the team. They were a cohesive group, mourning each other's losses and celebrating their wins. She would be forever grateful that they'd refused to accept her resignation from this job she loved when she'd first lost her eyesight.

"I've figured out the error in the automated inventory code. We don't need to keep it on our list of tasks." Dhruv tapped on his laptop screen. "I'm deleting it. I'll finish this task after lunch."

Emily's head snapped toward him. "Is that what you wanted to say?"

Dhruv nodded, then caught himself and said, "Yeah."

She cleared her throat. "Is there anything else you'd like to tell the group?"

"Like something personal?" Rhonda interjected. "That we'd all be happy about?"

Dhruv's cheeks suddenly reddened. "There is something," he said. He tapped his pencil against the tabletop. "Stephanie and I are having a baby," he blurted out.

A stunned silence was followed by an explosion of motion as his coworkers pushed back their chairs and rushed to shake his hand or pull him in for a hug. The room was filled with cries of congratulations. When everyone sat back down, Dhruv supplied the due date and answered the usual questions about how she was feeling and were they excited?

"Thank you, everybody," Dhruv said. "I'm glad you're happy for us."

"Of course we are," Emily said. "We'll have to figure out a date for your baby shower, but for now, we need to set goals for what we plan to accomplish this week."

"That's why I started the project list," Dhruv said, returning his attention to his laptop.

"Does that include items from the Denver team?" Emily asked.

"It's supposed to," Dhruv said. "Kari sent me a list of things to add to the list, but she didn't send much." Dhruv read aloud the list of twenty-three items.

"All but six of those are from our team," Emily said.

"How can Denver only be working on six things?" Mike asked. "Their team is as large as ours."

"They have to be working on more than that," Rhonda said. "Did you get everything from them, Dhruv."

"I asked Kari, and this is what I got."

"Denver has to be holding out on us," Mike said. "I know you and Kari and Dhruv work well together, Em," he continued, "but every time I ask one of the Denver team members for something, I always feel like they're replying with the bare minimum of information."

"I agree," Rhonda jumped in. "It's like cross-examining a witness when I talk to one of them."

"That's not productive," Emily said. "If we're going to merge our departments, we've got to cooperate. And be fully transparent."

"That's not happening," another team member agreed.

"Sounds like we've got people problems," Emily said. "We'll never be successful if both teams don't trust each other."

"What do you propose we do to make them...like us?" Dhruv asked.

Emily sat quietly, pursing her lips in deep concentration. "It's easier to ignore people you don't know...and like. Or respect."

"Being with us for part of a week won't change that," Rhonda said.

"No. It won't. So instead of assigning the projects on Dhruv's list by region, let's assign one person from each region to the task. You'll be forced to work with each other."

"Who will be the senior person responsible for each task?" Mike asked.

"We won't have a senior person. You'll need to proceed by consensus. That will force you to work together and compromise."

"You'll make the decision if the work group can't figure out which way to go?"

"Nope." Emily shook her head emphatically. "I won't review anything unless it comes to me with a recommendation signed off by both parties."

"But what if we can't agree with the person we're partnered with?"

"You can take your issues to Dhruv and Kari. They'll help you work things out," Emily said. "And I mean 'and.' You'll have to consult both of them, not one of them. If we're going to trust our new, combined team, we all need to feel that nobody is playing favorites."

The room became quiet.

"We've been recognized as the most collegial, productive team in the company for many years. We're now going to learn something new—we're going to figure out how to grow our team. The addition of the Denver group will double our size. We're going to keep and strengthen our working relationships and effectiveness—and we're going to do this with people who work remotely from us."

Emily pushed back her chair and stood. "This will be a challenge, but like everything else we've done, we'll accomplish this together. Before long, we'll wonder how we ever got along without our Denver counterparts."

Her team gathered their laptops and coffee cups and got up from the table without further comment.

"The dream team is getting bigger. That's something we can all be excited about."

Emily exited the room, unaware of the skeptical expressions on her team members' faces.

CHAPTER 20

Stephanie picked up Biscuit's working harness. "Office," she commanded. They exited her third-grade classroom, and she locked the door.

The pair set off along the now-deserted third-grade wing. Stephanie had stayed late, composing and editing her letter to the principal. She wanted to be crystal clear that she would return to the classroom after her maternity leave was over. Unemployment among blind adults was a shocking seventy percent nationwide. Stephanie had worked incredibly hard to secure this position—she wasn't going to give it up.

A grassy common area was on her left and classrooms on her right. They hadn't traveled more than six strides when a sound caught Stephanie's attention. She extended her right arm until she touched the wall, then found an open doorway. The classroom belonged to the room next to hers. Their rooms were linked by a connecting door in the back of the room that the other teacher had shut as soon as school was out.

"Rebecca?" Stephanie leaned through the open doorway and called to her again.

"Hey," came the soft reply.

"I'm surprised to find you here so late," Stephanie said. "Since you returned from maternity leave, you've gone home every day when school lets out. I heard you close our connecting door, too—like you do every day when you leave."

Rebecca snuffled.

Stephanie stepped closer. "Are you crying?"

Rebecca blew her nose. "Maybe a little."

"Oh, no. What's wrong? Is the baby all right?"

"Yes. He's fine. Perfect. I'm just exhausted and...well...I'm overwhelmed. Coming back to work has been harder than I thought."

"I'm sorry to hear that. Is he sleeping through the night yet?"

"In my dreams," she replied. "He still gets up twice a night. He goes right back to sleep, so it's not that bad. And my husband and I take turns giving him his bottle, so I shouldn't complain."

"Do you have anyone to help at home?"

"My mother is with him tonight. She said my husband and I need time to ourselves, so he's picking me up in a few minutes and we're going to dinner."

"That sounds like a great idea."

"It's just that," Rebecca paused and her breathing was shaky, "this whole motherhood thing has thrown me for a loop. I used to think I could handle anything. I really believed having a baby would be easy. I even looked down my nose at women who struggled with it."

She gave a derisive laugh. "You've seen the moms that come in here with their older kids after they've had a baby. They look like they've slept in their clothes and haven't washed their hair in a week."

Rebecca brought her hands to the sides of her head. "What's wrong with me? Of course you haven't seen them."

"I hear the fatigue in their voices, and I know they're struggling."

"I vowed I'd never be like them. Famous last words. I haven't worn makeup all week, and this is the outfit I wore on Monday. I picked it up off the floor of my closet this morning."

Stephanie sat down next to her coworker and patted her hand. "Sounds like you need to cut yourself some slack. As I see it, it makes no difference what you wore today."

Rebecca's head snapped up. "Were you making a joke?"

"Trying to. My point is this: you're in a very unusual situation. As a first-time parent, you're understandably stressed. He won't keep waking you up twice a night. Things will get easier. You'll adjust."

"You really think so?"

"I do. Have a nice dinner with your husband—and stay long enough to have dessert."

Rebecca chuckled. "Thanks for stopping in to cheer me up. You've really helped."

"I'm glad." Stephanie stood.

"I never asked about your doctor's visit last week. How

did that go? Do you have to have a colonoscopy? I know you dreaded that."

"It went great." Stephanie sat back down. "I don't have to have a colonoscopy."

"I'm relieved for you. Are you feeling better?"

"Yes. I'm only sick now a couple of mornings a month."

Rebecca pushed back in her chair. She stared at Stephanie.

"You're the first person here at school to know," Stephanie said. "I'm pregnant."

Rebecca drew in a quick breath.

"I stayed late, writing a letter to the principal to let him know." Stephanie patted the envelope in her pocket. "I was on my way to turn it in before Biscuit and I head home."

"When are you due?"

Stephanie told her. "I'll have a nice, long maternity leave before school resumes again in September."

"You're coming back to teaching?" Rebecca's voice rose an octave.

"Yes. I am." Stephanie straightened her back. "Why wouldn't I?"

"It's just that—like we've been talking about—it's so hard to do it all. I can barely manage everything and I'm not..." Rebecca cut herself off in mid sentence.

"Blind," Stephanie supplied. She got quickly to her feet.

"I'm sorry, Stephanie." Rebecca got up and reached for her. "Don't mind me. I'm projecting my problems onto you. You'll...you'll be fine."

"I'd better go. I want to put this on the principal's desk before the office closes." She and Biscuit headed for the door.

"We're the same height and coloring," Rebecca called after her. "Would you like to borrow some of my maternity clothes?"

Stephanie stopped in the doorway. "Sure. That would be nice."

"Great," Rebecca said, relief flooding into her voice. "You'll look cute in my things. I'll bring in a bag of clothes tomorrow that I think will fit you now."

Stephanie nodded.

"I'm happy for you—and Dhruv," Rebecca said. "Don't give a second thought to anything I said."

Stephanie and Biscuit arrived at the office just before closing time, her mind replaying her conversation with Rebecca as if it were on a repeating loop.

CHAPTER 21

We were working late. I didn't mind—but I was getting hungry. Emily had apologized to me over and over about running out the door this morning and forgetting my kibble. She'd thought she had a ziplock with at least one meal for me in her desk drawer. I could have told her I'd eaten that weeks ago.

The dinner at the fancy restaurant with the people from our office and some new ones I'd never met had been important to Emily. She'd been nervous when she'd stood up and talked to the group before dessert. Frankly, everyone had seemed on edge. They'd all smiled and acted friendly, but I sensed tension from both sides. One of the new people—a woman named Kari—was genuinely happy to be there. I liked her. The ones from our office were wonderful, of course. I was withholding judgment on the others.

The room had emptied out and the wait staff was efficiently clearing the tables. I thought I might be in luck when one of the servers stumbled and almost dropped a tray of half-eaten pieces of cheesecake. I'd never tried cheesecake but would have been more than happy to help clean up any mess. The man regained his balance and steadied the tray at the last minute, averting what would have been a disaster for him but a windfall for me.

I sat at Emily's feet while she and Dhruv continued their conversation.

Emily's phone announced our rideshare had arrived.

"We can finish this conversation tomorrow," she said to Dhruv.

"I'll walk you out," he said.

Emily pulled on my harness and directed me to take her outside. "I'm sorry I kept you out so late. Apologize to Stephanie for me."

"It's fine. She texted that she turned in her request for maternity leave to her principal and was tired. She was going to eat and go to bed early. She'll be asleep."

"Good. I'd like to tell you to come in late tomorrow, but our first meeting starts at 8:30 and I'd like to go over a few things with you first."

Dhruv verified that the car waiting at the curb was Emily's rideshare and opened the door for her. "I'll be in by 7:00."

"Me too," Emily said as we settled into the back seat. "See you then."

The rideshare pulled away from the curb. Emily checked her messages. The only one had been from Grant, telling her he was at a dinner meeting that would run late. He'd already talked to the girls after school and would connect with Emily in the morning.

Emily texted Martha that we were on the way home. She relaxed into the leather upholstery and dozed until the car made a sharp left turn, climbed a steep incline, and stopped.

The driver repeated her address.

"That's correct," Emily said.

"I'll wait here until I see you get inside," the driver said.

"Thank you," Emily replied.

We got out of the car and climbed the steps to the front door.

Martha opened it, and we were home. "The girls are asleep." She kept her voice low.

"Good. It's after ten, right?"

"Yes."

"I'm sorry I didn't get to tuck them in. Did they give you any trouble?"

"Those two? No. Never."

"I'm glad."

"You look exhausted," Martha said.

Emily removed my harness and hung it on its hook by the door. "I am. It's been a long day." She covered a yawn with her hand. "I need to feed Garth first thing. I feel terrible that he's waited so long for his supper."

I liked where this conversation was going and headed into the kitchen.

Emily scooped my kibble into my bowl with lightning speed.

I devoured it with my usual alacrity. I couldn't be sure,

but I think Emily gave me an extra scoop to compensate for the tardiness of my meal.

"Thank you for coming in to help with the girls," Emily said. "Weren't you hosting mah-jongg this afternoon?"

"I was supposed to, but most of us were sick and another woman had to take her dog to the emergency vet. We rescheduled."

"I'm glad you didn't cancel on account of us," Emily said. "You're a lifesaver. I don't know what we would have done without you."

"About that…" Martha put her hand on Emily's arm.

Emily yawned again.

"You're tired. Get to bed and we'll talk about this another time."

Emily straightened, suddenly alert. "What do you mean?"

"It's just that," Martha bit her lip, then continued. "Sylvia and I both adore spending time with Diedre and Zoe—we truly do."

"They think the world of you, too."

"Yes…well…we each have our own busy lives. Sylvia's got her book club and her volunteer days at the library. I love mah-jongg and spending time with my friends."

"Not to mention a certain dashing suitor by the name of Doug Roberts."

I watched Martha turn that pretty shade of pink that humans sometimes do.

"And spending time with Doug." Martha clasped her hands together. "We need to keep living our independent lives. Sylvia and I know how hard it is to regroup after a spouse dies. We've each finally built lives we're happy in."

"Grant and I understand and don't want to interfere with that."

"Good. Don't misunderstand—we're both happy to help when we can and will step in whenever there's an emergency."

"Are you trying to tell me that spur-of-the-moment business trips don't constitute an emergency?"

Martha was silent.

I looked from Emily to Martha. Based on the set of their jaws and the stiffness in their shoulders, I knew this silence was conveying a lot.

Martha finally spoke. "Given your careers, and the pace at which you both work, Sylvia and I think this sort of thing—like what happened today—will occur more and more. We can't drop what we're doing at a moment's notice."

Emily rested one hand on her waist and stretched back. "I understand." She blew out a breath. "We do not have our act together on this joint parenting thing," she replied.

"I'm not pressuring you," Martha said, pulling her daughter in for a hug. "Sylvia and I have you covered for this week while you've got your big meeting and Grant's out of town."

"I promise—Grant and I will talk this weekend. We'll figure out our childcare backup." Emily squeezed Martha tightly before letting her go.

"And maybe this was a one-off and you won't have to worry about it. At any rate, it's late. Let's go to bed."

I liked the sound of that.

Emily took me out for a comfort break. We checked on

the kids, asleep in Zoe's room with Sabrina snoring in her bed in the corner.

Emily got ready for bed with uncharacteristic speed.

I settled into my spot, but sleep eluded me. Things were unsettled for us at both our office and at home. I didn't like it, but I couldn't come up with solutions. Going with the flow and reacting in real time to whatever came my way was what I was trained to do. It would have to be enough to meet our challenges. I finally closed my eyes and slept.

CHAPTER 22

Zoe set her lunch tray on the table and slid into the seat across from Ava.

"Hi." A relieved smile flashed across Ava's face. "I thought maybe you weren't at school today."

"Sorry I'm late," Zoe said. "I was reading about the science fair on the bulletin board in the hallway."

"Are you going to enter? I think fourth grade works in teams."

Zoe nodded. "Three other boys in my class are doing a project and they asked me to join. I haven't decided."

"You're super smart. I'm not surprised."

"Have you done one?"

"Everyone in my class made models of the solar system last year." Ava continued eating her turkey sandwich.

"I'll bet you won," Zoe said, bending to make sure Ava could read her lips.

Ava nodded.

"That's cool. Will you enter again this year?"

"No. The projects are way too easy until you get to your grade."

"Working on simple stuff is boring," Zoe agreed.

They continued to eat in companionable silence.

"I'm doing something new," Ava said.

Zoe looked at her, raising one eyebrow.

"My mom says you should try lots of new things when you're a kid so you can find out what you like and what you're good at."

"That's what Sylvia says. She's Grant's mom."

"I'm a good dancer," Ava said. "I take lessons. Even though I can't hear the music, it's easy to learn steps and I memorize routines on the first try. I stay in time with everyone else by counting the beats, and usually I can feel the drum beats, too."

"That's so cool," Zoe said.

"My dance teacher says I'm very good." Ava sat up straighter. "She called me exceptional."

"Wow," Zoe replied.

"My teacher does choreography. Do you know what that is?"

"She makes up dances?"

"Yep. She does it for the youth theater. They're doing a musical called *Mary Poppins, Jr.* this spring. She said there's lots of dancing in it and told me I should try out for it. If I get a part, she said we'll work together on it, so that I nail it. That's what she said."

Zoe grinned at her friend. "I'm sure you will. Emily does almost everything people with eyesight can do—she just does things differently. I'm sure it's the same with being deaf."

Ava nodded her agreement.

"What about singing? Are you good at that?"

"Mom says so. I stay with the beat by counting when I sing."

"Then why not try out for the lead role?"

"No." Ava spread her hands on the table and splayed her fingers. She leaned toward Zoe. Her tone was firm. "I don't want to sing by myself."

Zoe leaned back and raised her hands in front of her, palms facing Ava. "Okay. I didn't mean to upset you."

Ava dropped her gaze to the table. "I'm sorry. It's just that most kids don't like the way I talk."

Zoe looked at her friend.

"I know I sound funny. Deaf people do. We can't help it. I don't hear what they say, but I can tell when someone's making fun of me."

"Emily says that she may not *see* people's reactions, but she can *hear* them by the way they move and breathe."

"Wow, she can hear people breathe? That's amazing." Ava paused, then said, "You're…you're my only friend who isn't deaf."

Zoe blinked rapidly. "You should definitely try out," she finally replied. "You'll be awesome."

"Thanks." Ava's eyes glittered with determination. "I've just decided. I'll get my mom to sign me up to audition."

"Good." Zoe paused before continuing. "I love Diedre— she's my stepsister—and hope she gets the lead role. She'll be wonderful. But I hate that stupid people make you afraid to try for it, too."

"Maybe I'll go for the lead next year."

The lunch bell rang, and Zoe walked with Ava to the girls' bathroom. She scanned the children filing past them, a fiercely protective look on her face.

No one paid them any attention.

Zoe released the breath she'd been holding. Maybe Ava was imagining things. She didn't think any of these kids would make fun of her new friend.

CHAPTER 23

*G*rant turned onto his side and pressed a kiss into Emily's neck.

She rolled over, pressing her back against his chest.

"It's nice that the girls are old enough to sleep in," he murmured, burrowing his face into the thick sheaf of her auburn hair fanned out on the pillow.

"It sure is. Monday through Friday I'm busy from the moment my alarm goes off until I hit the sheets."

"We've got ourselves over-extended, for sure."

"I'm not complaining. Busy is my normal state. I'm just thankful for the weekend."

"So you're not working today or tomorrow?"

"Well…I thought I'd look at the teams Dhruv and Kari put together for our projects. They finished them up right before the Denver group left yesterday afternoon. The new assignments will be announced on Monday morning. I need to approve them before those emails go out." She twisted her face toward him. "How about you?"

"Don't kill me, but I have to go into the office for a little while this afternoon. I need to check on a few things for this new project. I'll be gone two hours, tops." He hugged her closer. "I'll work around whatever we need to do for the girls. You shouldered all of that last week. I'll take the wheel now."

"They don't have plans to go anywhere," Emily replied. "Zoe's having a new friend over this afternoon and Diedre is learning lines and practicing 'A Spoonful of Sugar' from *Mary Poppins*."

"That sounds very low-key."

"Should be. I plan to look at those work groups on my laptop while they're busy." Emily pressed her hands over her head and extended her toes to the foot of the bed.

"I'm happy to hear Zoe's having a friend over. As an introvert myself, I remember how hard it was to make friends at a new school. Diedre is like Craig—neither of them has ever met a stranger."

"It's weird how different twins can be. You and your brother are identical physically but that's the end of the similarities. I was a shy kid, too. Never in a million years would I have auditioned for a part in a play—much less the lead."

"I'm happy she's trying out for it, but nervous if she gets a part."

"Why's that?"

"You saw the rehearsal schedule. Four nights a week until 9:00 and all day Saturday until tech week when rehearsals may go until midnight. Diedre's in fourth grade, for heaven's sake. That's a lot. We're finding it hard to manage the regular school schedule, without extracurricular activities."

"I've been thinking about all that, too. The bottom line is we want our girls to pursue their interests and take advantage of the opportunities that present themselves." She turned onto her side to face him. "We'll find a way to make it work."

Grant traced her chin with a finger and leaned in to kiss her. "I love your can-do attitude for everything, Em." He stretched. "I hope she isn't crushed if she doesn't get it."

"Learning how to handle disappointments is part of the process of growing up. Helping her find her way through them is part of our parenting journey." Emily pushed back the covers and stepped out of bed.

"True. And very wise." He rose and began making the bed.

"It is. And it's not from me." Emily smoothed the sheets and blanket on her side. "That's what Sylvia told me the other day."

"Sounds like something she would say."

"She's wise. Both of our mothers are."

They pulled the duvet cover into place.

"Speaking of which," Emily said, picking up a throw pillow from the floor. She felt the textured weave on one side and arranged the pillow in the middle of the bed with the textured side facing out. "We need to talk about backup childcare. Mom delicately pointed out that she and Sylvia have their own lives and can't always drop everything to help us."

"That's fair enough. We'd have been fine if I hadn't taken

this massive job in Southern California." He sighed audibly. "I'm sorry. I've messed things up before we even got started."

"You took that job for lots of good reasons. We made the decision together. You've got nothing to be sorry about." Emily walked around the end of the bed and circled him with her arms. "We'll figure this out. Are you in town next week?"

"I am."

"Good. Me too. We don't need an ironclad Plan B by Monday morning. We've got time."

An explosion of barking sounded from the girls' rooms, followed by the thundering of tiny paws in the hallway.

"Sabrina," they said in unison.

"That'll mean the girls are up," Grant said.

Emily walked the familiar path to their bathroom and grabbed her robe off the hook on the back of the door. "I'll take Sabrina and Garth out and feed them."

"I'm going to take a fast shower and then I'll make us all a big breakfast."

"Sounds like a plan."

"I'm looking forward to spending time with the girls this morning. I missed them. I want to hear all about their new school."

"They're excited to tell you. You can go to the office this afternoon while they're busy."

Grant said, "I'll stay here until Zoe's new friend comes over. I'd like to meet her."

"She'd love that. Did Zoe tell you anything about her?"

"Just that she's in third, a brainiac, and they eat lunch together."

"That's all?"

"Yeah. Why?"

"Nothing. You've got all the pertinent information. I'm glad you're going to meet her." Emily smiled to herself as she left the room. Deafness didn't define Ava, just as blindness didn't define her. She was glad that Zoe understood this truth.

CHAPTER 24

*T*he doorbell rang and Garth and Sabrina swarmed the door, barking in a fashion that was three parts welcome and one part warning.

Emily commanded them to sit and stay.

Grant checked the doorbell app before opening the door. "You must be Ava," he said to the tall, skinny girl with a plait of chestnut-colored hair that fell to her waist. He opened the door.

Ava stepped into the foyer, followed by her mother.

Emily stuck out her hand. "Emily Main," she said.

Ava's mother moved to Emily. "I'm Tammy," she said as they shook hands.

"Hi, Ava," Grant said again.

Ava didn't respond. She was accepting an effusive greeting from Sabrina, who had broken out of her sit-stay while Garth remained obediently in place.

"I'm sorry," Tammy said. "She reads lips, but only if she

knows you're talking."

Grant pivoted to look at the woman.

"Ava's deaf," her mother said.

"I...I didn't know that." He knelt next to Sabrina and looked into Ava's eyes. "I'm Grant," he said.

"My name's Ava," she said.

"Zoe and Diedre are in Diedre's room. Have you met Diedre?"

Ava shook her head no. "Zoe told me about her."

"She's looking forward to meeting you. I think they're working on Diedre's audition for *Mary Poppins, Jr.* I'll take you back to their rooms." Grant stood and gestured to a hallway that took a sharp turn to the left.

Ava swung to her mother and waved goodbye, then followed Grant.

Sabrina trotted after them.

Tammy sighed happily. "Your lab's very well behaved," she said. "Can I say hello to your dog?"

"That's what he's trained to do." Emily released Garth and called him over. "We're glad Ava could come over," Emily said. "Zoe's been looking forward to this afternoon."

"I'm thrilled about it, too. This is her first invitation to play at another child's house since she started at this school." Tammy's voice was thick with emotion as she bent to greet Garth.

"That's hard," Emily said, her own voice close to cracking. "People aren't always welcoming to those of us with differences."

"Ava said that Zoe understands and acts like Ava is normal."

"That's Zoe," Emily said, pride clear in her tone. "She was that way with me, too. Never saw me as any different or less capable."

Tammy tilted her head to one side. "What do you mean?"

"Zoe's never been bothered that I'm blind. In fact, she's the person who convinced me to get a guide dog."

Tammy took a step back, then looked down at the black lab whose muzzle rested under her hand. "You mean…this guy is a guide dog?"

Emily chuckled. "Garth isn't just any guide dog. He's the most outstanding guide in the whole wide world," she said, drawing out the last phrase as she reached out to rub his ears.

"I never would have guessed," Tammy said. She looked again at Garth. "That's why he waited patiently while Sabrina jumped all over Ava."

"Yep. Sabrina is Zoe's pet and definitely isn't well trained. Fortunately, none of her bad habits have worn off on Garth."

"How long…have you been blind since birth?"

"No. I lost my sight in an accident several years ago."

"That must have been hard."

"It was devastating, at the time. I was lucky enough to have supportive coworkers who forced me into rehabilita- tion training. Now I live a normal, independent life. I still work at the same company. In fact, I was promoted recently. Grant and I just got married, too. It's a long story, but Zoe became my ward shortly after I lost my sight. Grant has a fourth-grade daughter, so now I'm a stepmother, too."

"Congratulations. That's a lot of change in a short period of time."

"We're managing."

"Do you have help with your girls?"

"Not at the moment, but we're considering hiring a nanny. Grant may have to travel a lot."

"I guess you wouldn't want to be here with them by yourself."

"I take care of them on my own all the time. It's just that I have a demanding job, too. I can't always pick them up from the after-school program on time."

"I'm a dental hygienist and only work part-time. Ava has speech therapy once a week, and she's in dance classes two other afternoons. I'm lucky to have the flexibility I need."

"Being a working mother is way harder than I realized," Emily said. "Grant and I have been relying on our mothers for backup. We've decided we're imposing on them too much. That's why we need to come up with a better alternative."

"I don't know if you'd be interested, but my husband's cousin is a college sophomore who's looking for a part-time job. She used to be a full-time nanny before she went back to school. She's a kind, caring, responsible young woman."

"We'd love to talk to her! Can you text me her number?" Emily pulled her phone out of the back pocket of her jeans. "You and I should exchange numbers, anyway." She swiped at her screen. "Okay—I'm ready." She tapped in the numbers that Tammy gave her.

"Got it," Tammy said, and texted the nanny's number.

"I guess I should be going. I've got errands a mile long."

"Take as much time as you need. She'll be fine here. I'm not going anywhere."

"What about your husband? He's going to be here, too, isn't he?"

"Grant stayed so he could meet Ava, but he has to go into his office." Emily walked to the front door.

Ava's mother followed slowly.

"Ava's never been to a friend's for a play date before," her mother finally said.

Emily turned to her. "I understand you must be nervous about leaving her. Would you like to look around? We don't have guns and we don't have a pool."

"I'm sure your house is safe." Tammy bit her lip. "I guess I'm just being overprotective."

"That's understandable."

The women stood together in silence.

Emily took a deep breath. "If you're unsettled about leaving her with me because I'm blind, don't be. I'm as capable of keeping children safe as you are."

Tammy reached out to touch Emily's arm. "That's exactly what I was worried about. Please forgive me. I know you are."

Emily put her hand on top of the other woman's and squeezed it. "We're all entitled to be concerned about our kids." She leaned towards the door and opened it. "I hope you check off all the items on your list."

Tammy stepped through the door.

"You've got my number. Call me to check on Ava as often as you'd like."

"Thank you, Emily."

Emily and Garth stood in the open door as Tammy's heels clicked down the steps to the driveway.

CHAPTER 25

Sabrina burst into Diedre's room and launched herself onto the bed where Zoe lay sprawled on her stomach.

Zoe turned on her side, then sprang to her feet. "Ava must be here!" Zoe tapped the screen of her phone and the room fell quiet.

Ava stood in the doorway of Diedre's room, shifting her weight from foot to foot.

"Diedre was singing along to the soundtrack of *Mary Poppins*. We didn't hear the doorbell," Zoe said. She took Ava by the elbow and brought her into the room.

"I've got to go to the office for a while," Grant said. "Emily's here if you need anything."

The girls nodded absently as he made his exit.

"Hi, Ava." Diedre faced Ava, as Zoe had instructed her to do. "Zoe said you're trying out, too."

Ava nodded. "Not for the part of Mary Poppins, though."

"I've been looking at all the lines I'll have to learn. There's a lot. I'm not sure I want to try out for Mary Poppins, either."

"Sure you do," Zoe replied. "You sing as well as the girl on the recording."

Diedre shrugged. "I'm a good singer, but memorizing all those lines? I don't think I can do it."

"We can help you," Ava said. "You break the scenes into chunks and repeat the words over and over. Start by reading them and pretty soon you're saying them by heart."

"This is the way real actors learn lines," Zoe said. "I researched it." Zoe picked up the papers Grant had printed out for them earlier. "Let's use the audition scene. I'll go make two more copies of the script—one for me and one for Ava. We'll listen as you read."

Diedre cut her eyes from Ava to Zoe. "That won't be fun for Ava. I mean…"

"I'm really good at reading lips," Ava said. "If you mess up words, I'll know it."

"Are you sure this won't be boring for you? I thought you came over to work on science fair ideas for Zoe."

"We've got plenty of time to come up with our project," Zoe said. "Auditions are soon. We'll start with you and then you and I can help Ava."

"I like that," Diedre said.

"Be right back." Zoe raced out of the room, script in hand, with Sabrina at her heels.

"We'll help you learn your lines, too," Diedre said.

"I don't want a speaking part," Ava said.

"Why not?" Diedre waited, hoping Ava wouldn't say what she thought she would.

"Kids make fun of the way I talk."

Diedre crossed her arms across her chest. "That's mean."

"I just want to sing and dance. I'll keep my voice real soft so you won't hear me above the other singers."

Zoe and Sabrina reentered the room. Zoe distributed a stapled stack of papers to each of them. "Turn to page twenty," she said. "That's where the audition scene starts." She tapped a spot halfway down the paper.

Zoe and Ava perched on the side of the bed, facing Diedre.

Sabrina lay between them, her head resting on Ava's lap.

Ava stroked Sabrina from the top of her head to the tip of her rapidly wagging tail, but she kept her eyes on Diedre.

Diedre focused on the script and read her part, with Zoe supplying the lines from the other characters. Diedre repeated the process until she soon let the script fall to her side. Ava interrupted her twice with corrections; Zoe only once.

A satisfied smile washed over her face when Diedre had flawlessly completed her lines from memory for the third time. "I think I've got it."

"You do!" Ava agreed.

"If I get the part, will you help me like this? I think I can learn it if you do," Diedre said.

Zoe looked at Ava. They both nodded.

"Do you want to practice for your audition, Ava? We can help you."

"I already learned the words to 'Step in Time.' I count the beats in my head to make sure I'm with the music." She rose from the bed and Diedre took her place. "Will you clap your hands to the beat while I sing so I know how fast I'm supposed to go?"

"Sure," Diedre said. "We'll find the song on the sound-track and play it softly while you sing so we clap at the right pace."

Zoe found the song and tapped her screen while signaling to Ava to start. Ava's pace was far too slow at first. With repetition, she finally sang at the appropriate tempo.

"That really helped." She glowed with new confidence.

"What about the dancing?" Diedre asked. "We've both got to dance. I think they even want Mary Poppins to tap dance. I don't know how."

Ava scooted off the bed and rolled the rug off the center of the bedroom floor. She quickly demonstrated a shuffle-ball-change, a flap-toe-heel-toe, and a triple time step.

Diedre jumped to her feet. "That was perfect. You know how to tap!"

"Mom says I've been a good dancer since I started to walk. I love tapping because I feel the beat through my tap shoes, up into my whole body. I can't hear the music, but I can feel it."

"Will you teach me those steps?"

"Sure."

"I'm a beginner."

"The triple time step is the most difficult, but we can build up to it. All the steps are combinations of the same basic movements."

"Is that the name of one of the steps you did?" Zoe asked, picking up a pencil and paper.

"That last one, yes." Ava demonstrated it again. "Do you have tap shoes?"

Diedre shook her head. "I'll have to buy them."

Ava placed her foot on the floor next to Diedre's. "Your foot is a teensy bit shorter than mine. I'm tall for my age." She looked down at Diedre. "I still have my old shoes. We can see if they fit you."

Diedre grabbed Ava's arm. "That would be so cool."

"I'll teach you the basic steps now," Ava said. "You should practice them over and over until they're comfortable. You'll need to learn them starting on each foot."

"That's helpful," Zoe chimed in.

"We're going to start on our right," Ava said. "Pick up your right foot and brush your toes diagonally to the right, ending by bringing your toes to the floor." She demonstrated, and Diedre followed her lead.

They continued to work on the step while Zoe went to the kitchen and brought back a sleeve of Oreo cookies and three glasses of milk on a tray. The girls took a break for their snack, then got back to business.

By the time Tammy returned to collect Ava, Diedre had mastered brush-step-ball-change on each foot under the tutelage of her able teacher.

Emily and Tammy stood in the doorway while Diedre and Ava showed everything they'd learned.

Tammy put her hand to her heart as she watched.

"Sounds to me like you've had a wonderful time together," Emily said. "I walked by to check on them several times," she said to Tammy, "and they never noticed I was there."

"We need to do this again, Mom," Ava said. "Diedre's going to use my old tap shoes."

"Sure," she choked out.

"Can we get together tomorrow? It takes time to learn to tap dance," Ava said.

"You're welcome here," Emily said.

"Can Zoe and Diedre come to our house?" Ava asked. "I've got a tap practice floor we can use."

"We'd love to have both of you over," Tammy swiftly agreed. "I'd be happy to pick them up and bring them home."

"Girls?" Emily asked.

"Yeah!" the girls replied.

"It's settled, then," Tammy said. The mothers and daughters walked to the door.

"Keep practicing," Ava said to Diedre.

"You're going to get this part and be the best Mary Poppins ever," Zoe said to her stepsister.

Diedre put her arms around Zoe and Ava in a group hug. "Thank you, guys. You make me feel like I can do this."

Tammy put her arm around Emily's shoulder and leaned into her. "This is the best afternoon I've had in a very long time. I'm grateful your daughters are in Ava's life."

Emily's voice resonated with emotion. "I feel the same way. See you tomorrow."

CHAPTER 26

I waited by the door the next day until I heard the car back out of the driveway. The house was suddenly quiet after Ava and her mom had left with the girls. The mothers and daughters had been talking a mile a minute, all of them in high spirits. Now that they were gone, things were too quiet.

I padded into the family room to find Sabrina settling into her bed for a nap. Grant was stretched out on the sofa in front of the television, his eyes half closed. Neither of them would be any fun.

I stretched my front paws out in front of me and fought a yawn. Frankly, I was bored. We spent all week racing from our house to the office. That was fine, but weekends were made for long walks in the sunshine. Enjoying nature.

I went to the French doors leading to the backyard. The sky was overcast, and a fine drizzle wet the pavers. I didn't mind walking in this kind of weather, but humans didn't like it.

Emily had headed for her laptop as soon as the front door closed on the girls. I was about to resign myself to a nap when she pushed past me into the family room.

"Grant...honey?"

"Huh," he replied, pushing himself up on one elbow.

"Were you asleep?"

"No...well...just resting," he said, running his hand over the stubble on his chin. "What's up?"

"Stephanie just called. She and Dhruv are moving their stuff down the hall into the apartment I just vacated."

"That's nice." He still sounded half asleep.

"The cleaning crew apparently removed all the braille labels from the kitchen. Stephanie remembered I was pleased with how I had organized it and asked if I could come over to help her put on new labels."

"Now?"

"She said anytime, but the girls are out of the house, and I have time. Plus, I've got a couple of comments for Dhruv on the project assignments he and Kari came up with."

I made a beeline for Emily and rested my head against her thigh.

"I think Garth needs an outing, too," she said. "I'll bet he misses Biscuit and would love to see Sugar and Rocco, too."

My Emily was the best.

Grant picked up the remote and switched off the television. "This game is boring, anyway. That's why I was getting sleepy. Can Dhruv use my help moving furniture?"

"I'm sure he could." Emily paused. "I wasn't trying to get

you to come with me. I wanted to let you know Garth and I were going out. You've had a long week. If you want some home alone time, go for it."

"I'd rather be with you." He stood. "Let me get my shoes and keys and we'll be on our way."

The drive to our old apartment was fast in the middle of a Sunday afternoon. Emily took me out of my working harness as soon as we got near Dhruv and Stephanie's apartment.

My friends Sugar and Rocco were barking their special greeting for me before we got to their door. They were like Sabrina—not as well-mannered as Biscuit and me. It wasn't their fault—they weren't highly trained like we were.

The door opened and two arms I recognized shoved an armchair partially into the hallway.

"Here, let me help with that," Grant said as Dhruv moved around the chair and bent to pick it up from the front.

"Grant," Dhruv cried, straightening and extending his hand. "What are you—and Emily—doing here?"

Rocco squeezed through Dhruv's legs and jumped onto my front legs to greet me.

"I'm here to help Stephanie replace the braille labels in the kitchen," Emily said. "And Grant thought you might need help," she reached out and touched the arm of the chair, "moving furniture. Didn't Stephanie tell you we were coming?"

"We've been so busy, we've barely spoken since breakfast. She's feeling good and is acting like we need to get everything done right now."

"That sounds like her," Emily said. "No time like the present. Is she here?"

"She and Biscuit are in your old place," he replied.

"I can see that Sugar wants to say hello to this guy," Grant said, referring to me. He picked up the chair by one arm and Dhruv lifted it by the other. "Let's take this down the hall and then let the dogs run around out back."

"Good idea," Dhruv said. "We'll get Biscuit, too."

They soon deposited the chair near the fireplace in the window, its location carefully noted by both Stephanie and Emily. Everyone stepped to the grassy area behind the building reserved for dogs and the four of us ran, wrestled, sniffed, and peed to our heart's content. Our humans chatted amiably until the misty drizzle turned into solid rain.

"We'd better go in," Stephanie said, calling for Biscuit.

I turned and followed my guide dog bestie, anticipating the command from Emily that followed. Biscuit and I peeled off from the group when Stephanie and Emily entered our old apartment. Grant, Dhruv, and my other dog friends continued down the hall.

"I've got a pretty good idea of what should go where in the kitchen," Stephanie said. "I appreciate your coming over to help me fine-tune things."

Biscuit and I stood in the kitchen doorway.

"I'm happy to be here," Emily said. "I've missed you. And Garth loves spending time with Biscuit."

"They're great together, aren't they? Besties—just like us."

"I think so, too. Sometimes it's nice to be with a friend."

Emily and Stephanie reached out for each other and stood quietly, their arms around each other's waists.

Biscuit and I swung our muzzles to each other. The energy in the room had changed, and we both knew it. Our people were having big feelings. Instead of retreating to the living room for naps, we stayed put.

"Dhruv told me things are not going well with integrating the Denver team," Stephanie said.

"We're not off to the best start, but we'll get there. Kari, Dhruv's Denver counterpart, is committed to making this work. I think she and Dhruv are working well together." Emily turned to Stephanie. "Has Dhruv said anything different to you?"

"No...not at all. He really enjoys working with Kari."

"Good. It's going to take time. How about you? Was it fun telling people about your pregnancy?"

Stephanie faced forward. I could see her chin quiver.

Biscuit went to her side and brushed against her leg.

"It was odd, actually," came Stephanie's eventual reply.

"Odd? I don't like the sound of that."

"You know that both sets of parents are thrilled," Stephanie continued, "but Dhruv's extended family—especially his aunties—don't think a blind woman can be a good mother."

"What do they know about it? Just ignore them."

"That's what Dhruv said. Actually, he said that they're opinionated and bossy, and drive all the young mothers in the family nuts. They act like nobody can do anything right."

"There you are, then."

"It's not just them. I told the teacher in the classroom next to mine..."

"Rebecca? The one you like so much—who recently returned from maternity leave herself?"

"Excellent memory. Yes. She's completely overwhelmed by the entire experience. She doesn't think a blind woman can be a mother. At least not of a newborn."

Emily's spine stiffened, and she arched her back. She looked like a cat I once met whose tail got big when it didn't want to play with me. "Did she say that?"

"Not in so many words. And she apologized. But I know she thinks I can't do this." Her voice was barely audible when she finished.

"And now you're doubting your abilities, too."

Stephanie's ragged breathing was her answer.

Emily moved her hand up to Stephanie's shoulder and gave it a shake. "I want you to stop this right now." Her tone was firm. "We both know other blind parents—blind couples who are parents. They're all competent and wonderful."

Stephanie snuffled and wiped her eyes on her sleeve.

"You're one of the most loving and thoughtful people I've ever met," Emily continued. "That's a prime quality in any parent. You're a gifted and creative problem solver. All independent blind people are. We think outside the box and find ways to do things all day long. You're like...Ph.D. level in problem-solving."

Stephanie chuckled.

"Here's what I want you to do," Emily said. "Pay attention to all the things that you do this week better than if you were sighted. Write them down. I'll keep a list, too. We'll have coffee next weekend and compare lists. That'll give us both a boost of confidence."

"I'm not sure I'll have anything on my list," Stephanie said.

"Stop thinking that! Right now. I'll bet you'll be amazed. The person with the shortest list has to buy."

Stephanie chortled. "I know how competitive you are, Em. I'll have to really pay attention to what I do."

"There you go. This is going to be good. I can't wait to see what we accomplish this week."

"Speaking of which, let's get my kitchen done."

Biscuit glanced over at me. I nodded. The crisis had passed. We curled up together on the living room floor, in a sliver of sunshine that had just broken through the clouds outside the window.

CHAPTER 27

"*A*nd that concludes our first weekly meeting with the new teams." Emily faced the camera on her laptop. "Great reports, everyone. And solid progress. Thank you. We'll see everyone on zoom again next week." She held up a hand as the team members in the San Francisco office pushed back their chairs from the conference table. "Dhruv —can you and Kari stay on with me?"

"Sure," he replied, sitting back down.

"Of course," Kari chimed in from Denver.

"We'll wait until everyone else returns to work," Emily said.

She and Dhruv were soon alone in the conference room.

"Okay—it's just me here in Denver," Kari said. "Is there... a problem?"

"No. Nothing of the kind. I have some questions—and a few suggestions—after hearing the reports this morning."

"They were good, right?" Dhruv asked.

"Yes. And all were given by the most senior member of the two-person teams you put together."

"We built the teams of one person from San Francisco and one from Denver," Kari said, "and we paired the most experienced programmers with the newbies. We wanted to encourage mentorship."

"That makes sense," Emily said. "Who chose the person to give the weekly report?"

"We let each team decide," Dhruv said.

"And they all chose the most experienced person to present," Emily observed. "I don't know the Denver people very well yet, but the ones from San Francisco don't need practice making presentations."

Kari and Dhruv remained silent.

"What's our goal in combining the San Francisco and Denver teams?" Emily asked.

"Denver needed a shift to a collegial group who could work collaboratively," Kari said.

"That's one thing—a change in departmental culture. Dhruv?"

"We're developing a large group of programming experts who can function across a wide range of corporate objectives. If—when—there's another major issue, we'll be able to pull in programmers who will hit the ground running."

"And work together with transparency. We don't want anyone protecting their turf and withholding information from the others working on the same issue. That's what got us into so much trouble with the cyber breach," Kari said.

"Exactly," Emily said. "I'm sure the experienced programmers stepped in to make today's reports because they knew they could do it."

"At least two of the newbies from Denver are very shy and wouldn't volunteer to make a report. They'd be thrilled to always leave it to someone else."

"Fear of public speaking," Emily said.

"Making oral reports is part of our job," Dhruv said. "We all have to do them eventually if we want to advance. I used to hate them, but my manager made me do them—and helped me practice them and become comfortable speaking in front of other people."

Emily didn't see the admiring look he gave her, but she could hear the gratitude in his voice. "We want everyone on both teams to achieve mastery of everything needed to advance their careers," she said.

"So we should tell them that the weekly reporting needs to shift between team members," Dhruv said.

"Starting next week," Kari concluded.

"Is that what you wanted to talk to us about?" Dhruv asked.

"That's one thing. I also wanted to share my thoughts about two of the teams. One from Denver and one from San Francisco."

"You approved them," Kari quickly added.

"I know I did. I'm not saying that the pairing won't work, but I want you to pay special attention to their working dynamics in the coming weeks."

"Elaborate," Dhruv said.

"These two teams are made up of unique personality

types. One person is shy, retiring, and non-confrontational. The other is…" she paused, looking for words.

"Overbearing?" Kari supplied a name. "If you're talking about her, I can confirm she comes off that way. She's convinced she always has the right answer. If you challenge her, you can change her mind, but you have to be extremely pushy with her. At least that's what I found working with her. And underneath that obnoxious exterior, she's the nicest person."

"We combined and restructured these regional teams so that the company would have the full benefit of everyone's expertise," Dhruv said.

"We don't want anyone's opinions to be discounted or overlooked," Emily said.

"Good call, Emily. Dhruv and I put those two teams together based on subject matter expertise. We never considered personality dynamics."

"I agree—this isn't good. Should we reassign them?" Dhruv asked.

"Not yet," Emily said. "I'm only suggesting you monitor these teams. You're both supervisors now. You may have to work more closely with them to make sure they're functioning well together."

"Thanks, Emily," Kari said.

"The people part of the job is the hardest," Dhruv said.

"Always is," Emily replied. "Keep me posted and reach out whenever you need me. I'm always available to kick ideas around. Now—let's get back to work."

She closed her laptop and she and Garth walked with Dhruv back to their offices.

"One last thing," she said to him as she and Garth turned to her office. "The girls and I are throwing a baby shower for you and Stephanie."

"She told me. A couples' shower. I've never heard of one." His tone of voice contained more trepidation than excitement.

Emily smiled at her introverted coworker. "It'll be fun. Would you remind Stephanie that I'll need a couple of dates from her and a list of the people she'd like to invite?"

"Won't it just be you and Grant and the girls?"

Emily chuckled. "Of course not. They'll be there, of course. I'm going to invite both of your coworkers and your families."

"You mean—mine too? I have a lot of cousins." He inhaled sharply. "And my aunties?"

"All of them."

Dhruv was silent.

"What's wrong?"

"My aunties are...a bit much. They always want to control everything."

"It's just a shower. There's nothing for them to control. It'll be fine."

"Oh...okay."

"Just get me dates and those lists," Emily said. "And don't worry about anything else. I've got this." She and Garth proceeded to her office, leaving a pensive-looking Dhruv staring after them.

CHAPTER 28

*R*ebecca and Stephanie stood together along the edge of the playing fields at the far corner of the school campus.

"At least this fire drill was on a clear day," Stephanie said, raising her voice to be heard over the excited chatter of the third graders.

"That's true," Rebecca stretched her arms over her head. "I'm not sure we'll get them settled down in time to accomplish anything else today once we get the signal to return to our rooms."

"I think you're right. It took forever to bring their attention back to our language arts lesson after recess. And that subject is one of their favorites."

"You can't blame them. After almost two weeks of rain, it's wonderful to be out in the sunshine."

Stephanie tilted her chin toward the sky, enjoying the warmth on her cheeks.

The children in front of them continued to chase each other across the grass and call out to their friends.

"Who's whimpering?" Stephanie brought her face down and turned toward Rebecca.

"What do you mean?"

"A kid is in distress."

"I don't hear anything."

They stood still and listened.

"Nothing. Maybe some kids were fooling around," Rebecca said.

"There." Stephanie raised her right hand quickly. "Hear that?"

"I...I don't," Rebecca said.

"Can you watch both our classes for a minute?"

"Of course," Rebecca said.

Stephanie pulled on Biscuit's harness and commanded her forward. Their destination was the tall hedgerow in front of the fence that bordered the playing field.

The sound was more persistent now.

Stephanie commanded Biscuit to take her to the right. She slowed their pace and Stephanie located the sound. It was unquestionably the sound of a whimpering child.

"Are you all right in there?" Stephanie called.

The whimpering ceased.

"I know someone's in there." She reached out a hand and felt the dense shrub. She tried to shove her hand into the bush, but the growth was too thick. How in the world did anyone get back there?

Stephanie stood, thinking.

The whimpering started again.

Her kids had counted off for her when they'd gotten to the playing fields and Rebecca had accounted for all of her class. Who could be back there?

"I'm here to help you," she said in a soothing voice.

Stephanie dropped to her knees and felt along the ground. Twelve inches to her left, Stephanie noticed that the grass was matted down. Further exploration revealed a gap between the trunks of two large bushes. She told Biscuit to sit and stay, then dropped her harness and assessed the opening. It was large enough for a small child to crawl through.

Stephanie rocked back on her heels, suddenly sure she knew who was suffering on the other side of the hedge.

"Liam," she called in a calm voice. "I know you're back there. You're safe. There's no fire. The drill will be over soon, and you'll need to go back to your classroom."

Liam didn't respond but continued to whimper.

Stephanie thought of the neurodiverse boy in the third classroom down from hers. He was always excited to see Biscuit, and she allowed him to pet her guide whenever Biscuit wasn't working. Loud sounds were triggers for some children. The fire alarm, with its piercing noise and flashing lights, was the likely culprit.

"Liam," she tried again. "I'm here with Biscuit. You know Biscuit."

The whimpering stopped again.

"The thing is, she's scared. Biscuit doesn't like all the noise. It hurts her ears." At least that part was true, Stephanie thought. "Can you help me make Biscuit feel better? She needs someone special to pet her."

Stephanie held her breath and waited.

The snapping of twigs told her Liam was on the move. He soon burrowed out from behind the bush.

Stephanie stood and gave him her hand, pulling him to his feet. "Thank you for coming out, Liam. That was very brave of you. You can pet Biscuit now."

Liam knelt next to the dog and ran his hands gently along her back.

The school public address system crackled, and the principal announced that there had been no fire. They'd completed a successful drill and directed everyone to return to their classrooms.

"I need to go back to my class," Stephanie said. She grasped Biscuit's harness. "And Biscuit has to go back to work now."

Liam jumped to his feet. "I know. No touching her."

"That's right. Very good. Are you okay to go back to your class?"

"Yeah."

"Good. I want you to stay with me as we rejoin my class. You'll walk back to the third-grade wing with us and I'll drop you off at your room on the way to mine. Can you do that?"

Liam nodded.

"I can't see you, so you'll have to use words."

"I'll walk with you."

Stephanie touched his shoulder. "I know the alarm scared

you and it was courageous of you to come out to help Biscuit. Thank you."

Liam stood a little taller. Stephanie commanded Biscuit to find her classroom, and she and Liam made their way back.

CHAPTER 29

Zoe and her new friend Ava sat across from each other at the table in the school library. The third-grader sat at the edge of her seat, elbows propped on the table and her ankles crossed under the chair. She flipped through the last few pages of the notebook containing descriptions of previous science-fair-winning projects. "None of them are good enough," she whispered to Zoe. She closed the notebook and set it on top of the growing stack of discarded books at the end of the long library table.

"Look at this one," Zoe said, sliding a different notebook to her friend.

Ava turned in her chair and leaned across the table.

Zoe opened a folded diagram. She tapped it with her finger. "This one is sort of cool, but I'm going to ask the librarian if she has any other books."

Ava nodded. "You want to pick the best project." Ava leaned over the diagram to study it.

Zoe approached the young librarian, who was ferrying an armload of books back to her desk. She smiled at the usually friendly woman.

"Yes?" The librarian's tone was polite but curt.

"Do you have any more books with science fair projects?" Zoe asked.

"You've already got ten of them out. Surely you can find something you'd like to work on in what you've got."

Two books from the top of the librarian's stack began to slide.

The librarian groaned and shifted her weight to prevent the others from joining them.

Zoe stepped forward and grabbed the two escapees before they tumbled to the floor.

"Thank you," the woman said. "Zoe, is it?"

Zoe nodded.

"You're always so helpful." She made it to her desk and deposited the books into a rolling cart. "I never have to clean up after you."

"Thank you," Zoe murmured.

The librarian looked over at Ava and the tall stack of books and notebooks at the end of the table where she sat. "You really didn't find a project you'd like to work on?"

Zoe shook her head. "No, ma'am. They're all too easy."

The woman pursed her lips as she contemplated the girl. "You're in all the advanced classes, aren't you?"

"I am."

"Well...I guess it wouldn't hurt." She sat behind her desk and tapped at her computer screen. "I have one more book. It's for higher grade levels. Some of the projects are similar to the ones in those," she gestured to the table, "but are more detailed and complicated. Would you like to look at that book?"

Zoe nodded vigorously.

"They might be too hard for you."

"I understand."

"I don't want you to become frustrated with your project. Your parents and teacher have to sign off on it, so I guess the final decision is theirs." She got up. "Wait right here. I'll have to do some digging to find it."

Zoe smiled her thanks.

The librarian headed for a storage room in the back of the library.

Zoe busied herself straightening the books on the cart.

A loud, crescendoing thump broke the quiet in the room.

Zoe spun around in time to see the notebooks and books that had been at the end of their table now lay scattered across the floor. One of the notebook's rings had sprung open, and its pages were embedded in the mess.

Ava sat at the table, nose eight inches from the diagram, oblivious to what had happened behind her.

A girl who Zoe recognized as being one of the theater kids from Diedre's class was diving back into her seat at a nearby table. Two other girls at the table were snickering and pointing. A third girl was pulling at her ears and laughing.

The librarian reappeared, carrying an even larger notebook than the others. She halted when she spied the disheveled pile of books and notebooks on the floor.

Zoe blinked hard.

The librarian put the notebook on a shelf behind her desk. "You see—you had too many books out already."

"That wasn't our fault," Zoe said.

"What do you mean?"

"They didn't fall because we stacked them wrong."

The librarian sighed. "I know it was an accident."

"No. It wasn't an accident."

"What're you talking about?"

"Those kids at the next table." Zoe made a small motion with her head. "The girl in the blue shirt pushed them over."

"Why would they do that?"

"They wanted to see if Ava would jump. She's deaf and didn't react."

The librarian studied the table of girls who were now quietly reading.

"Did you see that girl push the books off the table?"

Zoe clenched her teeth. "I turned around at the sound. I saw her sitting down, and the others were all laughing. At Ava."

The librarian sighed heavily and turned her attention back to Zoe. "I believe you, but I can't do anything about this based on what you've seen." She continued. "It doesn't look like Ava knows anything about it. Let's pick up the books and I'll give you the new notebook." She grasped the rolling cart. "I'll help you."

"Thank you," Zoe said. She caught the eye of the perpetrator as they passed her table and glared at the girl.

The girl shrugged and turned away. The others at the table snickered behind their hands.

The librarian tapped Ava on the shoulder and pointed to the floor.

Ava shook her head in answer to the librarian's question, then got on the floor with Zoe and helped her gather all the materials.

"What happened?" Ava asked Zoe, keeping her head down while focusing on her lips.

"They just fell," Zoe lied. "No big deal."

Ava ran her eyes across Zoe's face, then nodded and helped complete the task.

"Thank you, girls," the librarian said. "I'll put that notebook back together in the proper order. You can come get the book of advanced projects I found for you."

Ava and Zoe were soon huddled together over a description of a roller coaster made of straws. One of the fourth-grade books had contained a description of a small, simple roller coaster. This one was three times the size and far more complex. The girls looked at each other and their smiles could have been mirror images.

"This is it!" Zoe cried, not bothering to whisper.

Ava's eyes telegraphed her agreement.

"Shhhhh…" came the exaggerated admonishment from the table of girls.

Zoe ignored them as she and Ava took the notebook to the librarian and asked for copies of the desired pages.

CHAPTER 30

I stretched my paws in front of me and dug my toes into my memory foam bed. We'd had a productive day, including a long meeting in the conference room. Very routine. Emily wasn't nervous about a thing, so I got a good nap.

Grant was home, and they'd had another of the thank-God-for-our-mothers casserole that they'd pulled out of the freezer the night before. The big excitement over dinner was talk about a baby shower for Dhruv and Stephanie. I knew they meant to include Biscuit, too.

Diedre and Zoe had a lot to say about that. Emily finally opened her laptop and began taking notes. I don't remember what a baby shower is, exactly. I *do* know that we're a family who loves to entertain. Grant said that—and that we're good at it. So it's sure to be fun.

The girls finished their homework, and Emily took Sabrina and me outside.

After we came back in, we headed to our room and Sabrina turned off as usual into the room where both girls slept. Tonight, they were in the twin beds in Diedre's room, talking to each other. Their tone of voice told me this wasn't their typical conversation.

I followed Sabrina into Diedre's room.

"I saw it, Diedre."

"You just said you didn't actually see it," Diedre said.

"Okay…well…I'm sure she did it. She pushed those books on the floor behind Ava to be mean."

"Oh—come on. I've never seen any of them do anything like that."

"They're bullies, Diedre. I know it."

Diedre remained silent.

"I wouldn't lie to you."

Diedre didn't respond.

"Why would I make this up?"

"I don't know." Diedre hesitated before continuing. "Maybe because they're my friends and I make friends easier than you."

Zoe shoved herself into an upright position. "What? You think I'm making this up—because I'm jealous of you?"

"I didn't say that." Diedre's tone was now sharp.

"That hurts my feelings. I'm not a liar. You should believe me, not them."

"I know you're not. But you've admitted that you didn't see her do it. Can't you be wrong?"

"She pushed those books. They were all in on it."

Diedre rolled away from Zoe.

"I'm going to sleep in my room tonight," Zoe said. She threw off the covers and stomped into the next room.

Sabrina and I exchanged glances. Sabrina got out of her bed and followed Zoe.

I stood in the middle of Diedre's room, listening. I soon heard what I feared I would. Diedre was whimpering.

I padded over to her and swiped the back of her neck with my tongue.

Diedre rolled to me and put her arms around my neck.

I didn't know how to resolve a misunderstanding between sisters, but at least I could provide comfort. I settled at the foot of her bed until her breathing told me she was asleep.

I got quietly to my feet and settled into my bed in Emily and Grant's room. Instinct told me Sabrina and I would soon be working overtime to restore peace in our family.

CHAPTER 31

*G*rant pulled the plastic lid off of his cup of coffee and blew across the surface of the steaming liquid as he walked to his gate. With any luck, his flight would be on time, and he'd be home before the girls went to bed. He needed this hit of caffeine.

He was exhausted from his week on the project site. The eighteen-hour days he'd put in would allow him to spend the following week at home. Being away from his family was like a festering wound for him, with no relief until he got home. He knew men who relished the opportunity to spend quiet time in a hotel room. He wasn't one of them.

He took the remaining seat in the packed waiting area for his flight. He was wedged between a woman who was wrangling three small children and an older man who was dozing in his chair, with a copy of a newspaper crumpled on his lap. One child sneezed, showering Grant's knee with droplets.

Grant rose quickly and found an open spot along a

column. He rested his back against it and checked his watch. Boarding started in another fifteen minutes. He took a swig of his coffee.

Diedre had been thrilled when he'd promised her that he would take her to her audition next week. And Zoe was eager to tell him all about her idea for her science fair project. Grant smiled, remembering the winning science fair projects he and his twin brother Craig had worked on together.

Grant didn't know much about musical theater, but science fair projects were right up his alley. He was excited to hear what Zoe had in mind. Maybe she and her classmates would let him help them. He shut his eyes briefly as he remembered how his dad had practically taken over their projects. Craig had gotten really mad at their father one year. Grant drank more coffee and made a mental note to rein himself in. This was Zoe's project, not his. He'd ask Emily to monitor his involvement, too. She'd tell him if he was over-stepping the mark.

The public address system at the gate crackled and a woman's voice announced that group A would board in five minutes.

Grant drained his cup and took his place in line. He might be tired, but he and Emily were making their combined lives work. They hadn't needed to hire a nanny, after all. In a few short hours, he'd be back to his happy, peaceful home.

GRANT ROLLED over in bed and groaned. His head was pounding from the three cups of coffee he'd had on the plane. They'd sat at the gate for two and a half hours before they'd been cleared for departure. He'd texted Emily to tell her not to wait up for him. The extra caffeine had been necessary for him to drive home from the airport.

The house had been quiet when he'd finally gotten there and he'd crawled into bed right away, but his over-stimulated brain hadn't let him fall asleep until almost five.

He opened one eye and looked at his phone on his nightstand. It was only eight-thirty. Why were his girls not sleeping in like they usually did on Saturdays? More importantly, why were they shouting at each other?

He lay back, willing for things to get quiet. When first one bedroom door and then the other slammed shut, he knew he had to get up.

Grant swung his feet to the floor, found the bottle of ibuprofen in the medicine cabinet, and washed two tablets down with a handful of water.

Doors opened in the hallway, and it sounded like the girls were coming his way.

Emily's voice was discernible above the others. "You're not going to wake up your dad. His flight was delayed, and he didn't get home until the middle of the night. We're going to let him sleep."

"But he always makes Saturday breakfast," Diedre whined.

"Yeah," Zoe said. "And he promised to talk to me about my project."

"You'll have plenty of time with him when he wakes up. He can make breakfast tomorrow," Emily said, her tone firm.

Grant pulled on a pair of sweatpants and a sweatshirt and opened the door to their bedroom.

"Or I can make pancakes right now," he said, forcing an energetic demeanor.

"Dad!" Diedre cried, throwing her arms around his waist.

He hugged her and held out an arm to Zoe.

She came to him slowly. He pulled her in tight.

"Was I dreaming, or did I hear the two of you arguing?"

Both girls remained quiet, nestled in the group hug.

"They've been upset with each other about a change in plans for the weekend."

"Really?"

Zoe nodded.

"Have you resolved things?" he asked.

"Not really," Diedre mumbled.

"Let's talk over breakfast," Grant said. "Are you hungry?"

Both girls said yes.

"Good. I'll make pancakes."

"And I'll scramble eggs," Emily interjected.

"Have you heard the term 'hangry'?" Grant asked.

"That's when you're mad 'cause you're hungry," Zoe said.

"I guess we're hangry," Diedre said.

"It's not a good idea to try to resolve a misunderstanding when you're hangry." He headed toward the kitchen.

"Grant's right," Emily said. "I want both of you to get dressed and make your beds. By the time you're done, we'll be ready to eat."

"You'll each have the chance to say what's bothering you. No shouting. No name-calling," he added.

Zoe and Diedre stepped out of his embrace and stalked off to their rooms.

"How long has this been going on?" Grant asked Emily as they headed into the kitchen.

"I sensed tension between them earlier in the week. The girls actually slept in their own rooms the entire time you were gone." Emily took eggs from the refrigerator.

"That's a first, but surely doesn't mean anything bad? They were going to grow out of sleeping in each other's rooms at some point." He cracked an egg into the pancake mix and stirred the batter.

"That's what I told myself. They were okay at bedtime but blew up at each other this morning. Diedre got a call from one of her friends at school, inviting her for a sleepover. Zoe got mad and they've been at each other ever since."

Grant poured rounds of batter onto a hot griddle. "They're each going to have their own friends. Zoe has to accept that."

Emily spun on him. "She knows that. I don't think Zoe's being jealous."

"It sure sounds like it."

"Let's wait to pass judgment until we hear the whole story, shall we?" Emily whisked the eggs with extra vigor.

Diedre entered the kitchen.

"Set the table, please," Emily said as she located the edge of a twelve-inch frying pan with her left hand and poured the beaten eggs in with her right. She held her hand above the surface of the stovetop to locate the hot burner, then slid the frying pan into place and began scrambling the eggs.

Zoe joined them and put milk and orange juice on the counter.

Stony silence replaced the easy banter of their usual Saturday morning conversation. Everyone filled their plates and took their first bites.

"Let's start at the beginning. I was woken by something I don't want to hear again: the sounds of the two of you fighting. Emily says you were fine when you went to bed. What's going on?"

Zoe swung to face her stepsister.

Diedre rolled her eyes.

"Actually, I think this started at the beginning of the week. On the night Zoe left Diedre's room to go sleep in her own," Emily said.

The room was silent except for the ping of icy rain pelting the windows.

"Let's try this," Emily said. "You both seemed fine this morning until Diedre told me she's been invited to a friend's this afternoon and to spend the night."

"Ava's coming over this afternoon to rehearse for auditions. We've made plans."

"She's nailed her part," Diedre said. "The rehearsal is more for my benefit."

"So why don't you want to rehearse with Ava and me?" Zoe asked. Her tone was sharp. "Isn't our help good enough?"

"It's not that. You've been great. But the girl who invited me over is one of the theater kids at school. She's done other musicals with the youth theater. Another girl will be there who's also been in shows. They know a lot about these auditions. I think they can help me with things you don't know about," Diedre replied firmly.

"That seems reasonable, Zoe," Emily said.

"What about Ava? Do I just call her and tell her not to come over?" Zoe retorted.

"Of course not," Grant said. "You said she helped you pick the science fair project, right?"

"Yeah."

"Would she like to work on it with us?"

"I guess."

"Invite her to spend the night here. We can make it very special for the two of you," Emily suggested.

Zoe shrugged.

"I can't see you, honey," Emily reminded her.

"That'd be fun. I'm sure she'd like that. Could we invite the boys from my group over this afternoon? All of us have to agree on the project and two of them think it might be too hard."

"Sure," Grant said with genuine enthusiasm. "The more the merrier."

"Does that solve the problem?" Emily asked.

Zoe glanced at Diedre.

"Zoe doesn't like my theater friends," Diedre blurted out. "She thinks they're mean."

Zoe lowered her gaze to the table.

"Zoe?" Grant leaned toward her. "Is that true?"

Zoe lifted her chin and nodded. "They made fun of Ava."

"You don't *know* that!" Diedre snapped. "You think you saw something, but you don't know."

"You'd better tell us what happened," Grant said.

Zoe described the scene in the library. "They were playing a prank on her because she's deaf. That's mean. At least I think it's mean."

"I do, too," Diedre retorted, "but we don't know that's what happened."

Emily and Grant swiveled to face each other. "So, you don't want Diedre to have anything to do with those kids?" Grant asked Zoe.

"She shouldn't want them as friends," she stated forcefully.

Emily addressed Diedre. "And you want to give them the benefit of the doubt, is that right?"

"Yes."

"Sounds like Zoe wants to protect her friend Ava," Grant said. "That's reasonable."

"She's my friend, too," Diedre said. "But I want other friends."

"Even if they're bullies?" Zoe's volume rose.

"They're NOT." Diedre shouted.

"That's enough," Emily said, slapping her palm on the table. "I know Diedre is a kind and caring girl. She would never be a bully or tolerate that behavior in her friends."

"Thanks, Emily," Diedre said in a small voice.

"We've got a plan for today that allows each of you to do something you want. That plan doesn't hurt anyone else." Grant looked from one girl to the other. "Diedre will go to this girl's house, and you can invite the boys over."

"And Ava can spend the night if she wants?" Zoe asked.

"Yes," Emily said.

"Then that's what we'll do. And I don't want to hear the two of you arguing about it."

"We won't," Zoe said in a deadpan voice.

Diedre turned to Zoe. "I'm not going to let anyone hurt Ava. I promise."

Zoe looked into Diedre's eyes. "If you go up against them, they'll be mean to you, too."

"That won't happen."

"I hope you're right." Zoe picked up her plate and began clearing the table.

Diedre jumped up to help her.

Grant leaned in to Emily. "Was this a success?" he whispered.

She shrugged. "Only time will tell."

"Being a kid is tough," he said.

"It certainly is. I'm glad we've got each other to help them through this."

"I shudder to think we've got the teen years ahead of us."

Emily groaned and got to her feet. "I can't stand to think about that right now. Let's clean up the kitchen and have another cup of coffee by the fire before we get too busy to have time for each other."

CHAPTER 32

Sabrina jumped out of her bed and raced to the door, barking her head off. She didn't even know if there was anything to bark about. That was my buddy, Sabrina.

I rose, stretched, and followed her to the door. A car had just pulled into our driveway. I soon heard footsteps on the stairs leading to the front door that I knew belonged to our new friend Ava. Tammy was right behind her.

Zoe threw open the door to greet her friend. "You're early," she said.

"Is that all right?" Tammy asked. "She insisted we get here while Diedre was home."

Ava stepped into the house, holding up a shopping bag. "I've got tap shoes for Diedre."

Emily joined us, telling Sabrina to sit with me. To my surprise, Sabrina understood and obeyed the command.

"That's so nice of you," Emily said. "We ordered tap shoes for her online, but they haven't arrived yet."

"She'll need these for her audition this week," Ava said. "I hope they fit."

"She's in her room. Let's go see if they do."

The two girls headed to Diedre's room.

"Come on in," Emily said. "Do you have Ava's stuff?"

"It's all in her backpack," Tammy said. She set it on the floor by the door, then quickly picked it up. "I don't want to leave this where you might trip on it."

"Thank you for thinking of that," Emily said. "Things left out of place are a serious problem for people like me. That's why my house always looks neat—it's not just a preference but a matter of safety."

"I can understand that."

"It's fine to deposit Ava's backpack by the door. I'll remember it's there."

Tammy set the backpack down. "I guess I'd better go." She hesitated by the door. "Ava's never stayed overnight at a friend's before."

"Grant and I will both be here—after he gets home from taking Diedre to her friend's house. She'll be safe with us."

"I'm not worried about that. She might get homesick and want to come home."

"If she does, Grant can drive her home."

"You wouldn't need to do that. I'll come get her. I just don't want Zoe's feelings to be hurt if Ava changes her mind about staying. Didn't you say this is Zoe's first time to have a friend over?"

"Other than Diedre, yes." Emily reached out a hand to Tammy.

Tammy took it.

"I'll try to help Ava get over any fears…" Emily began.

"She can always text me, and I'll encourage her, too," Tammy said.

"But if she needs to go home, that's what she should do. Zoe is a sensitive and mature girl. She'll understand. Don't worry about her." Emily squeezed Tammy's hand before releasing it.

"Good. I feel better." Tammy chuckled. "I think I'm more nervous about this than Ava is."

"That sounds par for the course."

I'd been following the conversation until now. Sometimes Emily made no sense.

"See you tomorrow morning, then." Tammy opened the door.

"Call me any time to check on things," Emily replied, closing the door behind Tammy.

She turned toward the annoying staccato tapping sound coming from Diedre's room. I'd have preferred to go back to the bed that molded to my body, but I stuck with Emily instead.

Emily paused in the open doorway. "Are those Ava's tap shoes I hear?"

"Yes! They fit perfectly!" Diedre's delight was palpable.

"She doesn't have to break them in," Ava said, turning to look at Emily.

"This is so nice of you," Emily said. "We'll return them as soon as the ones we ordered get here."

"Diedre can keep them," Ava said. "I've outgrown them."

Diedre continued to execute steps. "I love them. We can cancel the ones we ordered."

"I'll do that," Emily said.

Grant joined them in the doorway. "Those taps sound great, honey. I hate to interrupt, but we need to leave for your friend's house. I want to be here when the boys arrive so we can get started on the roller coaster project. Wait until you see what I've got to show you, Zoe."

"Really, Dad?" Zoe asked.

"Did Grant forget to mention that Mouse Trap was his favorite game as a kid? At least, that's what he told me."

"Mine too, Mr. Johnson," Ava gushed. "I love the seesaw part."

"That's a good one," he agreed. "My favorite was the cage at the end."

"The bathtub was always the best for me," Emily said.

"That blue slalom at the beginning is the most fun," Diedre said.

Zoe looked at the others. "What're you talking about?"

Everyone swung to face her.

"You've never played Mouse Trap?" Emily asked.

"Never heard of it."

"We'll rectify that right now. I'm sure my mom still has our game. I'll stop at her place on my way home to pick it up."

"We can all play it tonight, after dinner," Emily said. "If you want to."

"Sure!" Ava clasped her hands together. "Maybe you'll get ideas for things you can add to your roller coaster."

"It's supposed to be made of straws," Zoe said. "That's what I've read."

"I think Ava's on to something. We can use my firm's architectural software programs to design a larger structure with more complex details."

Emily patted his elbow. "You remember that this is Zoe's project, not yours?"

Grant blushed. I think his expression is what people call chagrined. Sometimes dogs look chagrined, too. Especially Sabrina, when she gets caught doing something she knows is wrong. That never happens to me.

"Okay, you two. You'd better go," Emily said.

Diedre slipped off the tap shoes and put them into her backpack, zipping it shut. "Thank you for the shoes, Ava." She pulled the girl into a hug.

"Good luck practicing," Ava said. "Those girls will help you. They know a bunch."

"If I find out anything good, I'll tell you. I want us both to get parts. That would be so fun." She slung her backpack onto her shoulder and followed her father to the car.

"Let's put your stuff in my room," Zoe said to Ava. "Emily changed the sheets on both beds so you can pick the one you want."

Emily brought one hand to her heart in a gesture I recognized as one that showed she was happy. That made me feel happy, too.

CHAPTER 33

"We can practice tapping in my garage," Tania said. "My mom left the car in the driveway so we could. We always rehearse for auditions in my garage," she added.

Diedre and another girl from their class slipped into their warm jackets. They picked up their tap shoes and followed Tania to her garage.

"You can practice in your regular shoes," Tania said to Diedre.

Diedre held up the shoes she'd received from Ava. "I've got shoes."

"Oh...good," Tania said.

The girls buckled on their shoes and lined up behind Tania.

"This is just like dance class," the other girl said. "Tania's a great dancer. She's going to go over basic steps with us."

Diedre nodded.

Tania tapped at her phone, and a snippet of music from the play filled the space. She led them through the basic tap steps that Diedre had learned from Ava.

"I thought you didn't know how to tap," Tania said.

"I just learned."

"You're good," Tania said.

Diedre flushed with pride. "Thank you. I'm not nearly as good as you. What part are you auditioning for?"

"I'm going for the main chimney sweep," Tania said. "He's got a big tap solo."

"You'll get it for sure," the other girl said. "You're the best dancer in the whole youth theater."

"Fingers crossed," Tania said.

"I'm auditioning to be in the ensemble," the other girl said. "I don't care what part I get. Being in the show is enough for me."

"Are you really going to try out for Mary Poppins?" Tania asked.

Diedre nodded. "I know I'm young. They'll probably cast a high school girl. But Emily found out that if they don't give me the part, they could still put me in the ensemble. I'm fine with that."

"You'd be with me—if I make it," the other girl said.

"That'd be fun." Diedre smiled at her.

"Can you sing?" Tania asked.

"I'm better at that than dancing."

Tania tapped at her phone again and found the accompaniment to "A Spoonful of Sugar."

"Want to sing for us?" the other girl asked.

Diedre cleared her throat, and the space filled with her clear, bright soprano.

Both girls stared at her. "You're great," Tania said.

"Better than the older girls in the troupe," the other girl said.

"I'm auditioning with a small clip from the middle of the song," Diedre said. "That's what the audition form says to do."

"Are you doing the part with high notes?" Tania asked.

Diedre nodded.

"Tania and I have to sing at our audition, but we're not all that good," the other girl said. "We're best at dancing."

"I'm getting cold," Tania said. "Let's go inside."

The three girls headed inside, depositing their shoes and jackets in a heap by the garage door.

"How'd it go, girls?" Tania's mom asked. "I've got hot chocolate for you in the crock pot." She began ladling the fragrant liquid into wide mugs. "There are plenty of mini marshmallows in a bowl on the counter."

"We're ready," Tania replied. "Diedre's new to the troupe —and she's good."

"That's wonderful. The girls have so much fun with the youth theater. And I'm always happy to share carpool duties with other mothers. If you get cast, be sure to tell your mom."

"My stepmom doesn't drive," Diedre said.

"Oh?" Tania's mother handed her a mug of the steaming treat.

"She's blind," Diedre continued.

"I'm sorry. I didn't know."

"It's okay. She does everything except that. My dad drives. I'll tell him."

"Excellent," Tania's mother said.

"Diedre just learned to tap dance, and she's good already," Tania said.

"My friend Ava taught me how," Diedre said. "You should see her. Those feet move so fast, and she hits all her taps."

Tania and the other girl exchanged glances. "The deaf girl from third grade?" Tania asked.

"Yep," Diedre replied. "She's auditioning for a chimney sweep part, too."

"You have to sing to be a chimney sweep," Tania said.

"I know," Diedre said. "She can sing. Zoe—she's my step-sister—and I helped her learn the song."

"That's so interesting," Tania's mother said, wiping a drip of hot chocolate from the counter.

"She counts the beats to stay in time with the music."

"Good for her," Tania's mother said, replacing the sponge in the holder by the sink. "I'm going to move the laundry along. You girls enjoy that hot chocolate."

"Thank you," Diedre said.

Tania stepped close to Diedre and lowered her voice. "What does she sound like?"

"What do you mean?" Diedre asked.

The other girl pinched her nose shut with her fingers and sang the audition song in the most nasal voice she could manage. "That's how she'll sound."

Tania and the other girl snickered.

"Nobody wants to hear her sing," Tania said.

"Stop it." Diedre took a step back and straightened her spine. "That's not nice. She can't help how her voice sounds."

Tania and the other girl stopped laughing and stared at Diedre.

"There's a deaf actress named Marlee Matlin. She's really famous. She sounds like that, and no one cares."

"We were just kidding," the other girl said.

Tania turned her back to Diedre, but not before Diedre saw her roll her eyes.

"Did you play a trick on Ava at the library?" Diedre asked.

"What're you talking about?" The other girl cast a nervous glance at Tania.

"No," Tania said. "Who told you that?"

"Zoe."

"What did she say?"

Diedre recited Zoe's version of the incident.

"You see," Tania said. "Zoe just thought she saw me push those books. Like I told you, I didn't."

"Maybe they were piled too high and fell on their own," the other girl said.

"Zoe said everyone at your table was laughing."

"Loud noises in the library are funny," Tania said. "You know it makes the librarian mad."

Tania and her friend trained earnest eyes on Diedre.

"I guess that could happen," Diedre replied after a long pause.

"It *did* happen," the other girl said.

"We aren't mean to your little third-grade friend," Tania said.

"Good." Diedre sighed in relief. "That's what I told Zoe."

"Since you helped Ava with the chimney sweep song, can you sing it with us?" Tania asked.

"Sure," Diedre said.

The girls refilled their cups with hot chocolate and headed to Tania's room to rehearse.

CHAPTER 34

*E*mily tucked her feet under herself on the sofa as she tapped at her keyboard.

"Can I get you a refill before I go?"

Emily picked up her mug from the coffee table and extended it to Grant. "You are the perfect husband. Where are you off to so early?"

"Diedre called. She wants to come home."

"I'm surprised she's even awake. Zoe and Ava are still asleep. Is everything all right?"

"She said she had a good time but is ready to go." Grant went to the kitchen and refilled Emily's coffee cup. "She's not too keen on sleepovers. Remember last year when our romantic dinner got cut short by her bailing on a sleepover?" He put the cup in its place on the coffee table.

"That's right. She wasn't really sick like she'd said she was. But she's older now, so it might be easier for her."

"I'll try to get her to open up with me on the way here. At

least she spent the night. Are you fine with me leaving you with Zoe and Ava?"

"Of course. Take your time. I'm making lists for Stephanie and Dhruv's baby shower. Garth and I are meeting Stephanie and Biscuit this afternoon at that coffee shop near my old place to make plans." Emily reached her arms over her head and stretched. "I wonder if the girls will want to come with me."

"Our pint-sized event planners would jump at the chance. I love watching them collaborate. We've teased them about it, but I believe they could run a successful event planning business when they grow up."

Emily chuckled. "When those two put their heads together, they can accomplish anything."

Grant bent to kiss Emily. "I'd better go. See you shortly."

"Why don't the two of you grab breakfast? Diedre hasn't had one-on-one time with her dad for ages."

"Great idea. I'll suggest it."

Emily continued her perusal of accessible online baby registries. Diedre and Grant surprised her when they entered the house fifteen minutes later.

Diedre walked to the sofa and slumped down next to Emily.

Emily reached out an arm and drew the girl to her. "I thought you and your dad were going to stop for breakfast."

Diedre shrugged. "I wanted to come home."

"Did anything happen at Tania's?"

"No." Diedre straightened. "They were great. We're all set for auditions next week."

Grant joined them. "If Diedre gets a part, we can carpool to rehearsals with Tania's mother."

"That's handy," Emily replied, closing her laptop. "Let's get breakfast started. I've got cinnamon rolls ready to go into the oven. I'm sure the aroma of baking bread will wake up your sister."

The three of them went to the kitchen. As predicted, the delicious smells roused Zoe and Ava. Breakfast was soon underway. Zoe and Diedre positioned themselves at opposite ends of the table.

"My mom will be here any minute," Ava said, polishing off the last morsel of her cinnamon roll.

"What are you doing today?" Emily asked her.

"We're helping my grandmother clean out her attic," Ava said.

"That sounds productive," Grant said. "I've always loved to poke around an attic."

"Hoping to find a long-forgotten treasure, like you see on TV?" Emily asked.

Grant chuckled. "Guilty as charged."

"Let's get your stuff together," Zoe said to Ava.

"I'll help," Diedre chimed in.

The three girls rose and took their plates to the sink.

"Would the two of you like to join Stephanie and me this afternoon to plan Stephanie's shower?" Emily asked what she thought was a rhetorical question, given the girls' love of event planning.

Zoe and Diedre stared at each other.

"No," Zoe said.

"I've got homework," Diedre said.

Emily's jaw dropped.

The doorbell rang.

"That'll be Ava's mom," Diedre said.

"I'll get her backpack," Zoe said.

"We'll talk about this later," Emily called after Zoe and Diedre as the girls left the kitchen.

EMILY LISTENED to the text message from Stephanie.

"We're at a table along the back wall."

Emily smiled and shook her head. She was ten minutes early and still hadn't beaten her friend to the coffee shop. "Find Biscuit," Emily commanded Garth.

He took her directly to their destination.

Emily and Stephanie hugged each other while Garth and Biscuit bumped noses and sniffed each other in an overly familiar way.

Emily hung her purse on the back of her chair and removed her wallet. "Can I get you something?"

"Already done. Your grande caramel macchiato is on the table at the six o'clock position from where you're sitting."

Emily resumed her seat. "You are a wonder! Thank you."

"It's the least I could do since we're meeting to talk about the shower you're throwing for us."

"I'm so excited about it."

"I expected the girls to be here, too," Stephanie said. "Is this new school piling on the homework?"

"They're both extremely busy." She told Stephanie about the science fair project and the youth theater production.

"But that's not why they didn't come. At least I don't think it is."

"What do you mean?"

"They're not getting along like they used to."

"I hate to hear that. They were so close. Did something happen?"

"They had a disagreement about one of Diedre's new friends, but they worked it out."

"Maybe it's just normal pre-adolescent stuff. Fourth and fifth grade kids can be extremely moody. One moment they're your adorable child and the next they're almost demonic."

Emily sighed. "I've heard that. I don't remember being that way, do you?"

"'Course not. We were both perfectly behaved, I'm sure. Any idea what tore them apart?"

"No. Grant and I have asked."

"Then I wouldn't worry about it. They're moody. I'm sure they still love each other, and things will get back to normal."

"You really think so?"

"I do. In the meantime, you're wasting time trying to fix something that isn't broken."

"Let's hope."

"They'll probably be all over you the minute you get home, wanting to go over every detail of the shower."

"Speaking of which." Emily pulled her laptop from her purse and set it on the small round tabletop, sliding her cup carefully to one side. "Here's what I'm thinking."

They put their heads together and by the time they'd

finished their drinks, they'd decided on food, selected decorations, planned games, and finalized the guest list.

"Now all you need to do is register your wish list, and I can get the invitations out."

"You're sure you don't mind doing old-fashioned paper invitations?" Stephanie's tone was apologetic. "Dhruv's extended family isn't techie."

"Which is so ironic, since he's uber talented in that area," Emily commented. "It's fine. Receiving a stiff paper invitation on good cardstock makes me feel special." She closed her laptop.

"I guess we should get going," Stephanie said.

"There's one more thing. Tell me about your accomplishments this week. The ones you were supposed to record, that remind you how capable you are."

Stephanie leaned across the table and grasped Emily's hand. "It worked! Wait until I tell you." She recounted the incident with Liam during the fire drill.

"Holy smokes, Steph," Emily said. "You saved that poor boy from being abandoned behind that hedge."

"It's not that big of a deal. His teacher would have taken roll call when they got back to their room and noticed he was missing. She would have reported it, and they would have found him."

"Eventually." Emily put her free hand on top of their clasped ones. "Do not downplay this. The fact that you heard him—and came to his aid—is huge! You should feel very competent about what you did."

"I *do* feel that way." Her tone brightened. "I'm proud of myself."

"As you should be." Emily said.

"What about you, Em? Tell me your successes this week."

"Nothing as dramatic as yours." She paused, thinking. "Honestly? I've just survived a busy week as a working mother—sighted or not."

"That's enough of a win for anyone," Stephanie said. She crumpled her paper napkin and shoved it into her empty cup. "It's gotten a lot noisier in here. It must be busier than when we arrived. People are probably waiting for tables to open up."

"I think you're right," Emily said. "Good work on helping Liam. Let's continue to keep lists of our accomplishments."

"I promise I will. And don't fret about the girls," Stephanie said.

"Okay. I'm glad we have each other to bounce things off of."

They rose from their table and allowed their guides to take them to the street, unaware of the admiring glances following their progress.

CHAPTER 35

J had almost caught up with that rabbit when a sound startled me awake.

I shifted my muzzle onto my paws and listened. Grant's low rumbling snore came at sporadic intervals. I was about to burrow back into my memory-foam bed when I heard it again.

I couldn't be sure, but I thought the footsteps in the hallway were Zoe's.

The girls never got out of bed at night. I thought I should investigate.

I rose and stretched, wishing I could go back to sleep. I'd had a busy day. Biscuit and I had enjoyed a good cuddle under the table at the coffee shop.

I loved a good coffee shop. Any coffee shop, really. The aromas made my nose twitch the whole time, preventing me from falling asleep while we were there. The absence of my afternoon nap must be why I was so tired now.

Or maybe it was the excitement after dinner. When we got home from our visit with Stephanie and Biscuit, we found Zoe and Grant hard at work on something called a prototype—for a roller coaster made of straws.

They'd spread out on the dining room table and moved between Grant's laptop and their model until dinner time. They'd resumed their labors as soon as Grant started the dishwasher. Structures collapsed and marbles bounced around the room. Sabrina chased them, but Grant put a stop to that. He was worried that one of us would choke on a marble. Zoe raced after them instead. The scene was chaotic and fascinating. Grant and Zoe persevered through failure after failure, making minor adjustments along the way, until Emily appeared in the doorway.

"We've got a big week ahead," she'd told them.

My tail wagged involuntarily. I loved big weeks. Going out into the world with Emily was my second favorite thing, after Crunchy Cheetos.

"We should all go to bed early. A good night's sleep is the best way to start a new week," she added.

"That's what Martha always says," Zoe said.

"And she's right," Grant said, shutting his laptop.

"But we almost had it," Zoe protested. "Can't we try one more time?"

"We'll work on it tomorrow night, after dinner. I'm in town all week," Grant said. "There's something I'd like to research that might help increase the stability…"

"You're about to go down a rabbit hole again," Emily interjected. "Time to get ready for bed, Zoe. Diedre's already asleep."

Zoe released an exaggerated sigh. "All right."

Emily had gathered Sabrina and me for our final comfort break of the day. By the time we got back inside for our bedtime treats, Zoe had climbed into bed. Her own bed in her own room.

I'd followed Emily into our room and settled into my bed. That the girls were now sleeping in their own rooms bothered me. Something still wasn't right between them. I'd put my head down and meant to think about the issue, but my mind was soon chasing rabbits into holes.

I padded into the hallway.

Zoe wasn't in her room.

I poked my nose into the partially open doorway to Diedre's room. I didn't have to go in to know that Zoe had climbed into the other bed in her sister's room.

I walked in, anyway.

Diedre's rhythmic breathing told me she was sound asleep. Zoe's was more of a sharp intake, followed by a heavy release. She was wide awake.

I went to her and put my muzzle under her hand. It worked its way along my muzzle to the top of my head. She rubbed the spot behind my right ear in the way I loved.

We stayed like this for a few moments.

Sabrina must have heard the soft jingle of my collar as Zoe petted me. She soon bounded into the room and flung herself onto the bed, displacing me.

I stepped back. Zoe was Sabrina's person. I knew my place.

Zoe rolled onto her side and pulled Sabrina into the

curve of her body. She'd be fine, now. Sabrina would get her to sleep.

I retraced my steps to my bed and settled myself again. Zoe's return to Diedre's room was a step in the right direction.

All would be right with my family. I hoped I could go back to those rabbits...

CHAPTER 36

*E*mily pulled her purse from her desk drawer and rose from her office chair. She was inserting Garth into his working harness when her computer notified her that she had an urgent message. It was from the head of a division her team serviced. She'd never communicated with the man before. She listened to his email.

"Emily—the solutions your team produced continue to fail. We've been dealing with this for three days. Every time, we're told that they work only to find they don't. We need your immediate attention to this matter."

She let her purse slide off of her shoulder onto her desktop.

"Dhruv's office," Emily commanded Garth.

Garth took her to his office, but Dhruv wasn't at this desk.

"Oh, come on," Emily muttered under her breath. She

tapped her watch to listen to the time. "I've got to be out of here in five minutes. Do you know where Dhruv is, Garth?"

Emily could feel Garth wag his tail.

"I'll take that as a yes. Find Dhruv."

Garth turned and took her to the break room where Dhruv was making himself a cup of coffee.

"Emily. Good. I was coming to see you as soon as I got my coffee."

"Would it be about an angry email I just received?"

"I was afraid he'd do that." Dhruv harrumphed. "I'm sorry about that, Em."

"We don't have time for being sorry, Dhruv. We need to fix it."

"We already have," he said. "Kari and I worked on the issue all afternoon. We solved the programming glitch."

"Does he know that?"

"We just emailed him the fix. Since he's in the Denver office, Kari is on her way to his office to make sure he understands what we've done."

Emily blew out a breath. "I'm glad the two of you fixed it, but you're not supposed to be doing the actual programming work. One of your teams should have handled this. I haven't looked at the problem they tasked you with solving, but it didn't seem like it was beyond the ability of anyone on our teams."

"You're right. This problem should not have festered and then been dumped in our laps—Kari's and mine—to solve."

Emily's watch alarm sounded.

"I need to get out of here," Emily said. "Tonight is

Diedre's audition for the youth theater. Grant's taking her, and I need to get home for Zoe. Walk with us back to my office."

Dhruv followed along.

"You're certain it's fixed?"

"Absolutely."

"That's the immediate problem, but not all the teams are working. What's going on?"

"Kari and I are going to spend tomorrow figuring that out. We thought that pairing a subject-matter expert with a newbie would be a great idea for mentoring, but those two old timers seem too set in their ways to listen to new ideas."

"Identifying the problem is crucial." Garth took them to Emily's office. She snatched up her purse and hung it on her shoulder. "Now—what are you going to do about it?" She spun around and directed Garth to the elevators.

"I'm...not sure. Kari's better at the people part of being a boss than I am."

"You're going to have to learn, Dhruv." Emily's tone was uncharacteristically curt. She stabbed at the down button.

The elevator arrived, and Garth and Emily stepped into it.

"I don't mean to be harsh, Dhruv," Emily said. "I'm in a hurry. You two have to fix this. I'm open tomorrow afternoon. Get with Kari and put something on my calendar for the three of us to discuss solutions."

The elevator doors closed before he could respond.

Emily stepped out of the elevator and retrieved the message that her rideshare driver had waited the allotted time for her and had just left. She poked at the screen of her phone and ordered another one. The voice-over told her it would be there in eleven minutes.

Emily bit her lower lip. If her ride was on time, she'd be ten minutes late getting home. She texted Grant.

His response was swift. "We've got a few minutes' cushion. It'll be fine."

Emily shoved her phone into her coat pocket. She and Garth stood in the thin sunshine of the late afternoon and waited.

Emily finally pulled her phone back out and checked the time. Thirteen minutes had gone by. The rideshare app said her driver was still six minutes away. She updated Grant.

"Still okay," was his response.

Emily and Garth paced along the curb until her ride finally arrived. They situated themselves in the back seat as quickly as possible and told the driver they were running late.

The driver assured Emily she'd do her best, but that there was an accident along the quickest route and her navigation app was directing them another way.

Emily called Grant. "I'm sorry, sweetheart. Traffic's a mess and the driver says it'll take thirty minutes for us to get home. You can't wait that long to leave for the audition."

"No. We've got to leave in five."

They were both silent, thinking about what to do.

Emily addressed the driver. "Could we make a stop on the way home?"

"Sure," the woman said.

"Is Sylvia home?" Emily asked. "You could drop Zoe there and the driver and I can pick her up on our way home."

"Mom's at her sister's house for book club. I texted her right after you first called—to see if I could drop off Zoe."

"Great minds," Emily murmured.

"Unfortunately, my aunt is a good thirty minutes in the other direction. That won't work."

Zoe and Diedre waited in the entryway, eavesdropping on Grant's end of the conversation.

Diedre shifted her weight from foot to foot. "We've got to go," she hissed in a stage whisper. "They said we can't be late, or they won't let us audition."

Zoe walked up to Grant and tugged on his sleeve. "I can stay home alone until Emily gets here."

"I don't know about that, honey. You've never stayed by yourself before. I think you'd better come with us."

"Sabrina's with me. I'll lock the doors and Emily will be here soon." Zoe looked at him with wide, imploring eyes. "I want to work on my science fair project. I can't do that at the theater."

"Did you hear all that?" Grant asked Emily.

"I did. And I think she'll be fine. Zoe is very mature. Will you make sure the doors are locked?"

"Of course."

"Tell her to call me the minute you leave, and we'll stay on the phone together until I get home."

"That's a good idea. We've got to get going. I'll text when we're on our way home from the audition."

"Hand the phone to Diedre, please."

Grant did as Emily requested.

"I'm sorry I'm not home to tell you in person," Emily said, "but best of luck tonight, sweetie. You've worked so hard, and I know you'll do your very best."

"Thanks, Emily," Diedre said. "I'm really nervous."

"That's natural," Emily said. "All those nerves will go away once you step on stage. You're going to be great."

"We're leaving. Zoe said she'll call you after she goes to the bathroom."

Diedre swiped to end the call and handed the phone to her dad.

"You know how to use the landline phone?" Grant asked Zoe as they rushed to the garage.

"Of course," Zoe called after him. She watched from the window until their taillights had disappeared from view.

The house was suddenly silent.

Zoe reached down to stroke Sabrina. The sun was dipping below the horizon. She looked at the French doors leading to the backyard. The covered patio was already dark.

The front door was wooden and massive, with a heavy lock. The French door was a wall of glass. She swallowed hard.

Zoe hurried to the French doors and pulled the drapes shut. At least a bad guy wouldn't see that she was home alone. She was on her way to call Emily when she spotted the large rectangular ottoman that always sat along the side of the fireplace.

Zoe got behind it and, with several mighty shoves, positioned it in front of the drawn drapes. If someone broke in through the French doors, they'd trip and fall over the ottoman. That would give her more time to escape out the front.

Satisfied that she'd done what she could, Zoe went to the bathroom and then placed her call to Emily.

CHAPTER 37

"Hi, sweetie." Emily answered the call on the first ring. "Are you all right?"

"I'm fine." Zoe checked to make sure Sabrina was at her heels, then began moving through the house, turning on lights in every room.

"Tell me about your day," Emily said as her rideshare snaked through rush hour traffic.

Zoe filled her in. "Not much happened, really. The boys are excited about the roller coaster."

"That's good, isn't it?"

"Yeah."

"How's Diedre? She told me she's nervous."

"Grant and I kept telling her she's going to do great." Zoe hurried past the ottoman and the drapes. "When will you be home?"

Emily asked the driver how much longer and then answered Zoe. "Traffic is a mess," Emily said. "We'll be another fifteen minutes."

Zoe didn't respond.

"Are you hungry?"

"No. Grant got us hamburgers when he picked us up from school. He left a salad for you in the fridge."

"That was nice of him. I'm famished," Emily said. Zoe wasn't a mopey child. She suspected being home alone—in their big house—was scarier than Zoe had thought it would be. "I never heard the scientific basis of your project," she said. "Can you explain it to me?"

"It's gravity," Zoe said.

Emily raked her hand through her hair. Getting the usually chatty Zoe to talk was proving difficult. She pulled her laptop from her satchel and opened the file she'd started for Stephanie and Dhruv's shower. "Would you like to know what Stephanie and I have planned for the shower?"

"Sure," Zoe said. "That'd be great." Her voice held only a modicum of enthusiasm.

"Wait until you hear our ideas." Emily inhaled deeply as she listened to her screen reader. She would draw out her description and distract Zoe until she and Garth got home.

Zoe settled herself on the floor by the front door.

Sabrina plopped down next to her and put her chin in Zoe's lap.

The girl kept an eye on the street as she and Emily discussed details for the upcoming shower.

Headlights finally turned into the driveway. When Emily and Garth got out of the car, Zoe flung the front door open. "Hi, Emily," she called in a voice that dripped relief.

Emily and Garth hurried from the driveway up the stairs.

Zoe flung her arms around Emily and hugged her tightly.

Emily smoothed the hair away from Zoe's forehead and planted a kiss on it. "Were you scared?"

"Kind of," Zoe said, clinging to Emily.

"I'm sorry that we put you through this." Emily patted her back.

"That's okay." Zoe's voice was muffled as she leaned against Emily. "I thought I'd be fine. But then it got dark."

"I understand," Emily said. "Did you say there's a salad for me in the refrigerator?"

"Yes. Want me to put it on the table for you?"

They stepped apart.

"No. I can get it. Would you feed Garth and Sabrina?"

Zoe called the dogs to follow her to the kitchen.

"I'm going to put my satchel in the family room," Emily called after them. She set her bag on the coffee table and proceeded on the route to the kitchen that she knew by heart.

Zoe placed the bowls on the floor in front of the dogs.

Emily took four steps before her shin connected with the edge of the ottoman. Her legs buckled and she went down. Her left knee took the brunt of the impact with the wooden floor.

A sharp pain radiated across her kneecap. Emily yelped.

Garth stopped eating and raced to her side.

"Emily!" Zoe was right behind Garth.

Emily lifted her left hand and placed it on top of the ottoman. Leaning heavily on her left side, she hoisted herself off the floor.

Zoe guided her onto the ottoman. "You're bleeding!"

Emily felt her throbbing left knee. The fabric of her wool dress slacks was torn and a sticky substance covered her kneecap. She brought her hand to her nose and sniffed. It was blood.

"What do we do?" Zoe asked.

Emily gingerly extended her left leg. "Nothing's broken."

"This is all my fault, Emily," Zoe said. "I moved the ottoman in front of the back door because it was getting dark outside and I wanted to...bad-guy-proof the house." Her voice broke. "I'm such an idiot."

"You are no such thing." Emily forced the words between clenched teeth. "You made a mistake."

"That really hurt you." Zoe began to cry. "I'm sorry."

"I know you are, honey. I'm going to need your help now. Can you look at my knee?"

"Yes."

"Is it still bleeding? It feels like it's getting worse."

"It is. There's a gash."

"How wide and deep?"

"Two inches wide. I can't tell how deep—there's too much blood."

Emily nodded. "I may have to get stitches. I want you to call Grant for me."

Zoe retrieved Emily's phone from her satchel and placed the call to Grant. "It went right to voicemail," she said.

"They probably made everyone turn off their cell phones during auditions," Emily said. She removed a tissue from the pocket of her slacks and held it over the wound. "Place a video call to my mom. Put it on speaker."

Zoe soon had Martha on the line. "Emily fell, and it's all my fault."

"Hey, Mom." Emily interrupted Zoe. "We've got a situation here—and Zoe is not to blame," she quickly added. She explained what happened.

"Let me see the gash," Martha said.

Emily lifted the bloody tissue, and Zoe centered the screen on the wound.

"Move the phone a little to the left," Martha said, "so I can see it at an angle."

Zoe did as instructed.

"It looks deep, honey," Martha said. "You'll need to have stitches."

"That's what I thought," Emily replied.

"Grant's at auditions, isn't he?"

"Yep. Sylvia is at her sister's for book club."

"Do you want me to drive in? I can be there in a little over an hour at this time of day."

"No, of course not. Thank you for offering, but Zoe and I can get to urgent care faster with a rideshare."

"I think that's best," Martha said.

"I'll get Garth's harness," Zoe said.

"We'll leave him home," Emily said. "You'll be my guide, Zoe."

"Will you text to let me know you got there safely?" Martha asked.

"Of course," Emily said. "And when we get home."

"You'd better get going," Martha said.

"I'll order our ride now. Don't worry. This shouldn't take long." They ended the call.

Emily directed Zoe to take the dogs out before they left.

The rideshare pulled into the driveway as Zoe and the dogs rejoined Emily. "Should I leave a note for Grant?" Zoe asked.

"Don't worry about it," Emily replied. "We'll be home before they are. I just want to get this taken care of."

After locking up, Emily hobbled down the stairs, using the railing for support, and Zoe guiding the way. They left two anxious dogs peering out the window after them.

CHAPTER 38

The door to the rehearsal room opened and a woman with a messy bun held in place by a pair of chopsticks poked her head into the hallway. "Ava?"

Tammy jumped out of a molded plastic chair in a string of chairs lining the wall like train cars.

Ava felt the straps of her shoes, double-checking that the buckles were secure, then followed her mother into the audition room.

The woman motioned Ava to the center of the space. Two other women sat on the far side of a rectangular table, clipboards in front of each of them. Chopstick bun woman took a seat between them. "You can wait in the hallway," she said to Tammy. "We find kids do better when their parents aren't in the room."

"I need to be here to let her know that her music has started."

The three women looked at Tammy with blank expressions. "She'll...know that when she hears it," one of the women said.

"Ava is deaf," Tammy said.

All three of them jerked against the backs of their chairs as if they'd slammed on the brakes.

"She counts the beats of the music when she dances. You'll see."

"All right," said chopstick bun woman. "Good luck, Ava. Show us what you've got."

GRANT AND DIEDRE consulted the diagram at the entrance to the youth theater building. Auditions for Mary Poppins were being held on the main stage. They found her name on the long list of girls trying out for the lead role. Diedre was in the middle of the pack.

They made their way along the corridor toward the stage entrance. As they passed an intersecting hallway, Diedre noticed a familiar mother/daughter pair rise from their chairs and head into an audition room.

"It's Ava and her mom," Diedre said, grabbing Grant's sleeve. "I'm going to watch." She pointed to the rectangular glass window in the door.

Before he could respond, Diedre had taken off down the hall, reaching the door as it clicked shut. She cupped her face with her hands and pressed it against the window.

Diedre watched as Tammy tapped at the screen of her phone with one hand while holding up the other. Tammy's head bobbed three times, then she brought her hand down like she was waving a flag to start a race.

Ava began to tap.

Diedre had to strain to hear the music, but Ava's taps were loud and crisp. She was in perfect time with the music and never missed a beat. Her arm movements were precise; her smile never wavered. She made the routine look effortless—and like she was having the time of her life performing it.

The thirty-second audition was over in a flash.

Diedre leaned to the right so she could see the judges behind the table. The three women sat, wide-eyed and transfixed, until one of them began clapping. The other two soon joined her. She couldn't hear what they were saying to Tammy and Ava, but she knew it had to be good.

Diedre stepped away from the door and threw her arms around Ava as soon as she stepped into the hallway. Diedre pulled back so Ava could see her lips. "You did it!"

Ava shrugged modestly, but her cat-who-ate-the-canary grin told Diedre what she wanted to know.

"You got the part, didn't you? They told you right now?"

"They were very complimentary," Tammy interjected, "but they have others who are auditioning for the part of Bert."

"They said I'll be a chimney sweep, for sure," Ava said.

"You looked perfect," Diedre said. "Your audition was even better than when you practiced it."

"Thank you for helping me," Ava said. She turned to her mother. "Can we stay for Diedre's audition?"

Tammy looked at Grant, who stood watching the happy scene. "When does Diedre go on?"

"I'm not sure, but I bet it'll be another hour," he said.

Tammy touched her daughter's back. "I have to be at work extra early tomorrow morning. I hope you don't mind," she looked at Diedre. "We'd better go."

"That's fine," Diedre said. "Mary Poppins is auditioning on the main stage, so I don't think you could watch me, anyway."

Ava patted Diedre's back. "You're going to do great."

"I just thought of this." Diedre brought her hands to the top of her head. "If you're Bert and I get Mary Poppins, we'll be the leads in the play."

"That'd be so fun!" Ava's enthusiasm was palpable.

"We'd better get to the stage," Grant said. "If you miss your audition, that'll never happen."

The girls exchanged a last hug and stepped apart.

"Good luck, Diedre," Ava called as they trailed after their parents in opposite directions.

GRANT PACED in the small area by the back door to the stage. Try as he might, he couldn't hear anything behind the solid metal door. He checked his watch. It seemed like a long time, but in reality, she'd only been gone for ten minutes. With a five-minute audition slot, it seemed like an eternity.

He shoved his hands in his pocket and resumed pacing. His back was to the door when she flung it open. Grant sensed, rather than saw, his daughter's beaming face.

"Dad." She crossed to him in three long strides.

He spun around, and they both stepped out of the way as the next girl was called to the stage.

"I gather by the size of that smile that it went well?"

Diedre closed her eyes and nodded. "I didn't mess up a thing. All that practice really helped."

"I'm so proud of you," he said. "Knowing you did your best is always the greatest."

They moved along the corridor. "Did they have any feedback?" He chose his words carefully; he didn't want to seem anxious.

"There were three judges. They told me I have a beautiful voice."

"Is that all?"

"The main judge said it's powerful. Another said I enunciate well, and she heard every word. The third one told me my tap dancing was what they were looking for."

"That's fantastic, sweetheart. You were in there longer than I expected." He hoped she would keep talking.

"I know. Before I started, they told me to wait until they dismissed me before I left the stage. When I was done, I just stood there. The judges were huddled together, whispering behind their hands or clipboards. I overheard them talking about me being in fourth grade."

"That's it?"

Diedre nodded. "They finally told me I'd done great and could leave."

Grant put his arm across her shoulders. Although he'd said nothing to Diedre, he and Emily had assumed she was too young for the role. The best she could hope for, for this production, would be to be in the ensemble. Now, he wasn't so sure. "Would you like to call Zoe and Emily to tell them about it on the way home?"

"They'll still be up when we get there, won't they?"

Grant consulted his watch. "Easily. We're going to be home earlier than I thought."

"Then I'd like to wait to tell them in person."

"Good idea," he replied.

They hurried to his car and headed for home.

CHAPTER 39

A chill ran down Grant's spine as he pulled into the driveway and pressed the button on the garage door opener. The house was in total darkness. He glanced at the clock on his dashboard. It was only 8:20. Maybe Emily and Zoe were in their bedrooms at the back of the house.

Garth and Sabrina greeted them as they entered. Sabrina was her usual exuberant self, but Garth was subdued.

"We're home," Diedre hollered as she ran into the house.

No one replied.

"Em?" Grant called, moving past Diedre. He rounded the corner into the family room, looking from the kitchen on his right to the bedroom wing on his left. Other than a lamp in the family room that was connected to a timer and came on every evening, the house was dark.

"They're not here," Diedre said, unable to conceal her disappointment.

"Were they planning to go anywhere?" he asked.

Diedre shook her head.

"Maybe they left a note." He entered the kitchen and turned on the overhead light. A scan of the countertops revealed no note. He opened the refrigerator to find the salad he'd left for Emily untouched.

"We know Emily came home because Garth is here," he said, more to himself than to Diedre. He pulled his phone from his pocket and checked for messages. There were three missed calls from Emily—two from earlier in the evening and one that came in right before they'd left the theater. Emily hadn't left messages.

His phone was still set to silent mode. He cursed under his breath as he turned notifications back on.

"Why would she go out without Garth?" Diedre asked. Worry replaced her jubilance.

"She's got Zoe with her as a sighted guide. She's supposed to go out without Garth so that he learns how to stay behind. Sometimes guide dogs can't go with their handlers." He entered the family room and turned on the other lamps.

"Like noisy concerts that might hurt their ears. I remember," Diedre said. "But they weren't going to anything like that."

"No," Grant muttered under his breath. He clicked on the floor lamp near the ottoman. The area jumped into illumination.

Grant stopped short and bent to examine a corner of the ottoman. His eyes followed a trail of blood onto the floor. He dropped to his knees and looked at the smeary residue.

Sabrina joined him and began licking the spot. He pushed

her back. "Leave it," he ordered with a firmness that Sabrina obeyed.

"Someone's hurt themselves." He looked at Diedre. "This is blood."

"The ottoman is out of place," Diedre replied. "It's always supposed to be over there." She pointed to the other side of the fireplace.

"Emily must have fallen," he said. "That would be what she called me about."

"Oh, no! Do you think she's hurt?"

Grant nodded slowly. "I'm afraid so."

Diedre put her hands to her cheeks. "Like a broken leg?"

Grant looked around himself. Other than the ottoman, everything else in their neatly ordered environment was in its place. If Emily had broken her leg, paramedics would have taken her to the hospital. The family room didn't look like multiple people had just tromped through it. The hospital would have called him as her emergency contact.

"I don't know, honey." Grant placed a call to Emily, and it went directly to her voicemail. He cursed again.

"Call Martha," Diedre suggested. "She might know."

"Great idea." Grant placed a call to his mother-in-law.

Martha answered on the first ring. "Are they home?" she asked without saying hello.

"No. And I have no idea where they are." Despite his best efforts, panic was taking hold of him. "Do you?"

"Yes. They're fine, Grant." Martha inhaled deeply and told him what she knew. "Em texted me when they pulled up to urgent care. She promised she'd text when she got home, too. When you called, I assumed you were reaching out to me on her behalf instead of her sending me a text."

"Do you know where she went? There are several in this area."

"She didn't mention which one."

"Why didn't she leave me a voicemail?"

"She probably didn't want you and Diedre to abandon her audition," Martha said, "and race to her side."

"That sounds like Em. If she was only getting stitches, wouldn't she be home by now? It's been over two hours."

"You know how busy those places can be," Martha said.

"Maybe they took an X-ray and her leg *is* broken."

"She could walk on it when we talked, Grant. I don't think she could have done that on a broken leg. She or Zoe would have called me if that was the case."

"I guess you're right," he said. "Now what do I do?"

"You wait. That's the only thing you can do. She's with Zoe. You can be sure that one of them will reach out to you soon."

Sabrina raced to the front door and barked. Garth followed her.

"There's a car in the driveway," Diedre said, peering out the window by the front door. "It's Uncle Craig. And Emily and Zoe!"

"They're here—with my brother," Grant said into the phone.

"I heard Diedre," Martha said. "Now that she's home, I won't worry. Go get your wife, and one of you needs to call me in the morning with all the details."

"Will do. Thanks, Martha." Grant ended the call and

tossed his phone onto the entryway table. He was down the front steps in a flash.

Emily was leaning heavily on her brother-in-law as they approached the short flight of steps to the front door.

Grant scooped her into his arms and carried her up the steps into the house.

"I thought we'd beat you home," Emily said.

"Well, you didn't." Grant's tone was curt. He helped her to the sofa.

Garth planted himself at her feet, and Emily instinctively reached out to rub his ears.

"Were you worried?"

"Of course we were." He turned to his brother. "I thought you were at a work dinner with Gina."

"I was, but unlike some people, I keep my cell phone on."

Grant groaned.

"I tried to call you when we were on our way home," Emily said. "Just in case you got here before us. I gave my phone to Zoe when we were done at urgent care to order a rideshare because the nurse rushed after us for one more signature on a form. Zoe called Craig instead of a rideshare." Emily swiveled around. "Just for the record, young lady, you should have followed my instructions. We didn't need to interfere with Craig and Gina's plans."

"I beg to differ," Craig said. "Whenever anyone needs a ride in an emergency, they are to call all available family members before resorting to a rideshare. That's a family rule. Full stop." He put his arm around Zoe's shoulder and pulled her in for a hug. "Gina and I agree you did the right thing by calling me."

"Thanks, bro," Grant said.

"Speaking of Gina, I'd better head back to the restaurant to pick her up. Dinner should be over by now."

"I'm sorry we messed up your evening," Emily said. "Apologize to Gina for me, please."

"Promise not to tell her, but I was glad to get out of there. All that shop talk is boring if it's not your industry. I was pinching myself to stay awake."

Emily laughed. "In that case, glad to be of service."

"I'll see myself out," Craig said. "I'm sure Gina will call in the morning."

Grant sat next to Emily and took her hand in his. "I'm so sorry this happened to you," he said. "Are you in pain?"

"I'm fine," Emily said dismissively. "This whole evening has been a series of misadventures, made worse by two people who had their cell phones turned off. Urgent care required it, too. If you tried to call, I didn't get it."

Zoe and Diedre drifted into the room and stood together in the doorway.

"The whole evening wasn't a disaster," Grant said.

Zoe turned to her stepsister. "Have you got good news?"

Diedre nodded vigorously. "For both Ava and me."

Zoe clasped her hands together.

Emily patted the sofa next to her. "You two come sit with us. I want to hear every detail."

Diedre settled next to Emily. Zoe and Sabrina nestled at their feet. The pain, fear, and anxiety that had recently taken over the evening were swept aside by the promise of Diedre's tale.

CHAPTER 40

"It's time for speed geography," Stephanie said. Her class had just come in from the playground after lunch. She always started the afternoon with fifteen minutes of something the kids loved.

"Who wants to spin the globe and pick our spot for this week?"

Hands shot up all over the room.

"I heard a hand go up over here, in the back." Stephanie pointed. "Were you first, Jeremy?"

"Yes," he said.

"Okay. You know the drill."

Jeremy got out of his seat and headed to the teacher's desk. He gave the globe a firm push and sent it spinning. His finger was poised over it to select the spot they would research that week when the public address system crackled and came to life.

"Lockdown. Lockdown. Lockdown." The robotic voice

reverberated around the space at high volume. Lights on the phone on Stephanie's desk flashed. *"Lockdown. Lockdown. Lockdown."*

"You know what to do, kids," Stephanie strode to her classroom door. The nerve at her temple pulsed. No matter how many times they'd practiced this drill, the combination of the voice and the lights sent her blood pressure soaring. "Line up along the wall to the left of the door." She locked the door. Running her hand to the right from the lock, she found the cord for the blind. Stephanie pulled on the cord and lowered the blind into place, obscuring the window.

They practiced this drill regularly, and her class took their participation seriously. Even third graders knew about active shooters on school campuses. She heard them abandon their desks and line up single file against the wall.

"Sound off," she said.

The children followed the procedure of giving their name, starting with the child closest to the door. Stephanie knew all of their names and she kept track with her fingers as each one said their name.

"I count all of us," she said. "Is anyone missing?"

"We're all here," a girl said.

Stephanie groped the wall and switched off the overhead lights. "Sit quietly until we receive the all clear."

She retraced her steps to her desk, where Biscuit remained next to her chair. Stephanie grasped her harness and directed her guide to take her to the back of the classroom.

Biscuit led Stephanie to the door that connected Stephanie's classroom with Rebecca's. During lockdown, the staff had to shut and secure this door, which was otherwise always open during school hours.

Rebecca was waiting for her. "Geez. We just had a drill last month. We'll never get the kids settled down after this. The entire afternoon will be a waste."

"I was thinking the same thing," Stephanie said. She pulled on the door to shut it, but it wouldn't budge.

"It's propped open with a doorstop, remember? It seems to be wedged in here." Rebecca stopped trying to dislodge the heavy rubber stopper with her foot and bent to remove it. "Press on the door to move it a smidge so I can get this thing out of here." Her voice reflected her exertion.

Stephanie put her shoulder against the door, moving it a quarter inch.

"That's it!" Rebecca rocked back on her heels, holding up the stubborn doorstop. "Just in time to close this before the all clear," she said, getting to her feet. The cell phones in both of their pockets buzzed with an incoming text.

Stephanie was closing the door when Rebecca put out a hand to stop her. "Liam's not in his classroom," Rebecca said. "That's what the text was about."

"Maybe he's in the bathroom?"

"His teacher had bathroom duty. He wasn't there." Rebecca sighed. "His teacher was checking to see if he was in any of our rooms."

"He's not in mine," Stephanie said.

"Nor mine. I guess he's out there, somewhere. I'll tell his teacher to report his absence to the front office." Rebecca sighed heavily. "That poor kid. These drills are so hard on him."

"If it's a drill." Stephanie said the words softly. "We can't be sure."

Rebecca began pulling the door shut again. This time, Stephanie stopped her. "I know where he is."

"What?"

"From the fire drill. He'll be hiding behind the hedge."

"I'll text that to the office," Rebecca said.

"They'll never find him. That hedgerow is at least three hundred yards long. I'm going to get him."

"No, Stephanie. How will you find him—much less get him out of there if he is hiding? He won't reply if you call his name. He'll be curled into a ball. Terrified."

"That's why I have to go to him. Biscuit will find him sooner than any human could. He'll come to us."

"Then what? You can't come back here. Once you leave, I have to lock the door behind you. You'll be stuck out there."

"I've got my passkey." Stephanie patted the pocket of her oversize cardigan. "The equipment storage room isn't far from where I believe Liam is hiding. We'll shelter there."

The two women sprang into action.

"I'll lock the door behind you and take your kids into my room," Rebecca said.

Stephanie directed Biscuit to take her to her classroom door. "Kids," Stephanie said in a commanding voice. "You are to go with Ms. Rebecca into her classroom. *NOW.*"

She and Biscuit sped across the room with Rebecca at their heels.

Her class followed her direction without question.

"Good luck, Steph," Rebecca said as Stephanie and Biscuit

slipped out the door into the corridor. The lock clicked behind them.

"Find the playing fields," Stephanie commanded. "Hop up," she added. They took off at a brisk pace.

Biscuit took them across the deserted exterior of the campus, directly to the playing fields, and then to the row of bushes along the exterior fence. After the blaring noise from the public address system, the silence enfolding them was eerie and unsettling.

A stiff breeze blew Stephanie's hair into her face. She clawed it away with her free hand. If Liam was whimpering somewhere behind the hedge, she'd never hear him over the sound of the wind.

"Find the boy," Stephanie commanded Biscuit. Her guide hadn't been trained with this command. Stephanie said a silent prayer that Biscuit would somehow know what she meant.

She needn't have worried. Biscuit instinctively understood their mission. Her guide moved so fast, Stephanie practically had to run to keep up.

They zoomed along the hedgerow until Biscuit stopped abruptly.

"Get Liam," Stephanie said, almost out of breath.

Biscuit lowered her stomach to the ground and armycrawled her way through a familiar tunnel between two large bushes.

Stephanie dropped to her knees and leaned into the gap

as far as she could. She heard Biscuit's collar jangle, followed by a faltering voice calling Biscuit by name.

She rested both arms on the ground and dropped her head between them, breathing hard. She'd been right. They'd found the boy.

Stephanie remained motionless, thinking. She had to convince Liam to come out of hiding and go with her. The equipment room wasn't far. They'd be lucky if they reached it before the announcement came through that it had been a drill and was concluded.

An icy chill ran down her spine. If this were a drill, it would have been concluded by now. The all clear hadn't been announced. The thought hit her like a slap in the face. This was an active situation. What if a shooter was some-where on campus? She had to act. *Now.*

Stephanie flattened herself to the ground and reached through the opening until she felt Biscuit's flank. She walked her hand along her dog's side until she grasped her harness. "Liam," she said in what she hoped was a calm voice. "You and Biscuit and I all have to get to a safe place. She'll take us to the equipment room and we'll lock ourselves in there."

She could hear him breathing. He wasn't whimpering, but he didn't respond.

"You can play with a soccer ball when we're in there," she said, hoping to entice him.

Still no response from the boy.

"It will only be the three of us in there, Liam. We have to go now. Biscuit needs you to help her get to safety."

The bush rustled from the other side, and a twig cracked. Biscuit backed out the way she'd come in, pelting Stephanie with small clods of dirt stirred up by her powerful hind paws.

Stephanie eased back, staying low to the ground.

Biscuit stood and gave herself a good shake. "Quiet, girl," Stephanie whispered. She was more convinced with each passing second that this wasn't a drill. Fear circled her like an ever-tightening vice.

Liam scrambled out after Biscuit.

Stephanie took the boy's hand. "We're going to run to the equipment room," she said. "Hunched over, so we stay low. Can you do that?"

She felt the boy nod. "Biscuit will take us."

"I know the way, too," Liam said softly.

"Good." Stephanie positioned him between herself and the hedge. If a shooter was anywhere near them, her body would shield the boy.

"Equipment room," Stephanie commanded Biscuit. Her guide didn't need the added direction to "hop up." They took off at a run and quickly reached a solid metal door.

Stephanie crouched and removed her key from her pocket. "Is this the equipment room?" she asked Liam.

"Yeah," he said.

Her hand was shaking as she raised the key to the lock. Stephanie took a deep breath and concentrated on the task. This was no time to fumble with the lock or, worse yet, drop the key.

It slid into the opening and turned easily. The door swung open.

Stephanie pushed Liam into the room, and she and

Biscuit followed him. She slammed the door shut and threw the lock.

Liam positioned himself along the wall to the left of the door and plopped onto the floor. "Can I pet Biscuit?"

"Yes." She joined Liam on the floor and released Biscuit to play with the boy.

Stephanie rested her hand on her pregnant abdomen and felt her baby kick. The sensation comforted her. They were all safe.

Liam and Biscuit wrestled on the floor next to her. She rested her head against the wall and pulled out her cell phone to text Rebecca that she and Liam were safe in the equipment room.

A call came in before she could dictate her text. The voice-over announced it was from Rebecca. Stephanie answered it.

"Are you locked in somewhere?" her fellow teacher asked.

"Yes. We just got to the equipment room. Liam was where I thought he'd be. I was pulling out my phone to text you when you called."

"Thank God." Stephanie heard Rebecca release a shaky breath. "It's not a drill."

Stephanie swallowed but her mouth was as dry as chalk. "The all clear was taking too long. I was afraid of that."

"How's Liam?" Rebecca asked.

"He seems fine. He's been playing with Biscuit. Any idea what's going on?"

"One of the other teachers found out from her sister-in-law, who's a police dispatcher. They found two people dead in a house close to the school. The police department activated the lockdown."

"So we haven't had..." Stephanie remembered Liam's proximity.

"Anything on our campus? No." Rebecca supplied. She lowered her voice to a whisper. "The police think it's a murder/suicide. As soon as they confirm that's the case—that a killer isn't roaming around the neighborhood—they'll end the lockdown."

As if on cue, Stephanie overheard on Rebecca's phone the robotic voice declaring the all clear.

The two women remained silent until the announcement concluded. "You heard that?" Rebecca asked.

"I did." Stephanie got to her feet and motioned for Biscuit to join her. "We'll be right there."

"I don't know about you, but I'm going to let the kids read for the rest of the afternoon."

"Solid plan," Stephanie said. "I'll do the same."

"You're a hero, Stephanie." Rebecca's voice cracked. "A true hero."

"I don't know about that," Stephanie protested.

"I do. And everyone else is going to know soon, too. I promise you that."

Rebecca disconnected the call and Stephanie, Biscuit, and Liam made their way back to their classrooms.

CHAPTER 41

*G*rant sauntered along the airport concourse toward his gate. Things were going so well at the job in Los Angeles that he'd felt comfortable leaving Dave on his own to handle all the details. Grant was gratified to see the young architect he'd hired straight out of architecture school two years ago doing so well.

He was even more grateful to be heading home mid-week. He didn't even have to run for his gate before boarding was discontinued.

A tall, older man rolling a carry-on suitcase approached him on his right. Trim and well-dressed, the older man seemed familiar. He swung his face toward Grant and it lit with recognition.

"Grant," the older man said, extending his hand as he walked up to him.

"Norman Klein." Grant greeted the man, and they shook hands.

"I haven't seen you since your wedding," Norman said.

"We're both so grateful that you agreed to walk Emily down the aisle," Grant replied.

"Being the recipient of her father's heart saved my life. Allowing a part of him to be with her on that special day was the least I could do."

"Still…a lot of people would have said no."

Norman shrugged off the compliment. "How are the newlyweds?"

"We're doing well."

"Combining two families can be challenging, especially with kids. Zoe and Diedre acted like they were best of friends, so that might not be a problem for you."

"They're very close, but they're pre-adolescents and that can spell trouble. I'm a twin and my brother and I are best friends, but we fought constantly when we were their age. Still, the biggest challenge Emily and I face is juggling our work schedules and family obligations. Both girls are extremely busy. We feel like we're pulled in a thousand different directions."

"I remember those days. You don't know how you're going to survive, but you miss the hustle and bustle when the kids are grown and gone."

"Then we only need to hang on for eight more years," Grant chuckled. "Where are you headed?"

"I'm addressing the urban revitalization conference that starts tomorrow."

"That's impressive."

Norman shrugged. "I'm speaking about energy efficiency.

I've been interested in the subject my entire career. When I attended architecture school, the field was in its infancy, but now it's at the forefront of design."

"How fascinating. I'm working on a large-scale project in Los Angeles right now where our suggested use of sustainable materials and energy efficiency were key reasons my firm won the bid."

Norman named the project.

"That's right. Did your firm bid on it?"

"No. We don't have the capacity to take on a project of that scale."

"I'm not sure we do, either. That's the thing that's made our home life so challenging—I've been out of town a lot."

"Are you here for the conference?"

"No. I'm on my way home, actually. I thought about attending, but couldn't spare the time. I'm sure I'd learn a lot that I could apply to this project, though."

"I'll be there the entire conference," Norman said. "Let's get together for lunch whenever you have an opening in your schedule and I'll fill you in on what I learn."

"I'd really appreciate that." Grant tilted his head in the direction he'd been walking. "I'd better go. For the first time in weeks, I'm going to be home early."

They shook hands again, and Norman clapped a hand on his shoulder. "Give my regards to your lovely wife. She's a very special woman."

"Will do."

"And don't forget about lunch. I'd enjoy it."

"I'll call next week to set it up," Grant said. "I'm glad I ran into you." He turned and continued on to his gate, not realizing how impactful this chance meeting with Norman would turn out to be.

CHAPTER 42

I knew Grant was home before we reached the first step. He was in a good mood, too. Not that he wasn't usually an upbeat guy, but tonight he was more so.

If left on my own, I would have bounded up the stairs. I was guiding Emily, however, and proceeded with appropriate guide dog decorum.

We opened the front door to a chorus of high-pitched cheers from the girls. Sabrina joined in with her signature yip-yip-yip.

I was tempted to add a woof or two of my own, but kept myself under control.

"You're home!" Emily turned in the general direction of the merriment. "You didn't tell me you got an earlier flight."

"I wanted to surprise you." Grant leaned around the chaos created by the girls and Sabrina to kiss her.

"I don't think all this is because you got in early," Emily

said, unwinding her scarf from her neck. "Have you got news?" She directed the question toward the girls.

"I got a part," Diedre cried. "Not Mary Poppins. I'm in the ensemble."

"But she's the Mary Poppins understudy! A high school senior is Mary Poppins and if she can't go on, it'll be Diedre." Zoe didn't conceal her excitement. "Imagine that—you're good enough to step in for a high schooler."

"That is impressive." Emily held out her arms, and Zoe and Diedre collapsed into them. "I'm glad you're so happy."

"I don't care that I didn't get the main part," Diedre said. "That would be kinda scary. I'm just happy to be in it."

"Guess what else?" Zoe asked.

"What?" Emily and Grant replied in unison.

"Ava is a chimney sweep and," Zoe paused for effect, "she's the Bert understudy."

"Isn't that neat?" Diedre said. "I watched her audition, and she looked like she could be a real dancer on Broadway."

"I hope you're Mary Poppins at least once. And Ava gets to be Bert. Wouldn't that be great?" Zoe's enthusiasm was at full wattage.

"I don't think understudies get onstage very often in shows like these," Emily said. "I'm not trying to be a wet blanket, but..."

"I talked to Ava after we got our emails from the theater," Diedre interrupted. "We're both fine with not being Mary or Bert."

"This calls for a celebration," Grant said. "I'm taking us all out to dinner. Diedre—you can pick the restaurant."

I knew in a flash where we'd go. The girls always picked

the same place. Without exception. We were going to the pizza parlor on the next street.

My tail swished of its own volition along the floor. I loved pizza parlors. Unlike the fancy places Emily and Grant favored, there was always food on the floor in a pizza parlor. I loved those crispy, almost burnt pieces of crust. It didn't matter to me if they contained residues of tomato sauce or cheese. I loved them all. And if I got really lucky, there'd be a piece of that round, spicy meat they called pepperoni.

A rivulet of drool dropped from my mouth onto the floor.

"Look at Garth." Zoe pointed to me. "He's hungry. I'll feed him and Sabrina before we go."

"Dad?" Diedre looked at her father. "Can we ask Ava and her parents to join us? We can all celebrate."

Zoe stopped in her tracks. "Can we?"

"That's a wonderful idea," Emily said. "They may already have plans, but I'll call her mother now."

I wolfed down my kibble and positioned myself by the door. I gathered from the snippets of conversation swirling around me that Ava and her family would join us.

I cast a surreptitious glance at Sabrina. She was as much a part of our family as I was. I knew she wouldn't come with us and I felt guilty about leaving her. Still, I didn't make the rules and there was no reason both of us should miss out on a delicious outing to a pizza parlor floor. I also suspected— although I'd never tattle on her—that Zoe would slip me a crust or two under the table.

We were soon loaded into Grant's car and headed to meet our new friends. All was right in my world.

CHAPTER 43

"Hey, Em, sorry I'm late." Gina pulled out the chair across the table from Emily and flung herself into the seat, hanging her purse from the back of the chair. "Good boy, Garth," she said, glancing under the table to where he was nestled, head on his paws.

"You're only five minutes late," Emily replied. "For the mother of an infant, I think that should count as being on time."

"I hope my employer sees it that way." Gina opened her menu, then closed it and tossed it on the table. "I'm going to order what you're having. The fewer things I have to think about, the better."

"Sounds like you're…" Emily paused to choose the right word.

"Overwhelmed? You bet I am. I go back to work on Monday. Sylvia showed up this morning—unannounced—

and practically kicked me out. She said I desperately needed 'me' time."

"That sounds like Sylvia. We've had the most wonderful luck with our husbands—and their mother."

"I couldn't agree more—she's the best. Since I go back to work on Monday, today is my last chance to be out on my own. It felt so odd to leave the house without Alex and a diaper bag. I'm happy you could meet up on such short notice."

"I'm glad you called. I miss this. We used to have lunch every week."

"Let's make sure we get back to that. It'll be good for both of us."

"What are you doing the rest of the week?" Emily asked.

"Our new nanny starts tomorrow, so I can spend a few days with her before I leave Alex with a stranger."

"I can understand why you'd be stressed, but surely this new nanny has great references?"

"Stellar. She gave us four families to contact, and I talked to all of them. At length."

Emily pressed her lips together to suppress a smile. Those families probably came away feeling like they'd been cross-examined by the defense.

Gina gave the name of the nanny and continued her saga.

Emily held up a hand to interrupt Gina. "Can you repeat that name?"

Gina did as Emily asked. She hunched across the table. "Why? Have you heard something about her?"

"She sounds familiar. Let me check." Emily pulled her phone out of her purse and navigated to her notes app.

Their server appeared at the table. "Have you ladies...?"

"We'll both have the farm greens salad with chicken and green iced teas," Emily blurted out.

"You've got it," the woman said. She'd been a server long enough to recognize when two women didn't want to be interrupted.

Emily tapped her phone and the screen reader voiced all the items in her notes app. She stabbed the screen to silence the app in less than a minute. "There! Did you hear that?"

"I think so. Honestly, Em—I don't know how you listen at that speed. It's like trying to make sense of what an auctioneer is saying."

Emily chuckled. "You get used to it. The screen reader just read off the name of your nanny."

"What does that mean?"

"The mother of one of Zoe's friends recommended her to us. Your new nanny is her husband's cousin."

"That's good, right?"

"Very good. You're getting confirmation of her qualifications from an independent source." Emily returned her phone to her purse.

The server placed their salads and teas in front of them. "Your tea is at two o'clock," the woman said to Emily before slipping away.

"Were you guys going to hire her? Did I steal your nanny?"

"No. Grant's turned over the day-to-day supervision of the Los Angeles project to someone in his office. He'll be in town for the foreseeable future."

"That's a relief," Gina said. "I was worried about how you were going to keep all the balls in the air."

"We want to stay directly involved with the girls." Emily told Gina about the science fair project and the play. "These are critical ages for them and we want to bond with both of them before we enter the teen years."

"That's wise," Gina said. "But holy cow, Em, you've got a lot going on. I've heard about the roller coaster thing for the science fair through Craig. He and Grant are texting each other about it constantly. Those kids will be lucky if they get to do anything on the project."

"This confirms my suspicions," Emily said. "I thought he and Craig were sticking their noses in too far."

"Has Zoe said anything?"

"No."

"Maybe you have nothing to worry about."

Emily stopped, her fork halfway to her mouth. "Based on what you know, do you believe that?"

Gina guffawed. "Not for a moment. I'll have a talk with Craig."

"Thank you."

"You'll have to text me the dates of the play. I'll ask our new nanny to babysit for us. We'll come to every performance we can."

"That's not necessary," Emily said. "Martha and Sylvia have already purchased tickets for the entire run. If you could come once, that would be terrific."

"We'll be there more than once," Gina said. "That's how this family rolls."

Emily set her fork down and slid her hand across the table.

Gina took it and gave it a squeeze. "I wanted to ask if you need help with Stephanie's shower. It's coming up, isn't it?"

"The week after *Mary Poppins* closes," Emily said. "Except I'm not giving it, anymore."

"What?"

"Stephanie called last week. Dhruv's aunties are taking it over."

"Without even asking you?"

"The whole thing was a big mess. Apparently, his aunts—on both sides of the family—have always thrown elaborate baby showers for all the babies in the family. Dhruv tried to broach the topic with me, but wasn't being very clear and gave up. So, Stephanie finally called me."

Emily took a long sip of her tea before continuing. "I could tell that Stephanie felt terrible about the whole thing. She'd told them 'no', but then Dhruv's mother called her. She loves his mom and doesn't want to have problems with her."

"So Stephanie caved?"

"I wouldn't put it quite that harshly. Stephanie's a people pleaser, Gina. She doesn't have a lot of pushback in her. I didn't want to make her feel worse about it than she clearly does. So, I told her it was no problem."

"That was generous of you, Em. Are Zoe and Diedre disappointed? They love to act as event planners." She chuckled. "I guess I got that started with my wedding. To this day, I'm convinced they prevented my reception from being a disaster."

"They've been too busy to help me with any of it," Emily said.

"I'm stunned," Gina replied.

"They don't seem that eager to work together on it. The dynamics between them have shifted. I can't put my finger on it and they're not talking to me, but something's not right between them."

"I haven't noticed anything at the family dinners," Gina said. "Maybe they really are too busy."

Emily shrugged. "I hope you're right. Anyway—if the girls had been working like mad, planning the shower, I would have protested. As it is, we'll be invited to the shower, and that's easier for me. I've already returned the decor items I bought online."

"I'm glad it's working out better for you," Gina said.

"Rhonda's organizing a potluck luncheon shower for the San Francisco team, and I'm going to take Stephanie for a spa day three weeks before her due date."

"A spa day is exactly what she'll need," Gina said. "Hearing about your schedule, you'll need one too."

"Speaking of schedules," Emily said. "I've got to get back to the office. Do you remember me talking about Kari?"

"She's the team lead of your Denver crew?"

"Yep. She's flying in for a meeting this afternoon."

"We haven't even talked about your work," Gina said.

"Let's leave that topic for next time." Emily raised her hand to summon their server. "I've barely touched this salad. I'm going to take it back to my office."

"Good idea," Gina said. "I'll have mine boxed up, too."

"Why don't you just sit here for a few more minutes and

finish your lunch in a leisurely fashion? You'll probably be eating at your desk every day as soon as you go back to work. May as well enjoy it while you can."

"Brilliant suggestion," Gina replied. "That's why you're zooming up the corporate ladder."

The server arrived at their table.

"My friend would like her salad in a to-go box. I'm going to finish mine here. And bring me the check," Gina said.

"You don't need to do that," Emily protested.

"You can treat next time."

The server returned with the boxed salad in a handled shopping bag.

"I'm looking forward to hearing all about 'boss lady Emily' next time we get together," Gina said.

Emily gathered her purse, her lunch, and Garth, and set out for her office.

CHAPTER 44

*E*mily felt Garth's tail swish from side to side as they stepped off the elevator. "Dhruv?"

"Right here," he replied. "Kari just arrived."

"Hi, Emily," Kari said. "My plane was early."

"Great. Let's get started," Emily said.

"Don't you want to eat your lunch first?" Kari asked.

"I'm fine. This is just leftovers," Emily lied, lifting the shopping bag by the handles. "I'll drop it off in the refrigerator on our way to the conference room. I appreciate your coming here," Emily added. "It's important that everyone knows we're working as a team."

"I think our integration of the San Francisco and Denver groups is going well," Dhruv said. "With two notable exceptions."

"I can guess who the problems are," Emily said, "but I'd like you to tell me."

"We've got one non-performing team in each location,"

Kari said. "All the others are working together beautifully. We both get compliments from the business units we service about how much quicker we are in responding to issues."

"Everyone on these teams tells us they love working with a counterpart in another part of the country. Having a person in another time zone working on a problem provides better coverage for the business units and has almost eliminated overtime. Team members collaborate while they're both at work. San Francisco continues to work when Denver goes home and Denver starts in the next morning where San Francisco left off."

"That's what you were hoping to achieve," Emily said.

"Our people say it's more fun to tackle a problem with someone else who is immersed in it, too. If one of them gets stuck, they can discuss it with their partner. In the rare cases where neither of them can come up with a solution, they consult one of us and we work it out together."

"That's why we're both so frustrated with these two teams that aren't working." Kari pressed her palms into the table. "The leads on both teams are the most experienced programmers from each office. We expected them to be the most productive teams."

"The junior members of the teams are exceptionally talented. Both of these teams should hit it out of the park. Instead, they're the least productive in either office. We receive constant complaints from the business people about them, too." Dhruv was reaching the boiling point.

"I agree with your assessment," Emily said. "If you hadn't requested this meeting, I would have."

"We need your help," Kari said. "We've each worked with both teams, to no effect."

"The problem is that the experienced programmers don't want to work with someone else. They like working alone," Dhruv said. "They think they're the smartest people in the room..."

"Which they probably are," Kari interjected.

"And they're not interested in anything the junior team members have to say," Dhruv added.

"The junior member of the team in my office stuck his head in my office last night to ask if he could submit for a job in another division. He said he used to love his job—but not now." Kari clicked and unclicked her pen in rapid succession. "He's the best new programmer we've got. I won't allow some arrogant old-timer to drive talented people away from our group."

"I agree." Emily's tone was firm. "What do you plan to do?"

"That's why we came to you," Dhruv said. "We'd like to reassign the talented newbies to another team in their office. We've identified a team in each office that is functioning so well—and has such a high workload—that it could easily take on someone else."

"Good idea. That's what I would do. What about the recalcitrant old-timers?"

"We'll scale down their responsibilities to particular business units and let them work on their own, like before." Kari sounded defeated. "It's difficult to hire talented programmers, so we don't want to let them go."

"No," Emily responded. "We've restructured our groups

to work in teams on all issues. Our strategy has worked well. Two employees aren't going to derail us. What kind of message does that send to everyone else?"

"So...we fire them?" Dhruv asked. "Even if we hire new programmers, it takes a while to get them trained on our systems. Will we work overtime until that happens?"

"I've got a better idea," Emily said, a smile playing at her lips. "Each of our offices has one of these old-timers, right?"

"Yep," Kari replied. "There's one in every crowd, as the saying goes."

"We'll team them up. They're both so headstrong that neither will let the other walk all over them," Emily said.

Dhruv swung to Kari. "Why didn't we think of that?"

"They may refuse to collaborate," Kari said.

"Assign them projects that aren't in their usual workload. Be sure to give them measurable performance goals, too. I know the man from our office. He's driven to succeed. I think he'll reach out to his cohort when he has to."

"There'll be a lot of hand wringing and gnashing of teeth when we implement this," Kari said.

"Stick to your guns and don't give them any slack," Emily said. "You both know that they can handle any issue that comes into our department."

"I agree with that assessment," Dhruv said. "They may not like it, but it's essential they learn to work with a partner."

"Exactly," Emily said.

"Do you mind if I go call the man who talked to me last night about a transfer within the company? I told him I'd be discussing his issues with you and that I'd report back," Kari said.

"Absolutely," Emily said. "We don't want anyone else in the company getting their hands on our talent."

Kari rose from her seat. She hurried to the conference room door, then turned back to them. "One more thing," she said. "I want both of you to check your calendars and tell me when you can come to Denver. Our office is planning a baby shower for Dhruv." She stepped out of the room without a backward glance at Dhruv.

Emily couldn't see him, but she knew his face had turned pink from ear to ear.

CHAPTER 45

*A*va deposited her dance bag on the floor in the corridor outside the rehearsal room. Unzipping the bag, she removed her tap shoes and placed them on the top of the bag. She took off her jacket and tossed it over her shoes before weaving her way through the crowded corridor to the ladies' room around the corner.

The other chimney sweeps stood in clusters, chatting and stretching.

Tania bumped shoulders with Ava as they passed. Then she plopped down on the floor and set her duffel next to Ava's. Tania rummaged in it until she found her tap shoes and buckled them on. She shoved her duffel out of the way, jostling Ava's shoes.

One of Ava's tap shoes slipped from its precarious perch on top of Ava's bag and landed, half in and half out, in Tania's duffel.

Tania reached for the shoe, then stood, suspended. She

kicked at her duffel. Ava's shoe slid all the way inside. She glanced around. No one was looking in her direction. Tania zipped her duffel shut.

The rehearsal door opened and the dance captain summoned them inside.

The dancers entered the room and took their assigned positions.

"Where's Ava?" the dance captain asked.

"She's here," one sweep answered.

"I think she went to the bathroom," offered another.

Ava burst into the room. Silence fell on the scene like a weighted blanket. The only sound was her steps—clicking on one foot with a tap shoe and a dull thud from the other, clad in a street shoe. She took her place in the center front of the group.

"Two things, Ava." The dance captain's tone tore through the blanket. "First, you're late. Which delays rehearsal. When you joined this troupe, you agreed to be on time. There's a saying in the theater: five minutes before curtain time is on time; curtain time is late. We follow that rule here so that it's part of your DNA by the time you go on to bigger things."

Ava's chin quivered. She kept her eyes glued to his lips.

"Second is that you have your shoes with you. *Always.* I see you're missing one tap shoe."

Tears puddled in Ava's lower lids.

"What if this was a performance night? We couldn't hold the curtain while you ran home to get your shoe."

Ava blinked hard and tears coursed down her cheeks. "I had both shoes with me," she said, choking on the words. "I put them on top of my bag before I went to the bathroom. Only one shoe was there when I came back."

"Did you look for it?"

Ava moved her head like a piston. "Everywhere. It disappeared."

The dance captain searched the eyes of the other dancers in the room. Tania was the only one who turned away from his searchlight glare.

"Do any of you know where Ava's shoe is?"

Tania shifted from foot to foot. Everyone, including Tania, shook their head no.

He inhaled slowly, then proceeded. "You've followed every rule to the letter, until now. I'll make an exception and allow you to rehearse with us this time. We're close to opening night and we've still got a lot to mark. Let's take it from the top. Cue music."

Ava waved to Diedre as her friend exited the rehearsal room where she had been working with the high school girl cast in the lead role and the voice coach. "My mom's waiting for me in the parking lot. I'll see you tomorrow."

"My dad and Zoe are here, too. Let me grab my stuff, and I'll walk out with you," Diedre said.

Ava fell in line with Diedre.

"How did your rehearsal go? I'll bet you're nailing that tap solo they've made for you."

Ava's expression fell like an Etch A Sketch. "I almost got kicked out."

Diedre grabbed Ava by the elbow and pulled her to a halt. "What are you talking about?"

Ava filled her in on the missing shoe. "I swear to you—I looked everywhere for it." Her voice wobbled. "Turns out it got into Tania's duffel. It was on the floor next to mine, and she found it there when she put her tap shoes away."

Diedre tilted her head to one side and narrowed her eyes.

"She said she didn't notice and zipped her duffel shut before she came into rehearsal. She was scared she was running late."

"Your shoe was in her duffel, and she didn't notice. You didn't find it because it was in her bag?"

"That's right. The dance captain was very stern with me. I thought they were going to remove me from the cast. I cried and everything."

Diedre released Ava's elbow, and they continued walking down the corridor.

"But he didn't. I ran through the entire routine with one tap and one street shoe. He told me I have to come with two tap shoes next time or I'm out."

"Tania found your shoe just now—when you were all getting ready to go home?"

"Yeah. Thank goodness for her."

Diedre harrumphed. She looked up to see Tania enter the ladies' room. "I need to go to the bathroom before we leave," Diedre said.

"Okay," Ava said. "I'm going to the car. See ya."

Diedre entered the ladies' room and checked for feet under the stalls. Only one was occupied. She waited.

Outside, Zoe and Ava met in the wide, double-glass door entry to the theater.

"Hey, Ava," Zoe said. "Grant sent me to look for Diedre."

"She went to the ladies' room." She pointed. "It's back there."

"Thanks," Zoe replied, and headed off in search of her sister. She found the bathroom. A toilet flushed as she began to push the door open. She stopped and hovered behind the door when she heard Diedre's voice.

"I know what you did." Diedre's eyes met Tania's in the mirror.

Tania lowered her gaze to her hands and rinsed them over and over. "What're you talking about?"

"You put Ava's shoe in your duffel."

Tania spun to face Diedre, her hands dripping on the floor. "Is that what Ava said? She's lying…"

"Ava didn't say that. I did." Diedre stood her ground. "There's no way that shoe slipped into your duffel, and you didn't notice it."

Tania dried her hands on her jeans.

"You wanted Ava to get kicked out of the play. She's a better dancer than you are and you're jealous."

Tania straightened and took a step back. "Geez. It was just a joke. I didn't think she could get kicked off."

"I don't believe you, Tania. You know the theater's rules. You're a mean girl and you were trying to hurt her. Zoe told me…"

"That freak sister of yours? What did she say?"

"Zoe is *not* a freak. She's my sister and best friend. I believe her. She'd never lie." Diedre's voice rose in volume.

"She told me that you and some of the others make fun of Ava behind her back because of the way Ava talks. She can't help that. It's so stupid of all of you."

"What're you going to do about it? Tattle on me?" Despite her words, Tania's bravado was clearly wilting like day-old lettuce.

"Not this time," Diedre said. "But I'm warning you. If you do it again, I'll tell my parents and the grownups here. I'll stick up for Ava. She's a really good person. She taught me to tap dance well enough to be Mary's understudy. I'd rather be friends with Ava than with you."

Diedre spun around and pushed through the door, knocking Zoe so hard her sister lost her footing.

"What're you doing out here?" Diedre asked.

Zoe grinned as she got to her feet and brushed herself off. "Listening to my sister being the best ever."

"Did you hear all that?"

"I sure did." Zoe linked arms with Diedre. "Grant sent me to see if you needed help with anything. He wanted me to hurry you up."

"Sorry I made you both wait."

"I'm glad you did." Zoe pulled up as they reached the door. "Thank you for sticking up for Ava. And me."

"You were right about those girls, Zoe. I'm sorry I didn't see it earlier."

"Doesn't matter. You do now."

"Do you think I should tell Emily and Dad, after all?"

Zoe pursed her lips. "Not now. You told her you wouldn't."

"If they do one more mean thing, we will," Diedre said. "You'll watch them, too?"

"Yep. The weird thing is that I don't think Ava knows they're making fun of her or being mean."

"I hope not. She doesn't deserve that."

"She's got us. If that's not enough, we'll tell the adults," Zoe said.

The girls exchanged a look that sealed the deal and headed into the night to their waiting parent.

CHAPTER 46

"Take as much time as you need, Dave," Grant said into the phone. "Family comes first. I'll contact HR for you to get the paperwork rolling for your leave." He listened to the young architect's reply. "Keep us posted. Emily and I will pray for you."

Grant punched off the call and noted the time on his phone. He was already ten minutes late for his lunch with Norman Klein. He'd make the promised call to the person who handled Human Resources for his firm after lunch.

Grant got out of his car and hurried into the restaurant.

The hostess guided him to a table along a window overlooking the bay.

Norman rose and extended his hand.

"I'm sorry to be late." Grant shook Norman's hand, and they sat. "One of my employees called to tell me his wife has been diagnosed with cancer and is slated for surgery on Monday. They have three young children."

"Oohh...that's rough," Norman replied.

"He didn't give me any details, and I didn't pry. He just said they don't have any family who can help with the kids, so he needs to go out on family leave."

"Understandable." Norman cocked his head to one side. "You're a small firm. Does that create...challenges?"

"At the moment—incredible challenges. Do you remember that huge project in Los Angeles that we're working on?"

"Sure."

"Dave's been shadowing me on the project and just took over as the on-site person. I'm paying him a bonus for taking this on."

"That's decent of you."

Grant shrugged. "I don't want to be away from my family Monday through Friday every week. He's got a family, too. He discussed it with his wife, and she was all for it. The bonus would give them enough money to buy a larger home."

"Can you send someone else from your office?"

"Eventually. This client's number-one priority for this facility is environmentally friendly design. Dave and I are the experts in our firm. No one else can just step into our shoes." Grant raked his hand through his hair. "I'll have to fly down there tonight." His face mirrored the clouds on the horizon. "I'm helping Zoe with a science fair project that's due next week, and Diedre is in a youth theater production that opens a week from Friday. She's got rehearsals every night next week."

"And you don't want to miss out on all that."

258

"No." Grant sighed heavily. "I'm going to have to. We already have my mom and Martha slated to help us. Even with two extra sets of hands, we were going to be pushed to the limit. And now I'm dumping all this on Emily."

The server approached and took their beverage order. After hearing about the daily specials, they each ordered the catch of the day.

"What about hiring someone to help you?"

"We should have hired a nanny weeks ago..."

"I meant with the Los Angeles project."

"I'd need an architect with a thorough understanding of environmental architecture. And I wouldn't be comfortable sending a rookie I'd never worked with. Experienced architects are hard to find, much less on a moment's notice." Grant took a sip of his water and looked at Norman. Their eyes met over the rim of his glass.

Norman raised an eyebrow.

"You?" Grant sputtered, choking on his water.

"I'm only suggesting it. You know what's best."

"You'd be perfect!" Grant recovered himself. "This would be the ideal solution. The client will love you—I'm certain of it. And with your expertise in the subject, you'll make improvements that can only be done on the fly."

"I think you're overestimating my credentials," Norman said modestly.

"Your reputation says otherwise." Grant rocked back in his chair. "We'd hire your firm as a subcontractor. Do you have time for this commitment? I know you're as busy as we are."

"My sons handle our firm now. I stay on to keep my hand

in. I love the field, but I try to stay out of the way. The practice will be theirs one of these days."

"Family firm dynamics can be challenging."

"To say the least. I'm not complaining. Both of my boys are talented architects and good business people. I was ready to step away from the firm when my wife died. We had plans to travel that I don't want to pursue now. Frankly, I'm itching to be part of a real project again."

"You'd have to be there all week, every week. Most days will be longer than eight hours and they'll be very fast paced."

"I miss that feeling of having my hair on fire."

Grant and Norman both laughed.

The server brought their plates of sea bass over cauliflower puree.

"Let's do this," Grant said. He offered a stipend.

"That's more than generous," Norman said. "There's just one additional condition before I accept."

Grant cocked his head to one side.

"You need to get Emily's approval. She and I haven't been in touch since the wedding. I was honored to walk her down the aisle since I was the recipient of her father's heart. That was a one-time event. Working for you is another thing. She may feel—I don't know—weird about it."

Grant inhaled slowly. "That's a good call. I'll ask her, but I know she'll be on board. She was excited that we ran into each other at the airport and thrilled that I was having lunch with you today."

"In that case, let's eat and you can tell me everything I need to know about the project."

"I'll confirm with Emily and let you know by this evening. When can you start?"

"If you're going to the project tomorrow, I can go with you."

Grant picked up his fork. "I walked in here feeling like my world had spun out of control. I'm going to leave knowing things are in better hands than ever."

CHAPTER 47

We were on our way to meet Grant. In the middle of our workday. Maybe for coffee. I wasn't too sure. All I knew was that Emily had woken me from my mid-afternoon nap and that's what she'd said.

We exited the building into a sunny and crisp afternoon, with a breeze that pushed the clouds along almost as fast as we were walking.

Emily commanded me to take her to our favorite coffee shop around the corner. I'd been right about that.

The tinkling bell sounded as we entered. My nose took off twitching like marbles poured from a sack. Almost nothing smelled better than coffee.

I spotted Grant and headed in his direction before Emily gave the command.

He rose. They kissed. I settled under the table. They sat.

"I got you a caramel macchiato," Grant said. He slid the cup into her hand.

"Thank you. I could use a treat."

"Tough day?"

"Not at the office. Did you see the email from the theater?"

"I haven't been back to the office since before lunch. What's up?"

"The boy playing Bert broke his leg last weekend. He's out for the entire production."

"Poor kid."

"That means his understudy—Ava—is stepping in."

"Wow. That's a lot for her, isn't it?"

"I should think so. And for us. They're starting rehearsals an hour earlier for Ava and Mary Poppins—including the understudy—to help her get up to speed."

"Holy cow. Does Diedre know yet?"

"Nope. Thank goodness our mothers are helping out next week. I'm so glad we bought a house with a guest room for my mom. We need her." Emily took a sip of her coffee. "I didn't think things could get any busier for us."

Grant snorted.

"Oh, no. What's your news?"

"Don't freak out. It has a happy ending—potentially." Grant filled her in about Dave's sudden absence and his discussion with Norman.

"Do I mind? Are you kidding?" Emily released the breath she'd been holding. "He's the answer to our prayers. Not just for this project, but maybe for others, too. You never know. I'd love to see you work less than sixty hours a week."

"You're on board?"

"Completely. He was so kind at our wedding. I'd love to get to know him better."

"You don't feel—odd about it? With him having your dad's heart and all."

Emily's answer was swift and sure. "Not at all."

"What about Martha?"

"She felt comforted by his presence, too. It's all fine. The only thing you need to do now is buy your plane tickets and get him up to speed ASAP."

"On it," Grant said.

"Thank you for asking me first." She secured the lid on her mostly full cup of coffee. "I'd better get back. The early rehearsals start tonight, so I have to leave work an hour early."

"I'm sorry you have to shoulder all the burden this week."

Emily stood and grasped my harness. "We'll be fine. I'm just glad it's only for five days."

They kissed, and I soon had us zooming along to our office.

CHAPTER 48

Garth shifted positions underneath Emily's desk, and his tail thumped the floor.

"Dhruv?" Emily asked.

"It's me," he said. "I wanted to let you know I'm leaving early."

"Doctor appointment with Stephanie?"

"No. That's tomorrow. I want to be there when she gets her award."

"What award?"

"Teacher of Extraordinary Distinction."

"That sounds very important."

"It is. Her district hasn't awarded it in over twenty years."

"*Dhruv!* How did I not know this?"

"Sorry. I came by your office twice to tell you, but you'd already left for the day." He fidgeted in her doorway. "I've got to go. I can't be late."

Emily sprang from her chair. "I'll walk you to the elevator." She grabbed Garth's harness. "Tell me more."

"Remember how she helped that autistic boy during the lockdown?"

"Of course I do!"

"That's why. They're announcing it at an all-school assembly. The superintendent of schools and the school board will be there, too."

They reached the elevator, and he pushed the button.

"I wish I'd known," Emily said, her voice full of regret. "I would have loved to come with you. As it is, I need to pick up Diedre early from school and take her to play rehearsal."

"We know how busy you are."

"Please congratulate her from us and tell her how proud I am of her."

The elevator chimed, and the doors opened. "Will do," Dhruv said. He stepped into the elevator and was gone.

DHRUV CIRCLED the parking lot for the third time before giving up looking for a spot and angled his car into a triangle of pavement crisscrossed with yellow lines in front of a trash dumpster. If he got towed, so be it. He would not be late for Stephanie's award.

He ran to the front office and checked himself in.

The school secretary nodded approvingly when she read his name on the sheet. "We've been waiting for you. I'll text to let them know you'll be there shortly. And I handled your request. Do you know where the auditorium is?"

Dhruv said he did and tore out the door.

The large room that doubled as the gymnasium was brightly lit from can lights in the ceiling. Bleachers had been pulled out from both long sides of the rectangular room and were filled to capacity. Children chattered excitedly, their voices creating a buzz like a brood of cicadas.

Dhruv halted in the doorway. He detested chaotic environments like the one in front of him. His eyes searched the room until he found her; the woman who calmed and comforted him: his true north.

Stephanie sat on a folding chair along the far wall, Biscuit at her side. Men and women in crisp business attire flanked her on either side. An older gentleman stood at a podium in the middle, polishing his glasses and flipping through his notes.

As if she could feel his need for her, Stephanie looked up and smiled in his direction.

Dhruv swallowed his dread and stepped into the room. He forced himself to ignore the bedlam around him and crossed to her side.

Just like with Garth, Biscuit's tail announced his arrival.

"I told them you were coming," she said as he took her hand and squeezed it. "This won't take long. I'm the only one who has a chair because I'm pregnant."

"Rightly so," Dhruv said. "A woman in her eighth month shouldn't be standing." He didn't tell her he'd called the school secretary earlier to make sure they had a seat for her.

The microphone on the podium crackled, and Dhruv moved to stand behind Stephanie's chair. The room gradually quieted.

The man at the podium informed the crowd that he was the superintendent of schools and introduced the members of the school board who surrounded him. He thanked the principal and began his remarks.

"I have the distinct honor today to grant an award that hasn't been issued for the past twenty-four years. The actions required to be considered for this honor are so exemplary that it's rarely awarded. Today's recipient is over-whelmingly deserving."

He threw his shoulders back and spoke with conviction. "This teacher left the safety of her classroom during a campus lockdown. She rescued a child who was hiding outside, in an unsecured location. By the time she reached him, she felt certain this was a live situation and not a drill. She convinced the child to go with her to safety—and shielded him with her own body until they had gotten to the nearest safe room."

He turned toward Stephanie. "As you can see, she did this while she was pregnant. And as a visually impaired person." The superintendent paused and scanned the audience. "If anyone has reservations about the capability of people in either of these conditions, you now know those concerns are not valid." He raised his voice. "I'd like all of you to welcome our Teacher of Extraordinary Distinction to the podium, Stephanie Patel."

The room exploded into applause.

Dhruv helped Stephanie to her feet, and he and Biscuit walked her to the podium.

The superintendent shook her hand, then placed an engraved crystal obelisk into it.

Stephanie thanked him.

He leaned in and spoke into her ear so she could hear him above the deafening applause. "Would you like to say a few words?"

Stephanie swallowed hard. "Yes."

Dhruv took the obelisk from her. The superintendent guided her to the podium and adjusted the microphone.

"Thank you." Stephanie's shy voice silenced the crowd. "I'm truly grateful for this honor. I assure all of you that every teacher in this school would have done the same thing in my shoes. But I have one advantage they don't. My blindness played a significant part in rescuing this child." She reached down to pat the top of Biscuit's head. "My acute sense of hearing helped me locate the boy and the irresistible attraction of my guide dog, Biscuit, lured him out of hiding so we could all move to a safe shelter."

Laughter rolled around the room. Stephanie waited until it died down before continuing. "I'd ask one thing of all of you today. As you resume your activities, remember that blind people are as capable as sighted ones. We simply do things in different ways."

Applause erupted again, even louder than before. Stephanie flushed and took a step back.

Dhruv put his arm around her shoulder. "You are the most remarkable person in the world," Dhruv whispered in her ear. "Our baby is incredibly lucky—and so am I."

Stephanie leaned into him as the applause thundered on.

CHAPTER 49

*D*iedre stood on her tiptoes to find Ava in the swarm of kids waiting for the all-cast-and-crew meeting, outside the main theater door. She spotted her friend as she entered on the opposite side. Diedre swung her arm over her head until she got Ava's attention.

Ava nodded in acknowledgment.

Diedre wiggled her fingers like they were walking.

Ava nodded again, and Diedre wound her way through the crowd to find her friend. "I thought you were right behind me when the dance captain dismissed us to come to this meeting. Where did you go?"

"I stayed behind to talk to him."

"Why? He said you were doing incredibly well—you can handle the entire part."

"I wanted to ask him about stuff they're cutting out."

"But they aren't cutting anything from Bert's part."

"I was talking about my tap solo when I was a chimney sweep."

Diedre narrowed her eyes. "You can't still do that."

"I know, but one of the other sweeps could."

"Like who?"

"Tania."

"She's not the tap dancer you are."

"She'd do great."

"Does she know the part?"

"No. But I could easily teach it to her," Ava said. "Like I taught you to tap."

Diedre struggled to find her voice. "You'd do that for Tania? Teach her your routine."

"Sure. She's okay."

"She hid your tap shoe." Diedre shot back.

"We don't know that." Ava's voice was resolute. "Even if she did, my mom says everyone deserves a second chance."

Diedre looked away and blinked hard. When she turned back to Ava, her eyes were full of admiration. "That's about the nicest thing I've ever heard."

"You know Tania. Would she want to learn it?"

"I'm sure she'd jump at the chance. What did the dance captain say?"

"That I could work with her until dress rehearsal."

"Which is next week," Diedre interjected.

"If she can do it by then, he'll leave the solo in the show. They're going to make the announcement about me stepping in as Bert at this meeting, then we go straight into rehearsals. Will you help me talk to Tania?"

271

"Sure. I'll snag her on our way to the rehearsal room." Diedre looked at her friend. "You're a nice girl, Ava."

Ava had turned away to join the cue lining up to enter the theater and didn't register the compliment.

The brief announcement was greeted with a ripple of surprise that ran through the kids in the seats. The director had called upon Ava to stand and wave to the assemblage. He then sent everyone on their way.

Diedre spotted Tania ahead of them as they filed out of the auditorium. She called to her.

Tania turned and waited for them to catch up to her. She glanced at Ava and murmured, "Congratulations."

"Thank you. I wanted to ask you..." Ava's words raced ahead. "Would you like to learn my tap solo as lead chimney sweep?"

"What're you talking about? They've cut it from the show."

"I talked to the dance captain, and he said if I could teach it to you by Monday, he'd leave it in."

"Why would you want to do that?"

"Because it's a terrific part and makes the show better." Ava looked directly at Tania. "And I know you can do it. It's simply a matter of learning the routine."

Tania's eyes expanded like pancake batter poured on a griddle. "You really think so?"

Ava nodded. "You know all the steps individually. All you have to do is put them together."

"And you'll teach me?" Tania glanced at Diedre, then turned her gaze to the floor. "That's awfully nice of you—especially after..."

"The two of you should practice in your garage, Tania," Diedre interrupted. "Like we did before auditions." Diedre faced Ava. "She has a lot of space in there. Would your mom let you go to Tania's?"

"I'll ask her," Ava replied.

"Can I come, too?" Diedre asked. "I'll do the Mary Poppins part so you can practice Bert."

"And I can read the script while you do that, so you don't miss lines," Tania offered with enthusiasm.

"My mom will say yes," Tania said. "I'm sure she can pick us all up after school, too."

"If it's okay with our parents, let's start tomorrow," Ava said. She pointed down the hallway. "The director is holding the rehearsal room door open, scowling at us. We'd better get in there." She hurried ahead of them.

Tania and Diedre followed her. As they reached the door, Tania turned back to Diedre. "She's *soooo* nice. I'm sorry I was mean to her." She brushed the sleeve of her sweater across her eyes. "I'm ashamed of myself."

"She *is* the nicest. And we all make mistakes." She put her arm through Tania's and pulled her into the room.

CHAPTER 50

"We're getting there early enough to snag front row seats—or there'll be hell to pay." That's what Emily had yelled from the foyer, where we waited. Emily had her coat on, and I was in my harness. I'd earlier heard Grant whisper to Zoe that Emily was "in a mood." I had to agree.

Martha was with us, and we picked up Sylvia from the curb in front of her house. We were the first ones inside the theater and got those seats. I settled myself in front of Emily's feet. Front row center is what I believe they called it. I expected her to relax, but her nerves kept ratcheting up. We'd attended all the previous performances, and she hadn't been this nervous. I didn't yet know why this one was different.

People streamed in until they filled every seat for the last performance of *Mary Poppins, Jr.* Gina and Craig had walked in right after Stephanie and Dhruv. The only seats left for them were in the back. I was glad to see them—Diedre would be happy.

The lights flickered and eight chimes sounded. People who had been making their way to their seats increased their pace. The hubbub of conversation died off.

Emily leaned in to whisper to Grant. "I can't believe Diedre's going on as Mary Poppins! I'm sorry that the other girl has food poisoning—truly I am—but I'm thrilled our girl has this chance."

"I know. I'm *so* excited."

"Was she nervous when you dropped her off earlier?"

"Very. But Ava was terrific with her—telling her she knew every line as well as the lead girl and was a better singer."

"Diedre believed her?"

"Yep. If we had told her that, she would have discounted it because we're her parents."

Music started and the long red velvet drape in front of us opened. The lights in the audience dimmed even further.

When I stretch out on a cool floor in a dark room, there's generally only one outcome. But I didn't sleep at all tonight —not one wink. Our girl Diedre was on that stage. With her friend Ava. I kept my eyes glued to them every time they were on stage.

My family clapped throughout the entire performance like they were paid to do it. I joined in with my tail. When the show was done, the actors came out and lined up on stage. We clapped and thumped even harder. When Ava ran from the back of the stage to the center of the line, we increased our volume to a level I didn't think was possible.

And when Diedre followed Ava and walked through the line of actors to take her solo bow, we jumped to our feet. Everyone in the auditorium rose, too.

Grant put his fingers in his mouth and gave an ear-splitting whistle. I didn't like it, but I couldn't blame him. Diedre deserved every bit of this adulation.

Things eventually quieted down. We made our way outside to wait for Diedre. First Gina and Craig stopped to congratulate us. Emily and Gina hugged, and Craig slapped Grant on the back. They wanted to stay to see Diedre but had to get home so the babysitter could leave. It was a school night for her. We understood.

Gina handed Zoe two bouquets of flowers. One was for Diedre and one for Zoe. She'd won the science fair with her straw roller coaster project. I was proud of my talented family.

Dhruv and Stephanie were next in line. Two more bouquets were handed to Zoe. Stephanie and Emily did the swaying-hugging thing, while Dhruv and Grant chatted amiably. Biscuit and I stood companionably together, basking in the warmth of our happy humans. They finally said their goodbyes. Pregnant women need to get off their feet.

Martha and Sylvia were busy recounting to each other every stellar moment of Diedre's performance. I now understood the term "proud grandparent."

Diedre finally pushed through the stage door, her coat flung haphazardly over her shoulders and her backpack stuffed to the gills.

Zoe dropped the flowers and flung her arms around her

sister. The hug they shared made the ones I had observed moments earlier look like amateur versions.

I swung my muzzle from Emily to the rest of my family. I thought the day Emily and I met had been the happiest of my life. I learned a valuable lesson: happiness could always get happier.

CHAPTER 51

*D*iedre removed the last wrapped package from the gift table. She brought the large, flat rectangle to Stephanie and leaned it against the sofa, where she sat with Dhruv.

Zoe was busy balling up the wrapping paper from the last gift and placing it in the trash.

Emily and Grant leaned against the wall in Dhruv's aunt's modest apartment. Emily lifted the cut-glass punch cup to her lips and took a sip of the frothy concoction. "This is delicious," she whispered in Grant's ear. "Remind me to make punch, once in a while."

Grant chuckled softly and shifted his weight against the wall.

"How many more?" Emily whispered again.

"Last one," he replied. "Are you tired of standing? I can find you a chair."

"No. It's hot in here and I'd like to get some air. Garth and I will step outside when she's opened it."

Stephanie reached down and felt the package. "Ohhh...I wonder what this could be."

Six older women of Indian heritage scooted forward on the edges of their chairs.

"Who is this one from, honey?"

Dhruv read off the names of his aunts.

"But each of you've already given us gifts," Stephanie directed the comment into the room.

"This one is a joint gift—from all of us," one aunt said.

Stephanie carefully tore off the paper to reveal a two-foot square piece of poster board. One side was blank, and the other contained a color-coded, hand-lettered table. Columns with days of the week for a 60-day period ran along the top, while times from 7:00 a.m. to 7:00 p.m. in 30-minute increments marked rows along the left. Each box was filled in with the name of one of the six aunts, in both neat calligraphy and braille. A unique color was used for each aunt.

Dhruv leaned in to examine it while Stephanie read the braille with her fingertips.

"Daily Schedule for _____." Dhruv read the words above the table.

"We'll fill in the name when you have the baby," the first aunt said.

The aunts exchanged glances and leaned forward in their seats even further as Stephanie ran her fingers over the board.

"I'm not sure I understand," Stephanie said, keeping her voice level.

"This tells you who's going to be at your apartment to take care of the baby while Dhruv is at work," the second aunt supplied. "We'll do a new table every sixty days. We've got our phone numbers on the bottom, too, in case you need us to stop at the store for anything."

The room fell silent.

Emily's spine stiffened. Dhruv's aunts had clearly implied that a blind woman couldn't care for her baby. She felt for Stephanie and contemplated speaking up. Her friend hated confrontation.

Stephanie's gentle voice broke the silence. "This is incredibly thoughtful and generous of you," she said.

The aunts shared congratulatory glances.

"But we won't need all this help," Stephanie continued in a tone that hinted the aunts were approaching a submerged iceberg.

"What do you mean? Dhruv said you weren't hiring a nanny."

"We're not," he inserted himself into the conversation. "Stephanie will take care of our baby while I'm at work. Just like other families with a baby."

An emotional chill accompanied the silence this time.

"Is that…is that safe for the baby?"

"Of course it is." Emily's curt response landed in the room like a cannonball into the pool. "You saw the other gifts. Many are designed for blind parents—like the medicine droppers with raised marks and the baby carriers that won't interfere with her cane or guide dog use. And Stephanie is one of the most capable people I've ever met."

Dhruv's mother spoke up. "I told you about the award

Stephanie got for helping that child." The pride in her voice was unmistakable. "She did a lot of that because she is blind —not despite it."

The aunts deflated like popped balloons.

"We're grateful that you're as excited about our baby as we are," Stephanie said. She passed her hand over the chart. "We've got the parenting part handled, but we'll want babysitters, for sure. This is very helpful. Now we'll know which one of you is available when we need a sitter. Saves us calling around."

The aunts all sat up straighter.

"I'm the one you should be more worried about," Dhruv said. "I don't know a thing about babies. I'm terrified of being alone with our baby."

"Everyone feels that way at first," an aunt said. "You'll pick it up in no time. We're here to help you too, Dhruv."

The group around her nodded their agreement.

"I'm happy you're going to love our baby," Dhruv said, a catch in his voice.

"Who wants another piece of cake?" One aunt got out of her chair. "I'll bet you girls would. You've both been so helpful managing these gifts."

Zoe and Diedre followed her to the buffet table and were soon handing around second slices of the delicious cherry chip layer cake with buttercream icing.

The shower wound down. Grant and the girls helped Dhruv stow the gifts in the back of his SUV. Emily and Stephanie took Garth and Biscuit outside for a comfort break.

"That was a lovely shower," Emily said. "You've got everything you need. Grant offered to help Dhruv put the crib together. It's the same one that he assembled for Gina and Craig's baby, and he said it's tricky. The directions are hopeless, and it didn't come with all the necessary hardware."

"That would be really helpful," Stephanie said. She rested her hand on top of her huge abdomen. "I can hardly believe she's almost here."

"Time is flying. I can't wait for our spa day next Saturday."

"Me, too. I plan to get all these gifts settled into place before then. The spa will be a nice reward. Thank you for treating me to it, Em."

"I'm getting as much out of the day as you are," Emily said. "Now that the science fair and the play are done, I realize how ridiculously crowded my schedule was." She reached out her hand and found Stephanie's arm, giving it a squeeze. "I'm so proud of you for the way you handled yourself back there."

"What do you mean?"

"With Dhruv's aunts and that schedule of theirs."

"They mean well."

"I know. But assuming you can't take care of your own baby because you're blind? That must have hurt."

Stephanie inhaled deeply. "We get a lot of that, don't we? People assuming we're not capable—thinking they know best?"

"We sure do. Those subtle messages that you're not enough can get under your skin."

Stephanie placed her free hand on top of Emily's. "Most

of it comes from a good place. People care about us and want to help. I try to remember that."

"I need to be more like you. Stand my ground without coming unglued."

"Emily Main? I think you're perfect as you are. I don't want my bestie to change one little bit." She squeezed Emily's hand, then released it. "We'd better get back inside. I've had a wonderful time but now I want to go home, get into my pj's, and put my feet up."

Emily laughed. "I think that's always a solid plan."

They rejoined the others. After a prolonged goodbye with multiple hugs for the expectant parents, Emily's family walked Stephanie, Biscuit, and Dhruv to the car.

"See you Saturday," Grant said to Dhruv. "We'll put the crib together while Emily and Stephanie are at the spa."

"Perfect plan," Emily said as they headed with Garth and the girls to his SUV. "Everything will be in order before the baby arrives."

CHAPTER 52

"*D*hr*UV*!" Stephanie's voice picked up volume as she called his name.

He raced from the kitchen, where he'd been feeding Biscuit and their two other dogs, to the bedroom.

Stephanie stood in the doorway of their en suite bathroom, clutching her nightgown with one hand. The other gripped the door frame. A puddle of water lay on the tile between her feet.

Dhruv's eyes expanded like an ink stain. "You're..." His voice failed him.

"In labor, yes." She looked at the floor. "My water broke."

Dhruv crossed the room until he was at her side, then turned back to the bed, before switching directions and going to the closet—ricocheting around the room like a pinball shot from a spring.

"Honey," Stephanie said.

He stopped and faced her.

"We're going to the hospital."

"Okay," he replied but remained rooted to the spot.

She walked slowly to the hamper and pulled on the sweatshirt and sweatpants she'd worn the day before. "Will you get my sneakers from the closet?"

Responding to her clear direction, Dhruv retrieved her shoes and helped her slide her feet into them. He put his arm around her waist, and they headed for the door.

"Grab my hospital bag from the hall closet," she said when they reached the doorway.

He retrieved it and slung it over his shoulder.

"And Dhruv," she said.

"Huh?"

"Breathe. Everything's going to be fine. Instead of going to the spa, I'm having our baby today."

EMILY'S PHONE vibrated on her nightstand. She rolled onto her side, turning her back to it. She and Grant were picking up Stephanie at ten for their spa day. His muffled snore came from the other side of the bed. He'd promised to get up with the girls and let her sleep in. Since he was still in bed, surely it meant she could go back to sleep.

The phone quieted and Emily nestled deeper into her pillow. Probably a spam call, she thought, as she drifted toward sleep.

The vibrating started again, catapulting her back to consciousness. Maybe something had happened to her mother? Emily threw back the covers in a frustrated jerk and swung her feet to the floor. She groped for the phone and took it into the bathroom, where she could listen to the screen reader without disturbing Grant.

The two calls in quick succession had been from Dhruv. He left her a message on the second one.

"Her water broke. We're on our way to the hospital."

Emily heard Stephanie's moans of pain in the background.

"She's not going to the spa today," he continued. "We're having our baby!"

The message cut off.

Emily clasped her phone to her chest and offered a silent prayer for a safe and easy delivery, and health and happiness for the new family.

"Do you know where we're supposed to park?" Stephanie asked. "You read the papers from the birthing center?"

"I do," Dhruv lied. He thought he had another month to read all that stuff. If he read it too far in advance, he'd forget everything, anyway. He wasn't going to tell her that. After all, how hard could it be? The hospital would have good signage. He'd figure it out.

After driving around the extended campus of the hospital, Dhruv spotted a figure dressed in green scrubs a hundred yards ahead. He drove up to the woman and powered his driver's side window down.

Stephanie was alternating between groans and deep

breaths. She let out a low wail when they reached the woman.

Without being asked, she pointed ahead of them and then gestured to the right with her thumb. "Delivery is the next right, then two buildings over. Short-term parking is to the left of the birthing center entrance."

Stephanie screamed and Dhruv sped off in the direction the woman indicated.

He pulled into the only remaining short-term parking spot and helped Stephanie extricate herself from the car. She draped herself over his shoulders and they took a few halting steps toward the entrance before a set of automatic doors opened and a person in scrubs raced to them with a wheelchair.

The man asked their name.

Dhruv told him.

Stephanie dug her nails into Dhruv's shoulder, threw her head down, and screamed.

Dhruv turned terrified eyes on the man.

"That'll be a contraction," he said, for Dhruv's benefit. "Perfectly normal." When it had passed, he helped a heavily panting Stephanie sit in the wheelchair and quickly began pushing it toward the automatic doors.

"We've already registered with the hospital for the delivery. Our insurance information is on file, and they have approved coverage," Dhruv supplied. He walked next to them with the gait of someone traversing hot coals.

"Excellent," the man said. "How far apart are your contractions?"

Stephanie hinged forward in her chair and let out a scream worthy of a horror film.

"Not even two minutes," the man said, propelling the chair even faster. "How long has she been in labor?"

"Not long. Maybe an hour. We came as soon as her water broke."

He whisked them through the automatic doors.

"I'm taking them directly to a delivery room," the man spoke to a woman sitting in front of a computer. "Which one's open?"

The woman tapped at her keyboard with lightning speed and told him.

The wheelchair picked up speed on the smooth floor as the man headed for their destination.

"Sir," the woman called to Dhruv.

He turned back to her.

"Can you please give me your information? It'll only take a moment and then I'll take you to your wife. They'll get her onto the delivery table and take her vitals."

Dhruv stopped and turned to watch his wife and the man disappear around the corner. He bit his lip but did as the woman requested.

True to her word, Dhruv was in the delivery room, at Stephanie's side, when the doctor entered the room.

Stephanie sunk her nails into Dhruv's arm like a hawk taloning its prey and released another blood-curdling scream.

"She wants an epidural," Dhruv told the doctor. "We talked about it."

"It's too late for that. She's fully dilated and effaced. A few pushes and your daughter will be in your arms."

Stephanie squeezed Dhruv's arm and screamed again.

Dhruv's color drained from his face.

"Are you going to be okay, sir?" A nurse asked him.

Dhruv's mouth was as dry as set concrete. He nodded in the affirmative.

The doctor rolled his stool into position at the end of the table. "Stephanie—with the next contraction, I want you to push as hard as you can."

Stephanie writhed in pain.

The nurse on the other side of the table from Dhruv caught his attention. "Help me lift her shoulders." Dhruv followed the nurse's lead.

Stephanie grimaced and pushed with all her might. When the contraction passed, she slumped back against the table.

"That was perfect," the doctor said in encouragement. "The baby is moving down the birth canal."

Stephanie moaned.

Dhruv and the nurse lifted her shoulders, and the doctor called for her to push. There was still no baby.

"One more time," the doctor said to Stephanie.

She flung her head from side to side. "I can't. I'm too tired."

The nurse blotted the sweat out of Stephanie's eyes. With a narrowing of her eyes and a slight gesture with her head, she signaled to Dhruv that he should say something to his wife.

Dhruv swallowed his own horror at seeing his beloved Stephanie in labor and put his hand on her cheek. "You can do this, Stephanie. You're the woman brave enough to step into the line of fire to save a child. Just once more."

Stephanie nodded her head against his hand. When the next contraction started, she leaned forward before Dhruv and the nurse lifted her shoulders. She sucked in a deep breath, bore down, and pushed.

The baby slid into the doctor's waiting hands. Within moments, the high-pitched angry cries of a newborn reverberated around the room.

"Congratulations," the doctor said. "It's a girl."

Stephanie collapsed against the table, panting.

Dhruv leaned in to her. *"I. Love. You. Stephanie."* Every word was hurtled over the high wall of his emotion. He planted a kiss on her sweaty brow.

"Would you like to do the honors?" The nurse asked, pointing to the umbilical cord. She helped Dhruv cut the cord of the wailing infant.

Moments later, the nurse placed the baby, wiped clean and swaddled in a blanket, in her mother's arms.

Dhruv stared in amazement at the red-faced bundle. She had a full head of black hair, like his own, but her features were refined, like Stephanie's.

Stephanie ran her fingertips over the baby's face, exploring the delicate ears and button nose.

"Fingers and toes?" she asked the nurse.

"Five of each on each side. Would you like to look at them?" The nurse began to unwrap the blanket.

"I believe you. What color is her hair?" she asked.

"Black, like mine," Dhruv said.

"Good. Black hair is lovely."

The nurse looked confused.

"Stephanie is blind," Dhruv said.

"I didn't realize," the nurse said. "I see newborns all day long. Would you like my observations?"

"Yes, please," Stephanie said.

The nurse talked while the others finished their tasks. The doctor dictated notes into an iPad, congratulated the couple again, and went on to the next delivery.

Still, the nurse continued. She described the shape and color of the baby's eyes, the fullness of her lashes and the scarcity of her brows, the point of her chin and the roundness of her ears—all the while opining that this baby was by far the prettiest she'd seen since her own children had been born.

Through it all, the baby showcased her impressive lung capacity.

The nurse concluded her description. "I'll be right back to take you to your room."

Dhruv stared down at his infant daughter, nestled against his wife. He felt like his heart had super-sized itself in that moment—like in the *How the Grinch Stole Christmas* movie. He now understood that scene.

"I know what we should call her," Stephanie kept her chin tilted to the crying baby. "Based on her obvious tenacity and determination, she's a lot like Emily."

"So we'll name her Emily?"

"That might be confusing. When she and Grant have children, we'll probably get together all the time with our kids," Stephanie said. "I was thinking Amelia. It sounds like Emily, but different."

"Amelia." Dhruv drew the name out. "I love it. Like the famous American pilot."

"Exactly." Stephanie held the baby out to Dhruv.

He took her into his arms. "Welcome to the world, Amelia."

Her crying subsided, and she looked into her father's eyes.

He planted a gentle kiss on her forehead. "It's me—your dad. I will care for you; protect you; teach you when that's what you need from me. I will somehow let you go off on your own when it's time for that, too. I will care for you and love you, always." Tears rolled down his cheeks and splashed onto her blanket.

Two nurses entered the room. "Let's get you into your room."

A third nurse approached with a rolling bassinet. "I need to take her…"

"Amelia," Dhruv supplied.

"For tests."

Dhruv didn't want to let Amelia go.

"I'll bring her right back to you."

Stephanie said, "It's okay, honey. We've got the rest of our lives with our daughter."

Dhruv reluctantly handed Amelia to the nurses and followed Stephanie.

CHAPTER 53

*B*iscuit and I waited in the foyer by the front door. Sabrina sat with us, even though she knew she wasn't going anywhere. Rocco and Sugar were closed up in the basement after the fiasco with Rocco chewing the baseboards. Grant had said that the little dachshund was just nervous and wouldn't do it again. Emily had said better safe than sorry, and that Rocco would be happier if Sugar was with him.

We were keeping those two with us for a few days to let Stephanie and Dhruv get settled in with the baby. Stephanie had gone into labor a few weeks early and whoever was supposed to take care of "the dogs" couldn't. I had no idea what any of this was about.

The past twenty-four hours had been confusing for everyone.

Right after lunch yesterday, all of us (except Sabrina) had piled into Grant's SUV and raced over to Dhruv and

Stephanie's apartment. Which used to be our apartment. A man who looked like Dhruv but wasn't Dhruv met us there with a key.

We went in and brought Biscuit, Sugar, and Rocco home with us. Emily put Biscuit's harness on her and used her as her guide! That completely unnerved me—for about five seconds. I quickly got hold of my racing thoughts. Emily would never replace me with another dog. We were bonded with superglue. I felt ashamed for ever doubting her.

We were now bringing Biscuit back to Stephanie and Dhruv because they were home. With Amelia.

The whole scenario was like one of those hard balls that bounces so high you can never catch it.

We loaded ourselves into the car and were soon in the hallway outside our old apartment. Dhruv and Stephanie were home—and I detected a new smell that must be Amelia. Equal parts milk, poop, and baby lotion—I liked it.

Biscuit waved her tail with a ferocity I didn't know she possessed.

The door opened, and a disheveled-looking Dhruv stepped back to let us in.

"Perfect timing. Amelia just woke up. She and Stephanie are in the living room."

Emily took the working harness off Biscuit and allowed her to bound ahead of us. My people followed her.

Dhruv waited for them to enter the living room. He looked down at me and his face shone like a saint in a renaissance painting. He exuded love and contentment—whitewashed with fatigue.

My tail swished from side to side of its own accord,

hitting the pocket of his cargo pants. A small, orange foil bag teetered precariously, then fell to the floor.

"Dhruv," Stephanie called from the living room.

He strode toward her without noticing the almost-empty bag of Crunchy Cheetos that lay at my feet.

I looked after him. Leaving this bag on the floor could be a hazard for Stephanie. As a guide dog, I knew this to be true. At the very least, if someone stepped on the snack, they would track an orange mess on the carpet.

I weighed my options and decided the best solution was for me to remove the potential hazard. I stuck my nose inside the bag, hoovering up the three remaining orange cylinders, and carried the empty bag to the kitchen trash. Dogs always know where the trash is located—especially kitchen trash.

I licked the last orange crumbs from my lips and joined the others. It was time to meet Amelia.

THE END

THANK YOU FOR READING

If you enjoyed *From the Heart*, I'd be grateful if you wrote a review.

Just a few lines on Amazon or Goodreads would be great. Reviews are the best gift an author can receive. They encourage us when they're good, help us improve our next book when they're not, and help other readers make informed choices when purchasing books. Goodreads reviews help readers find new books. Reviews on Amazon keep the Amazon algorithms humming and are the most helpful aide in selling books! Thank you.

To post a review on Amazon:

1. Go to the product detail page for *From the Heart* on Amazon.com.

2. Click "Write a customer review" in the Customer Reviews section.

3. Write your review and click Submit.

In gratitude,
  Barbara Hinske

ACKNOWLEDGMENTS

I'm blessed with the wisdom and support of many kind and generous people. I want to thank the most supportive and delightful group of champions an author could hope for:

The many visually impaired people who have willingly shared their stories with me so that this series is accurate and honorable of their lived experiences. I want to specifically thank Kaila Allen for her insights on motherhood and Ron Kolesar for his thorough and helpful beta read;

Steve Pawlowski for starting me on this most gratifying path;

My insightful and supportive assistant Lisa Coleman who keeps all the plates spinning;

My life coach Mat Boggs for his wisdom and guidance;

My kind and generous legal team, Kenneth Kleinberg, Esq., and Michael McCarthy—thank you for believing in my vision;

The professional "dream team" of my editors Linden Gross, Kelly Byrd, and proofreader Dana Lee; and

Elizabeth Mackey for a beautiful cover.

RECURRING CHARACTERS

Recurring Characters

Amelia: Dhruv and Stephanie's newborn daughter in *From the Heart.* Dark hair.

Ava: Zoe's friend at new school. Third grader. Deaf. Brainiac. Tall, skinny with long, chestnut-colored braid. Excellent tap dancer. Mother is Tammy.

Connor Harrington III: highly successful sales executive; Emily's ex-husband.

Dhruv Patel: genius senior programmer on Emily's team; husband of Stephanie; father of Amelia; dogs are Sugar (golden retriever) and Rocco (dachshund).

Garth: Emily's black lab guide dog.

Gerald: Executive Vice President at Connor's employer.

Howard Kent: Executive Vice President of Systems and Programming at Emily's employer; a champion of Emily.

Irene: Zoe's grandmother.

JOHNSON

Alexander Johnson: son of Craig and Gina Roberts.

Craig Johnson: twin brother of Grant; married to Gina Roberts; father of Alex; veterinarian.

Diedre Johnson: daughter of Grant.

Grant Johnson: twin brother of Craig; love interest of Emily who becomes her husband; widowed father of Diedre; architect.

Sylvia Johnson: widowed mother of Craig and Grant; grandmother of Diedre and Alexander; her cat is Tibs.

Julie Ross: counselor at the Foundation for the Blind; her guide dog is Golda.

Karen: works at makeup counter at Nordstrom.

Kari: senior programmer on the cyber security team at Emily's employer in Denver office.

Katie and John: Garth's puppy raisers; their children are Alex and Abby; their cat is Liloh.

MAIN

Emily Main: department head of a top-notch programming team at a technology giant; lost her eyesight when her retinas detached in a riding accident on her honeymoon; divorced from Connor; daughter of Martha; Zoe is her ward; love interest of Grant who becomes his wife; Gina is her lifelong best friend: Garth (black lab) is her guide dog.

Martha Main: widowed mother of Emily.

Michael Ward: supervisor in Emily's team of programmers.

Norman Klein: recipient of heart donated by Emily's father (Martha's husband) after he was killed in an auto accident.

Rebecca: third grade teacher in classroom next to Stephanie's. New mother of a baby boy.

Rhonda: programmer in Emily's team.

ROBERTS

> *Doug Roberts:* uncle of Gina; love interest of Martha.

Gina Roberts: lifelong best friend of Emily; married to Craig Johnson; mother of Alex; parents are Hilary and Charles.

Hilary and Charles Roberts: Gina's parents (retired); Gina's mother is a breast cancer survivor.

Roger Foley: Connor's boss and Asia Region Senior Vice President.

Ross Wilcox: director of cyber security team of programmers at Emily's employer in the Denver office.

Scott Dalton: Connor's best friend.

Spencer Chamberlain: orientation and mobility specialist at the Foundation for the Blind.

Stephanie Wolf (now Patel): close friend and classmate of Emily at the Foundation for the Blind; third grade teacher; wife of Dhruv; mother of Amelia; guide dog is Biscuit (yellow lab).

Tania: fourth-grade classmate of Diedre.

Zoe: parents killed in a car accident; lives with her grandmother and becomes Emily's ward when her grandmother (Irene) dies, leaving Zoe in Emily's care; dog is Sabrina (miniature schnauzer).

PLEASE ENJOY THIS EXCERPT FROM COMING TO ROSEMONT

PROLOGUE

Frank Haynes spotted the forlorn-looking creature in the trees at the side of the road. He quickly pulled his Mercedes sedan off the highway and buttoned his cashmere sport coat against the icy fog as he stepped out onto the grassy berm. He walked gingerly in his slick-bottomed dress shoes as he approached the thin calico lurking in the underbrush. The wary animal rose up on her front legs, ready to take flight, and eyed him uneasily.

Haynes crooned softly to her. He pulled his collar up against the biting wind and wished he had grabbed his topcoat out of the backseat. But he dare not move now. The cat gradually relaxed and cautiously picked her way to him over the frost-stiffened grass. The cat rubbed against his legs in the familiar figure-eight pattern and began to purr—a tiny, tentative whisper that ripened into a deep, throaty rumble.

He reached a cautious hand down to her. She stretched into him, and he knew the bond had been made. He scooped her up and cradled the filthy creature against his chest, shielding her from the cold and stroking her gently, unconcerned about his expensive coat. When she was content, he returned to his car and placed her carefully in the blanket-lined crate that lived in his backseat for just such occasions. "You're safe now," he whispered the assurance. "You won't have to worry about food or cold anymore."

He shut the mesh grate of the cage and was surprised when the cat curled up and went to sleep. Most strays meowed and screamed all the way to the no-kill shelter that Haynes had founded and currently funded.

As he slipped behind the steering wheel, Haynes automatically checked the cell phone left behind in the console and was shocked to see he missed six calls during the short time he had been rescuing the cat. All from Westbury's idiot mayor, William Wheeler. He punched the return call button as he swung back onto the highway. Wheeler picked up on the first ring.

"Frank—where have you been? All hell's going to break loose around here," Wheeler shouted into the phone.

"What's up?" Haynes replied calmly.

"The town treasurer just called and told me the town can't cover the December payments from the pension fund. We're in trouble, Frank."

Damn, Haynes thought. This was coming two months earlier than he predicted. They wouldn't have time to get any of the condos sold by December. "Have you talked to either of the Delgados?"

"I called Chuck to tell him to move money from the reserve account you guys told me about. He said to talk to Ron about it. Ron thinks the reserve account has been 'depleted.' Some accountant and financial advisor he is! How did you guys let this happen? What have you been up to? If the town doesn't make those payments, we're sunk."

"Don't worry about it. I'll call Chuck and we'll get it straightened out. We always do, don't we?" Haynes disconnected the call over Wheeler's sputtering response.

Damn this faltering real estate market and those greedy, care- less Delgado brothers. How had they drained the reserve fund so quickly? They must be siphoning money for their own use from the tidy sum that the three of them had "borrowed" from the town worker's pension fund. Fleecing the faceless public was one thing. Double-crossing Frank Haynes was quite another. Wheeler was set up to take the fall, if it came to that. He could make the trail lead to the Delgados, too. Haynes vowed to find out where every nickel had gone. He executed a sharp U-turn and headed back to Town Hall.

CHAPTER 1

Maggie Martin settled herself in the back of the cab as the driver pulled away from the airport and into the thin sunshine of a late February afternoon. She nodded when he leaned back to tell her that Westbury was an hour's drive, and turned her attention to the countryside streaming by her window. She was in no mood for idle chatter with a taxi driver. The dormant farmland lay still and expectant. Occasional clumps of leafless trees were silhouetted against the storm clouds that soon filled the sky. Maggie was glad she had carefully folded and packed those extra sweaters.

She shivered in spite of the heat blasting from the vents and wondered how anyone could live in a cold climate. *Southern California might not have four seasons, but who in their right mind wanted winter?* Maggie chastised herself once again for even making this trip. She was behind in her work—she needed the billings—and she probably wouldn't find any answers, anyway.

As the monotonous scenery sped by, Maggie relived her final moments with Paul in the cardiac ICU. Wired and tubed, he was hooked up to the best equipment modern medicine had to offer. Their children, Mike and Susan, were both frantically making their way through traffic, but neither arrived in time. It had been Maggie and Paul at the very end. In his final moments, Paul rallied. He feebly squeezed Maggie's hand and repeated breathlessly, "Sorry. So sorry. House is for you." At least, that's what she thought he said. She had been crying, and the beeping monitors and wheezing oxygen machine made it impossible to hear.

She had been over this a million times. It hadn't made any sense because she knew their house was hers. Hadn't they just paid it off and thrown a burn-the-mortgage party with the kids? She had tried to reassure Paul, to quiet him, but he had been desperate to make his point. Maggie now understood Paul's deathbed confession. That's why she had decided to come to Rosemont before she listed it for sale. She needed to get answers; to make some sense of her life.

Maggie planned to go straight to her hotel in Westbury to try to get a good night's sleep before she and the realtor toured the house and signed the listing papers the next day. But her plane had arrived forty-five minutes early, the only advantage of the bumpy flight through strong tailwinds. God knows she was exhausted, having spent another sleepless night rehashing her sham of a marriage. But she was far too curious to get a glimpse of Rosemont to wait any longer. As they passed the highway sign announcing the Westbury exit fourteen miles ahead, Maggie retrieved her house key from the zippered compartment of her purse, leaned forward, and instructed the driver to take her directly to Rosemont.

The cabbie, as it turned out, didn't need directions. "Everybody in these parts knows the place," he assured her. "It's been vacant for years," he continued as he caught her eye in his rearview mirror. "Do you know the owner?"

"I am the owner," Maggie replied with an assurance in her voice that surprised her. "Actually, I just inherited Rosemont. I'm going to put it on the market, but I'm awfully curious to see it. Since it'll still be light when we get there, I thought I'd like to see it on my own, before the realtor and I get together tomorrow."

The cabbie nodded slowly, digesting this news, as he flipped on his left-turn signal and turned into a long, tree-lined drive that wound its way up a steep hill. They rounded the final corner and Maggie gasped. At the end of a deep lawn was an elegant manor house of aristocratic proportions. Built of warm limestone, with regal multi-paned windows, a sharply pitched tile roof, and six chimneys, Rosemont had the kind of gracious good looks that never go out of style. Dazed, she handed him his fare, with a more-than-generous tip, and secured his promise to drop her luggage at her hotel and return for her in an hour.

Maggie dashed through the now falling sleet to the massive front door. The key fit smoothly into the lock but wouldn't turn. She tugged and jiggled the handle, to no effect. It wasn't moving. Maggie looked wistfully over her shoulder as the taxi took the last turn at the end of the drive and vanished beyond the trees. Why did she have to insist on coming here tonight? Impatience did her in every time.

She buttoned the top button of her coat, fished the cabbie's card out of her pocket, and unzipped her purse to retrieve her phone. She'd have to call him to come back now. It was too cold and damp outside to even walk around and look in the windows. Maggie tugged off one of her gloves with her teeth and punched in his number on her phone. She brought it to her ear and idly tried the lock one more time. She felt something shift under her hand and the sturdy lock yielded. The door creaked open. Maggie abruptly ended the call and stepped over the threshold.

Even in the gloomy light of a stormy dusk, the beauty of the house overwhelmed Maggie, and she knew, for perhaps the first time in her life, that she was home. And that nothing would ever be the same again.

The mahogany front door opened to a foyer that gave way to a generous living room. A stone fireplace with an ornately carved mantel dominated one side of the room, and a graceful stairway swept up the opposite wall to the second floor. An archway led to a room lined with bookcases. *An honest-to-goodness library, for Pete's sake,* Maggie thought.

She inched forward slowly, like a dog expecting to come to the end of its leash, and peered into the library. Although all of the furniture was draped in heavy muslin covers, the room was stunning with its six-foot-high fireplace, French doors to a patio, and a stained-glass window. "I've been transported to a movie set of an English manor house," Maggie whispered. She set her purse on a round table in the middle of the foyer and unbuttoned her coat.

The fatigue and apathy that had been Maggie's constant companions since Paul's death began to dissipate as she examined this elegant old house she had inherited. Paul had never mentioned owning an estate on fifteen acres in Westbury. At least not until his final moments. Maggie had learned there were a lot of things that Paul had never mentioned. Unlike the others, this one was a pleasant surprise.

The remainder of the first floor was comprised of a large dining room, butler's pantry, kitchen, breakfast room, laundry, maid's quarters, and a large, sunny room whose function she couldn't identify. It had a herringbone tile floor and was lined with floor-to-ceiling windows along one wall. A conservatory, maybe? *Holy cow*—did she actually own a home with a library and a conservatory? The perfect lines of the house were evident at every turn.

With mounting excitement, Maggie found the switch for the chandelier that lit the staircase and raced to the second floor. A spacious landing gave way to six separate bedroom suites. She opened the first door carefully and proceeded with increasing confidence. Each suite was lovely and distinct in its own way, with huge windows and a sitting room and bathroom for each bedroom. One had a balcony, two had fireplaces. "I actually own this place," she murmured to herself in shock. She was considering which bedroom she liked best when she thought she heard a door close below. Was it already time for the taxi to return for her? Could she possibly have been here for an hour?

Maggie tore down the stairs as surely as if she had been running down them all of her life and came face to face with a solidly built man wearing tidy work clothes. With a pounding heart but steady voice, Maggie demanded to know who he was and how he got into her house.

He stepped back and held up his hands. "I'm sorry to startle you, ma'am. I'm Sam Torres. Your realtor expected you tomorrow, and he asked me to come by today to air the house out a bit and make sure that everything was in working order. I've been in the basement for the past three hours fiddling with the furnace. I've got it going now. I'm surprised we didn't hear each other. I didn't mean to frighten you."

He paused a moment to wipe his hands on a rag. He was never very good at guessing ages; he figured she must be in her fifties, but couldn't tell which end of that age range she leaned to. She was wrapped in a down-filled coat and wore those enormous Australian boots that were so popular. His wife lived in hers from October to May. She had a pair of glasses perched on her nose and was now regarding him imperiously through them.

"Welcome to Rosemont," he continued. "I understand you plan to put it on the market right away?"

Something about his polite, calm manner soon put her

at ease. Judging by his weathered skin and full head of gray hair, she guessed he must be a few years her senior. She extended her hand to introduce herself and told him that she was most definitely not going to sell this place. Sam looked at her sharply and started to reply but stopped himself. Then, to her own astonishment, she announced, "As soon as my taxi returns, I'm going to check out of my hotel and move in here. Tonight. Permanently." She reached for the banister, as if to steady herself, and turned aside. *What are you doing?* she thought to herself. *You can't just up and move here. Are you nuts? What do you need with a six-bedroom house? Your family is in California, and so is your work.*

Maggie glanced back; Sam Torres was regarding her carefully. She wondered if he could sense that her decision to move into the house that night had been made impetuously on the spot.

"In that case," he said, "I'd better give you a complete tour. You'll need to know where all the entrances, switches, and thermostats are located." He gestured toward the library and began by showing her how to unlock and open the cantankerous old French doors. Sam nodded in the direction of the fireplace. "You won't want to start a fire until all of these chimneys have been cleaned and checked. This house hasn't been lived in for more than a decade." Sam paused and turned to Maggie. "Are you sure you want to move in here tonight? Once the plumbing is in use again, you'll find almost everything leaks. And the place hasn't been cleaned in years. Wouldn't you like to get it fixed up first?"

"No, I can live with all of that for a few days. As long as

the furnace works and the electricity and water are turned on, I can cope."

"This sleet is supposed to turn to snow. You might get stranded up here," he cautioned as he produced a business card that read, "Sam the Handyman." "Here's my card. My cell phone number is on there. Why don't you call me when you get back tonight, and I can stop by to make sure that the furnace is still running and you're all set?" he offered.

"Thank you—very kind of you—but no need to drag out here later. I'll be fine," Maggie assured him with a confidence she didn't feel. For some reason, she felt completely comfortable with this concerned stranger. "Truthfully, this is a rash decision on my part."

Sam nodded.

"I can't explain it. I've never done anything like this in my entire life. But every fiber of my being tells me this is the right thing to do. For once in my adult life, I'm going to follow my intuition."

Sam regarded Maggie intently, and a slow smile lightened his worried expression. "In that case, moving in is exactly what you should do. Sounds like divine intuition. You should follow it. And you can always call me if anything comes up. My wife and I live about ten minutes away."

"Thank you, Sam. That makes me feel more comfortable." As they resumed their tour, Maggie was secretly relieved that Sam was making sure all the windows and doors were locked and all the thermostats were set. His instructions were thorough and helpful. It was evident that he knew the house well. The first floor had warmed to room temperature by the time they returned to the front door.

"I appreciate all you've done," Maggie said. "I'm not a dab hand at home repairs, so I'm sure I'll need your help on a regular basis. What do I owe you for today?" she asked as she turned toward her purse.

"Don't worry about that now," Sam said as he reached for the door. "We can settle up later. Would you like me to have the driveway plowed tomorrow?" She gratefully accepted. They said goodnight, and he headed out the door.

***

Later, in the eerie brightness of the nighttime snowstorm, Maggie and the taxi driver wrestled her suitcases and three bags of groceries to her front door. The driver helped her get them all inside and cautiously inquired if she would be okay there. She assured him she would be just fine, but she knew he doubted it, and, frankly, so did she. He had glanced at her in his rearview mirror occasionally on the drive out there and must have seen the waves of emotion surging through her. She went from feeling confident, intuitive, courageous, and spontaneous one moment to terrified, impulsive, incompetent, and irrational the next. She was known for her level-headed, depend-able (and ultimately predictable) nature. Paul said he never wondered what she was thinking, and her kids swore they knew what she would say before she said it —and they were usually right. At times Maggie felt proud of this—she was understood, knowable, transparent. At other times, she felt dull and unimaginative. Well—this decision would surely make jaws drop.

As the taxi crept up the driveway toward her new life,

fear and doubt were gaining the upper hand. She cleared her throat and was about to instruct the driver to take her back to the hotel when they again rounded the corner, and there it was. The house. *Her* house. Imposing, dependable, welcoming, strong. She would craft a happy future here.

She paid the driver, walked up the stone steps, and shut and locked the front door behind her. She toyed with the idea of phoning one of her children to let them know she changed her plans but decided against it. They could call her cell if they needed her. She wanted to savor her brave decision and her first night in her new home without the intrusion of their opinions.

Maggie picked up her groceries and headed in the direction of the kitchen. Dusty and in need of a thorough cleaning to be sure, but what a glorious kitchen! Beautiful walnut cabinets adorned with furniture-maker details soared to the twelve-foot ceiling. A huge window over the antique French sink and a smaller window over an old-fashioned copper vegetable sink would make the room irresistibly cheerful in daytime. The appliances and fixtures were outdated and would need to be replaced, but it was still the most beautiful kitchen she had ever seen—much less owned. *People will really have high expectations of a meal fixed here,* she mused. *I used to be such a good cook. I wonder if I can still muster up anything that does justice to this kitchen? I'll practice and get back on my game,* she decided with a bit of her characteristic determination.

Maggie stashed her groceries and dug into the rotisserie chicken and coleslaw that she bought for her dinner. She began a systematic reconnaissance of the kitchen. To her delight, it was equipped with every specialty pot, pan, and utensil imaginable. *I've been lusting after some of this stuff in catalogs for years,* she thought. *What great fun to cook in this kitchen.*

Along one wall was an enormous antique hutch. Maggie found it contained five complete sets of china, including specialty pieces like eggcups, double-handled soup bowls, and tureens. She recognized Colombia Enamel by Wedgwood and Botanic Garden by Portmeirion, but had to check the bottom of a plate to see that she had place settings for twelve of Derby Panel by Royal Crown Derby and a lovely blue-rimmed favorite called Autumn by Lenox. A set of cheerful yellow Fiestaware completed the collection. *Good Lord*—she felt faint. Maggie was a self-described china addict; now she had the collection to prove it. She vowed to use the good dishes every day.

Maggie made herself tea in a Wedgwood cup and wandered through the house to find a place to tuck herself away to enjoy it. The long day had taken its toll; she was exhausted. As she passed through the archway into the library, she found an overstuffed chair in the moonlight by the French doors and knew she had found her spot. Maggie dragged the sheet off the chair with one hand while waving away a cloud of dust with the other and settled into the chair's protective embrace.

An unblemished blanket of snow in the garden looked like frosting on a cake. At least four inches already, and it was still coming down hard. For the first time in months, everything around Maggie was quiet and still, and she felt peaceful. Thoughts of Paul were always crowding her, and they gradually settled on her now. Who was the man that she had been married to for over twenty-five years?

On the surface, Paul Martin was the charismatic president of Windsor College. Charming and handsome, with a killer smile. And laser focus. When he turned his attention on you, you felt like you were the most interesting and important person in the world. She had felt that way for years; had never doubted his integrity or fidelity. Mike and Susan, now both grown and out of the nest, adored their father. Paul's unexpected death at the age of sixty-two had unearthed a number of betrayals. *Were there others yet undiscovered?* He evidently thought he had plenty of time to cover his tracks. Now Maggie was left to cope with it all.

The first shoe to drop was his embezzlement from the college. The interim president discovered suspicious receipts in Paul's desk, receipts that he had been careless enough to leave sitting in a drawer. An audit was hastily done and the results discreetly fed to her. Paul had been submitting fraudulent expenses as far back as they could trace, in excess of two million dollars. Where in the world had he been spending all of this money?

At first, Maggie wondered if Paul had a gambling problem. As she pored through the college's audit, however, it became very clear that the money was being spent in one location: Scottsdale, Arizona. And another fresh hell was born. She would never forget that day, last September, when she had summoned the courage to uncover the identity of the other woman.

Her short flight had been turbulent, and wedged into a middle seat between an overweight man with a dripping nose and a sprawling teenager; she was queasy by the time they landed. Taxiing to the gate seemed interminable. She snatched her carry-on from the seatback in front of her the moment they came to a stop, and shoved past the teen, jostling the woman in the seat across the aisle as she attempted to stand up. "Getting a bit claustrophobic in there," she muttered in a half-hearted apology. The woman huffed and fixed Maggie with an icy stare. She didn't care what anyone thought; she needed to get off of that damn plane. The line in front of her inched along to the door. Why in the hell were people so slow and clumsy with their luggage? Why did they insist on stuffing bags into the over-head bins that they couldn't handle on their own? *Just breathe deeply*, she told herself.

The rental car was waiting for her. Thank goodness for the perks of being a frequent traveler. She settled into the seat and turned the air conditioner on full blast. Maggie fumbled in her purse for the report the private investigator had given her. She double-checked the address, but didn't need to; it was seared into her heart. Maggie punched it into the GPS system, adjusted her mirrors, and began her journey.

It was only ten o'clock in the morning, but near-record temperatures were predicted and heat waves shimmered off the highway. The GPS was reliable, and she was close to the address in under thirty minutes. Maggie decided she needed something to drink and turned into a convenience store to get a giant diet cola and a bottle of cold water. No one was behind her in line, so she took her time fishing out the correct change. Now that she was here, she wasn't so sure she wanted to pick at this scab. She lingered over the rack of tabloid magazines by the door. What was the matter with her? She was just going to drive by a house. She probably wouldn't even see "her." She had come all of this way—she needed to hitch up her britches and do this thing.

Maggie coiled herself into the now oven-like car and burned her hands as she grasped the steering wheel. She took a long pull on her diet cola and set off once more. She drove slowly as the ascending street numbers indicated she was getting close. *Undeniably a swanky neighborhood,* she brooded. *Nicer than ours.* Spacious, new stucco homes with red-tile roofs and soaring arches. Intricate iron gates and ornate light fixtures. Manicured lawns tended by efficient landscapers. No signs of life on this oppressive day. Everyone was safely tucked away.

And there it was. Bigger than the rest—or was she imaging that? It was unquestionably the nicest house on the street. Bile rose in Maggie's throat. If you had lined up photos of all of the houses on that street and asked her which one Paul would have selected, Maggie knew it would have been this house. More grand than their home in California. Maggie drifted across the centerline and caught herself before she hit the other curb. Thank God she was the only car on the street. She needed to get hold of herself; she didn't want to get into an accident right outside the other woman's house. How cliché would that be? She was acting like a stalker, for goodness sake. No one could ever know she had done this.

She turned around in a driveway five houses down and drove past to view it from the other direction. It looked even better. *That bastard.* She tightened her grip on the steering wheel and turned the car around again, trying to find a shady spot along the curb where she could discreetly watch the house. A couple of palm trees provided the only shade available, and she pulled to the curb. The air conditioning was no match for the midday sun, and she felt like one of the ants that her brother would fry under a magnifying glass on the sidewalk when they were kids. Why in the world had Paul done this? Why hadn't they just divorced? Was he that concerned about the effect it would have on his career? Divorce wasn't a stigma anymore. And he evidently had plenty of money, so splitting what they had in California wouldn't have posed a problem. Surely he knew that she would never have gone digging for more. *Or was he addicted to the thrill of living a secret life?* She instinctively knew she had hit the mark dead center.

Her soda was long gone and she was taking the last swig of water, chiding herself that it was demeaning to be sweltering in a rental car outside of the other woman's house—then she appeared.

Maggie crouched over the dashboard, the air conditioning blasting her hair out of her face, and focused on the other woman like a laser. Tall, thin, and pretty—with shoulder-length blond hair and long, tanned legs—she was laughing with two school-aged children as she herded them into her Escalade. She pulled out of the driveway and glanced in Maggie's direction as she turned to say something to the children in the backseat.

Maggie clutched the steering wheel as nausea overwhelmed her. She tried unsuccessfully to choke it back and grabbed frantically for the empty soda cup and heaved violently. Sweating profusely, she fumbled in her purse for some tissues and a breath mint. The tears she had been holding back for months now broke free. This had been a stupid, crazy thing to do. Why had she expected it to turn out differently? She was a mess. Vomit on her cuff and in her hair. The last thing she wanted to do was spend the day here and get back on a plane later. To hell with the one-way drop-off charge for the rental car. It was only a six-hour drive. She'd be in her driveway about the same time as her scheduled flight was supposed to land. And she wouldn't have to see anyone or talk to anyone along the way. She swung the car around and set her course for home.

The minute she uncovered the Scottsdale connection, Maggie had a gut feeling about what she would find. Paul had supported a second family there. The investigator found that the two children weren't Paul's, thank God. But it had been a long-standing relationship and by the looks of the financial records, he had been supporting her handsomely. The most difficult part of Maggie's situation was bearing this knowledge alone; she dared not confide in anyone she knew.

Paul had been acting strangely after he took the post at Windsor College eight years ago. And Maggie had done her best to contrive an innocent explanation and rationalize Paul's odd behavior. But everything now made sense: the weekends away, when he was ostensibly too tied up in "strategic planning sessions" to call home; his trendy new wardrobe and haircut; and his younger, more "hip" vocabulary. When Susan pointed this out, Paul laughed and passed them off as his way of relating to the student body.

He had also become increasingly critical of Maggie's blossoming consulting business as a forensic accountant. At first, she believed he was genuinely concerned she was taking on too much and spreading herself too thin. He was emphatic that he needed her by his side for the numerous social engagements required by his position. Somewhere along the way she realized that he resented her success and her growing independence from him. Paul loved to tell his amusing little story about meeting the shy, studious, plain girl in college and turning her into the beautiful, polished, accomplished woman she was now; that their love story was a modern-day *My Fair Lady*. *Ugh!* She might not have been a sophisticate, but she hadn't been a country bumpkin, either. Even Eliza Doolittle outgrew the tutelage of Professor Higgins.

The turning point in their relationship was that horrible fight about the black-tie fundraiser he wanted to chair. He would turn up at the event in his tuxedo and make a nice podium speech, and she would work tirelessly on it for almost a year. She had begged him not to volunteer, told him that she simply didn't have the time, that just this once she needed to focus on herself first. She was about to land a lucrative expert witness engagement she had worked so hard to get. It was a fascinating case and would demand all of her time. And would undoubtedly lead to more such work. She simply could not turn it down.

Paul had railed that he couldn't turn the fundraiser down, either. He started on his usual refrain of "whose job pays more of the bills around here" when Maggie quietly pointed out that her income had exceeded his for several years. For the first time in their more than twenty years of marriage, Maggie had put her foot down and told Paul no. Paul had exploded and they had gone to bed angry. This time, however, Maggie didn't give in or apologize just to keep the peace.

They didn't speak for a week. When they tentatively resumed communication, Paul was derisive and demeaning, constantly criticizing Maggie in matters both large and small. But his opinion of her appearance, her job, and her social skills didn't matter much to her anymore. Maggie's friend Helen summed it up nicely: Paul had lost control of Maggie and he didn't like it. She had half-heartedly defended Paul, saying he was a leader and not a control freak, but she knew Helen was right.

Her lawyer negotiated a settlement of the college's claim against Paul's estate in exchange for his million-dollar life insurance policy. The board of regents hadn't been anxious to have their lax oversight of the college's finances exposed, and Maggie didn't want Mike and Susan hurt by a public discrediting of Paul's memory. She needed to get to the bottom of the mystery that was Paul Martin before she brought Mike and Susan into this nightmare. Maggie hired a private investigator that quickly uncovered the truth.

Revisiting these horribly hurtful revelations—so frustrating because Paul was not there to question, cross-examine, rage at—was like watching a tornado relentlessly obliterate her lovingly crafted life. The pain, loss, and desolation were constant companions. But tonight, sunk into this massive chair within the perfect stillness, Maggie removed herself from the starring role and felt like she was watching someone else's tragedy. She let her mind go blank and watched the snow slanting down across the trees outside her window. And she surrendered to a deep and dreamless sleep.

***

Having his office above his liquor store had its advantages; Chuck Delgado was well into the bottle of Jameson he grabbed from behind the counter as he waited for Frank Haynes to arrive on this Godforsaken night. Shortly after two in the morning, someone tapped quietly on the back door below. Delgado checked the security camera and buzzed him up.

Haynes firmly climbed the steps into Delgado's lair and found him slumped in his chair just outside the pool of light supplied by the green-shaded lamp on his desk. Haynes scanned the room, allowing his eyes to adjust to the dimness. The rest of the room was in shadow, and Haynes was glad of it. He didn't care to be accosted by Delgado's collection of crude, pornographic trinkets and toys.

Delgado shoved the open bottle and a highball glass in his direction. Haynes firmly declined. He didn't need to get lightheaded now, and God knows when that glass had last been washed. He cast a dubious glance at the two chairs across the desk from Delgado, and moved a stack of newspapers and a hamburger wrapper onto the floor. *At least he's eating at one of my restaurants,* he thought.

They regarded each other intently. Haynes remained silent.

Delgado nursed his drink and Haynes sat, brooding and

impassive. Delgado finally sucked in a deep breath and began. "Okay, Frank, here's the thing. We ran into an unexpected situation."

Haynes raised an eyebrow.

"Not with anything here. Operations in Westbury are fine. In Florida. It's hard to keep your finger on things from a distance. I sent Wheeler down to check on things, but the bastard spent all his time with the whores in the condos. I understand a guy's gotta have fun, but he didn't do jack shit down there. Bastard lied to me when he got back. If this all goes down, he deserves to take the fall." Delgado gave a satisfied nod and sank back into his chair.

Haynes leaned rigidly forward, resting his elbows on his knees, and locked Delgado with his glare. He waited until Delgado, hand shaking, set his drink down.

"We aren't going to let this 'all go down,' Charles, now are we? We aren't going to let that happen. We had plenty of cushion built in to survive even the Recession. If you hadn't dipped your hand in the till, we wouldn't be having this unfortunate conversation."

"I had stuff to take care of. Those cops down there are expensive and—"

Haynes slammed a fist on the desk and roared, "Silence! I don't care what situation you got your sorry ass into. You know that you were not to bring your sordid business interests into our arrangement. Those condos were supposed to be legitimate investments, not whore houses or meth labs or whatever other Godforsaken activities you've got going in them."

Delgado held up a hand in a gesture of surrender. "You're

right, Frank, I know you are. But stuff happens. I'll get this figured out. I may have buyers for a couple of the condos. And I'm expecting money from another associate next week. Enough to fund the shortfall in the next pension payments. Don't go gettin' yourself into an uproar. We'll get things straightened out. I'm on it," he slurred.

"You've got ten days to get this handled," Haynes growled. "I'm going to watch your every move from here on in. You won't want to disappoint me." His tone sent a wave of fear and dread through Delgado.

Haynes rose slowly, turned on his heel, and walked down the stairs, allowing the echo of his steps to recede before he opened the back door and was swallowed by the night.

Delgado held his breath until he could no longer hear Haynes' car retreating. "That guy is seriously unhinged." He reached for the bottle and didn't bother with a glass.

From *Coming to Rosemont*

ABOUT THE AUTHOR

USA Today Bestselling Author BARBARA HINSKE is an attorney and novelist. She's authored the Guiding Emily series, the mystery thriller collection "Who's There?", the Paws & Pastries series, two novellas in The Wishing Tree series, and the beloved *Rosemont Series*. *Guiding Emily* was made into a Hallmark Channel movie of the same name in 2023 and her novella *The Christmas Club* was made into a Hallmark Channel movie of the same name in 2019.

She is extremely grateful to her readers! She inherited the writing gene from her father who wrote mysteries when he retired and told her a story every night of her childhood. She and her husband share their own Rosemont with two adorable and spoiled dogs. The old house keeps her husband busy with repair projects and her happily decorating, entertaining, and gardening. She also spends a lot of time baking and—as a result—dieting.

ALSO BY BARBARA HINSKE

Available at Amazon in Print, Audio, and for Kindle

The Rosemont Series

Coming to Rosemont

Weaving the Strands

Uncovering Secrets

Drawing Close

Bringing Them Home

Shelving Doubts

Restoring What Was Lost

No Matter How Far

When Dreams There Be

Novellas

The Night Train

The Christmas Club (adapted

for The Hallmark Channel, 2019)

Paws & Pastries

Sweets & Treats

Snowflakes, Cupcakes & Kittens

Workout Wishes & Valentine Kisses

Wishes of Home

Novels in the Guiding Emily Series

Guiding Emily (adapted for The Hallmark Channel, 2023)

The Unexpected Path

Over Every Hurdle

Down the Aisle

From the Heart

Novels in the "Who's There?!" Collection

Deadly Parcel

Final Circuit

CONNECT WITH BARBARA HINSKE ONLINE

Sign up for her newsletter at **BarbaraHinske.com**
   Goodreads.com/BarbaraHinske
   Facebook.com/BHinske
   Instagram/barbarahinskeauthor
   TikTok.com/BarbaraHinske
   Pinterest.com/BarbaraHinske
   BookBub/Barbara Hinske
   Twitter(X)/Barbara Hinske
   Search for **Barbara Hinske on YouTube**
   bhinske@gmail.com

Made in the USA
Las Vegas, NV
31 October 2024

10852122R10201